She glimpsed something out of the corner of her eye. What was it? She moved closer and saw pale limbs, the sheen of hair. Where in the world would Claude g... mannequin to hide here in his secret room?

But then, in horror, she realized that what she saw was no mannequin. It was a real body, a girl, dressed in blue jeans and a bright pullover, dead for sure, a snakebite on her outstretched arm. Now she knew the source of the scent she'd smelled when she pushed open the door with Claude's warning, DO NOT ENTER ON PAIN OF DEATH!

She had to get out. She turned, banged her head, could not see for a moment. The room had become suddenly darker. But that was because Claude was standing in the entranceway blocking out the sunlight, a look of dismay on his face.

It was at that moment Mavis began to scream.

DEAD AND BREAKFAST

ROBERT NORDAN

W☉RLDWIDE®

TORONTO • NEW YORK • LONDON
AMSTERDAM • PARIS • SYDNEY • HAMBURG
STOCKHOLM • ATHENS • TOKYO • MILAN
MADRID • WARSAW • BUDAPEST • AUCKLAND

DEAD AND BREAKFAST

A Worldwide Mystery/August 2003

First published by Five Star.

ISBN 0-373-26465-8

Printed in U.S.A.

For Tom Adair

The author would like to thank D. C. Brod, Ed Gorman, Douglas Rhone, M.D., Steve Gilbert and Vasssi Minervino for their help in the publication of this book.

ONE

You are my sunshine, my only sunshine,
You make me hap-py when skies are gray,
You'll never know, dear, how much I love you
Please don't take my sunshine away...

THE SOUND OF WAVERING voices lingered on the air, then faded. For a moment it was quiet on the bus except for the *thwamp* of the windshield wipers going back and forth and the swishing sound of water on the expressway. Well, *somebody* certainly took the sunshine away from this day, Mavis thought. Ever since they had left Markham early that morning the rain had poured down, and now, nearly three hours later, it still showed no sign of stopping.

"Honey, is something wrong? You've been quiet the whole time. I thought you would have enjoyed the sing-along. You're not sick are you?"

Mavis looked over at Zeena Campbell sitting in the seat beside her and for a moment wasn't sure who it was. She still couldn't get used to Zeena's hair. For as long as she could remember, it had been unnaturally black, but two Sundays ago Zeena had walked into their Sunday school classroom with her hair red as a house afire and said, when everybody turned to stare at her, "I thought it was time for a change. I wanted a new me, and Shirlee down at the beauty shop came up with this color. It's called 'Flaming Passion'—how do you all like it?" Fingering her own gray curls, Mavis had thought to herself that Zeena looked like a flaming something else but she didn't say it.

"I can't carry a tune in a tin bucket," she told Zeena. "Even when I was a girl and they tried to make me sing in the choir, they soon found out I didn't have a voice. Now, when I'm in church, I just mouth the words. Nobody knows the difference and I don't throw everybody else off key."

Zeena shrugged her shoulders, opened the large canvas bag she had brought onto the bus and took out her makeup kit and checked her face. I suppose she's had to buy a dresser full of new cosmetics to match her hair, Mavis thought, not to mention clothes. Zeena was wearing a bright purple jumpsuit that Mavis hadn't seen before, and she had three huge suitcases in the luggage compartment below that the bus driver had to struggle to get on that morning.

"Now, wasn't that *pretty?*" It was Cassie Branch, the tour director, who stood up front beside the driver, calling out in her chirrupy voice. "Anybody have a request for another song?" There was dead silence and Cassie got a hurt look on her face. "Well, I guess everybody wants a little rest before lunch," she said and tried to smile. She looked out the window. "Maybe the rain'll let up soon. I'm sure the Lord will give us sunny days for the trip ahead. He's just washing His earth clean for us right now."

Cassie sat down and Mavis gave a sigh of relief. Maybe they'd have some peace and quiet for a little while. Ever since they'd left, Cassie had been up there at the front of the bus talking about how much fun they'd have at Dollywood, what good food they'd eat while they were there, how nice the motel was going to be. It was a wonder the bus driver hadn't driven right off the road, listening to all that. When Cassie had started passing the song sheets around, Mavis had almost groaned aloud.

Of course, she had to admit, Cassie was just trying to do her job. Cassie Branch worked for the Happy Holiday Travel Service in Markham, and her specialty was arranging trips for seniors and religious groups. A small woman, no bigger than a minute, she had boundless energy, herding people on and off buses, getting them in line in restaurants, listening to a million complaints about food and bathrooms—with a smile that rarely faded and unending praise on her lips for the Lord's good works on earth.

Maybe it's just me, Mavis thought. Everybody else seemed to be having such a good time—why was she feeling so irritable? Maybe it was because she hadn't slept well the night before. She'd had no reason. After finishing up the supper dishes (something easy, a salad and a bowl of soup—no need to cook up a lot of food since she was going to be away), she had packed her bag, laid out her clothes for the morning, checked the house one last time to be sure all the windows were locked, and then had gone to bed. But all night long she tossed and turned, waking to go over in her mind again and again every item she had packed, worried that she might have forgotten something. "It's not the African jungle I'm going to," she finally said out loud in the darkness. "If I've left out anything, I can always buy it when I get there." After that, she had finally

fallen asleep, waking groggy and tired when the alarm
went off at six o'clock.

She had to admit it, she didn't like to travel. Getting
on and off buses and trains, trying to get used to an
unfamiliar bed with a pillow that was always too soft
or too hard, changing her diet so that she had to chew
milk of magnesia tablets half the time she was gone—
it wasn't for her. Worst of all was having to room with
someone. She didn't like intimacy with near strangers,
embarrassed by the noises they made in the night,
strangely upset when she saw their deodorant on the
edge of the sink. Even though she was only going part-
way on the tour, mainly for the ride, she had almost
told her nephew Dale that she'd changed her mind
when he pulled up in front of her house that morning
to take her down to the church to join the group.

"My, don't you look pretty!" he said when she
opened the front door.

"Pshaw," she answered him, but couldn't help but
smile when she saw his sweet face. "In all this rain,
I'll look half drowned before I even start out. Such a
shame. Shirlee worked me in special yesterday afternoon so I could get my hair done before I left—now,
it's all a waste of time and money."

"Don't you worry," Dale said and held up a huge
green-and-white-striped umbrella. "This'll keep you
dry. Your slacks may get a few spots but they'll dry
in no time."

Those slacks! Mavis almost blushed. Zeena had been
the one who had talked her into buying them. "Why,
Mavis, honey," she had said, "they're the perfect thing
for traveling. You know what a pain it is getting on
and off a bus in a skirt. And you've still got your —

figure, no need to hide it a-tall.'' Mavis hadn't answered, but what Zeena said about stepping up on the bus *was* true, so she had bought the slacks, a pretty peach color, the first she'd ever owned in her life. That morning, after she had pulled them on, they felt strange only for a little while, and, looking in her dresser mirror, she had to admit that they did look nice with the cream-colored blouse Zeena had helped her pick out.

"Well, I guess I'm ready," she told Dale, then picked up her purse and the sweater she had decided to carry along in case they had the air conditioning turned up ice-cold on the bus. He reached inside and picked up her bag, and Mavis, taking one last look around, went outside onto the front stoop and locked the door.

"We're off!" Dale said and flipped open the umbrella, as if he was escorting royalty. Taking his arm, Mavis walked carefully down the wet steps to the front walkway, and they hurried through the rain, giggling together, out to Dale's little red sports car parked at the curb. Just his presence had cheered her up, even though a few minutes before she had been thinking that she didn't want to go on this trip at all.

Dale was her sister Florence's boy, her only child. After his daddy disappeared, early on before Dale was even potty trained, Mavis and her husband John helped to raise him, and she came to love him like her own. Later, it seemed, death threw them together. Mavis lost her own daughter in a freak accident, John had a heart attack still young, and Florence died of cancer while Dale was in college. After his mother's funeral, he had taken Mavis's hands and said, "I guess we're the only family we have left now. We'll have to take care of each other."

And they had, up to this very moment, calling each other nearly every day, eating together several times a week, sharing the mystery novels they both enjoyed. Looking over at Dale now, his rumpled hair shining despite the darkened day outside, she thought, Lord, he looks sleepy as a two-year-old up way past his bedtime. I bet he didn't have three hours of sleep last night, out gallivanting.

Dale started the car. "You excited?" he asked her.

"Not one bit," she said. "A four-hour ride on a bus full of old women is not my idea of a good time."

"Too bad you aren't going all the way with the rest of the group. You'd probably enjoy Dollywood."

"No thank you!" she said, brushing her hand in front of her face as if an insect had just sailed by. "I can see all I care to see of Miss Dolly Parton's bosom on the covers of those magazines at the checkout counter without having to travel halfway across North Carolina to Tennessee and pay good money to see more. I just needed a ride in a hurry up to Monroeville, so I called Cassie Branch at Happy Holiday Travel Service and asked her if she had an extra seat on this trip everybody had been talking about. Right way, she said, 'Yes, ma'am, we sure do,' and quoted me a price that was better than the Greyhound I'd already checked."

"I'm sorry I can't take you."

"Don't be. It's good enough of you to drive up next week to bring me back. You've got your work to do."

Dale laughed. "Yeah, photographing the Summer Fun Fair out at the Cherry Hill Mall. There'll be a fashion show put on by the 4-H Club with all the little darlings done up in their homemade fashions, a Bible verse spelling bee, and the battle of the country music

D.J.'s—and God knows what else." He turned to her
and winked. "Maybe I'll get involved in a murder,
too."

"Don't say it!" Mavis touched his arm, then drew
her hand away. Dale sometimes was called in by the
police to photograph a crime scene, and he and Mavis
would pour over the pictures together hoping that they
could solve the mystery. "I don't want to have to
worry about you while I'm off on this trip."

"Don't worry. Nothing will happen. I'll take my pictures at Cherry Hill, develop them and turn in the
prints, and hurry off to see you in the mountains. By
then, I'll need some nice refreshing air."

Mavis smiled. She was glad Dale was coming. Ever
since she'd received the call from her friend, Eileen
Hollowell, she had thought how nice it would be to
have Dale come up, too. The two of them could ride
back home together. She could have taken the Greyhound, of course, but just the idea had made her feel
a little trembly inside. A perfectly nice person might
sit beside her, but you never knew—it could just as
easily be somebody drunk or doped, or worse, and then
what would she do?

By the time they reached the church, the bus was
half-filled, shadowy faces Mavis couldn't recognize
peering through the shaded glass of the windows. Before she even got out of the car, she could see Zeena's
flaming head bobbing up and down as she instructed
the driver how to arrange her three big bags in the
luggage compartment of the bus. "I spent a day packing," she was saying to no one in particular as Mavis
and Dale walked up to the bus, "and I don't want to
open up my suitcases in Dollywood and find a mess of

wrinkles." She spoke to the driver again. "Put them on top so nothing will mash them down."

Dale dropped Mavis's bag in front of the driver, and he picked it up and slid it over one of Zeena's bags. She didn't notice, already batting her eyelashes faster than a moth 'round a candle flame at the sight of Dale. "Why, my goodness, aren't you out early this morning," she said. "Mavis is just the luckiest thing I *know* to have her own personal escort to see her off on this journey, particularly one that's so good-looking."

"Not this morning," Dale laughed. "I probably look like something the cat dragged in, didn't even have a chance to shave."

Before Zeena could say something else silly, Cassie Branch came over and introduced herself. "I've heard so much about you," she said. "I hope you'll encourage your aunt to go on one of our little trips," she laughed, "*all the way,* I mean. She'd be a real addition to the group."

Dale gave her a dazzling smile. "Oh, I have," he said. "But I haven't had much luck. I guess I'll just have to take her off on a trip myself."

Cassie pulled one of her rare frowns and said, "Well, we'd still like to have her." Then, brightening, she said, "Maybe *you* can come with us sometime. Now that would be something!"

Mavis drew back and looked towards the bus. "He'd be bored out of his mind with these old ladies," she said.

"Well, I don't know," Zeena gave a little pout. She would have gone on, but the bus driver called out to ask if there were any more bags, else they were about ready to go, and Cassie hurriedly handed out envelopes to Mavis and the other passengers who hadn't, as yet, climbed onto the bus.

"It's your tickets," she said, and then called out, "come on now, everybody get on. We're going to have the *best* time."

Mavis put her envelope in her purse and slowly turned to Dale. "Well, I guess this is it," she said, the feeling of reluctance returning. She'd give most anything to be back in her own kitchen sitting in her nightgown with the newspaper and a second cup of coffee.

"I know you're going to have a great time," Dale said, "and I'll be up to see you in just a few days. You won't even miss me."

"Ha," Mavis said, then leaned over for him to kiss her cheek, turned and started up the steps of the bus. The slacks did make it easier after all. By the time she got down the narrow aisle to her seat and had settled in beside Zeena, the bus was already pulling away, and she had only one quick glance of Dale, standing with his hand half raised as he peered up at the bus trying to see her through the shadowy windows. She waved frantically at him but could tell by the look on his face that he couldn't see her. Lord, she prayed, just let this trip go along without any trouble.

MAVIS'S HEAD SLID ACROSS the headrest of her seat as the bus turned off the expressway. Suddenly awake (she had fallen asleep, lulled by the sound of the wheels, and the remnants of a vague dream still clouded her eyes), she looked around quickly to see if anyone was staring at her, afraid she might have been snoring. But nobody seemed to be paying her any attention, and when she reached up to check her hair, she found that the thin net she wore was still in place and the curls Shirlee had combed out on the back of her neck were still bouncy. She took a deep breath and relaxed.

"Feel better, honey?" Zeena said with a smile. "You seemed kind of grouchy earlier. Maybe your little nap will help."

"Maybe," Mavis said. "I guess I got up a little too early."

"Anybody hungry?" It was Cassie Branch up at the front of the bus again, as perky as ever. "Well, I hope so. Soon as we get to the mall, we'll have our lunch." She bent down to peer out the window. Mavis looked, too, but all she could see were filling stations and fast food signs, wavery through the rain. "We'll be here about an hour, so you can take your time. Lunch is included in the price of your ticket. I just know you're going to enjoy it."

The driver pulled into a special lot marked BUSES AND TRUCKS, stopped, and then opened the doors. "Mercy, it's wet," Cassie said. "You'll have to run for it." She pointed to a sign across the way that said THE BOUNTIFUL BUFFET, ALL YOU CAN EAT. "Come on."

They struggled out of their seats, grabbing jackets and sweaters and fanning out plastic bonnets to cover their hair, then ran stiffly across the wet asphalt, afraid they might slip and fall, to the door of the restaurant. "Where's the ladies room?" somebody called out to the woman at the cashier's desk, and they all trooped in the direction she pointed. Another reason not to travel in a group, Mavis thought, long lines for the bathroom. After she'd finally had her turn and was at the lavatory washing her hands, Zeena came up beside her and flopped down her purse. "I don't know which is worse," she said, pulling at her jumpsuit, "wearing pantyhose inside your girdle or out. Something binds either way."

"I wouldn't know," Mavis said, finished wiping her hands on a towel, and walked outside into the restaurant.

It *was* a lavish buffet. Mavis had trouble making up her mind but ended up with a pile of shrimp on her plate—goodness knows they cost a fortune in the store—and enough pickled artichoke hearts to sate her for days. "Iced tea," she said when the cute little waitress asked her what she'd have to drink, then unfolded her napkin and placed it in her lap.

"Shall we say grace?" asked a woman at the end of the table, folding brown-spotted hands beneath her chin, just as Mavis had the first shrimp halfway to her mouth. The others murmured yes and Mavis bowed her head hoping they'd ignore the shrimp while the woman said a brief prayer. She really didn't see the need for public display—surely the Lord knew they were glad to be off that bus and eating—but she'd go along with whatever the others wanted to do.

They all began to eat then. Mavis looked around the room at the bent-over white heads and pink scalps. Only Zeena, sitting at the table with Cassie and the bus driver, stood out, her red hair gleaming. Mavis knew a lot of the women on the tour, some from her church, some from the exercise classes she attended at the YMCA. Most were widows, some few single or divorced, lonely, most of them, though they never talked of their disappointment and loss. Three or four, maybe, like Zeena, still seemed to harbor some hope that they might find a man to round out their lives again, so dependent on husbands to take care of things for so many years that they hadn't known how to write a check for the funeral expenses. Unlike most, Mavis had lost John early and had been taking care of herself a long time. And never, in all those years, even though she had appreciated the attentions of a few men, had she found anyone who came even close to entering that special place in her heart where the memory of John still lingered.

"My goodness, Mavis Lashley, you look like you're a thousand miles away. What in the world are you thinking about?" It was Iva Mae Johnson, one of Mavis's neighbors, just a street away, always the first person in the neighborhood to hear bad news and the most eager to share it.

Mavis turned to her. "Nothing," she said. "Just day-dreaming. My, isn't this a fine lunch?" she added, hoping to change the subject.

"It sure is," Iva Mae said and the others murmured assent. "It's too bad you won't be having any more meals with us."

"I'm sorry, too," Mavis said, hoping the Lord would forgive her that little lie. "I was lucky to get a ride this far with you all."

"Now just where is it you're going?" Iva Mae asked, curiosity apparently getting the best of her.

"To Monroeville, just up the road a piece. I've got a good friend there—Eileen Hollowell, known her for years—and she called all of a sudden and asked me up for a visit."

"Well, isn't that nice," Iva Mae said with a look that indicated she thought there might be more to the story. Mavis didn't add anything, however, and Iva Mae went back to her gossiping.

The dessert buffet provided still more choices, and

Mavis finally made up her mind to get the fresh peach cobbler, though most everyone else slid several desserts onto their plates, no doubt planning to wrap up the extras in a paper napkin and put them in their bags along with any artificial sweetener packets left in the holders. "It all looks so fattening," Zeena called out with a moan, but it didn't keep her from loading her plate like the others. Mavis ate her cobbler, then asked for a little more tea from the friendly waitress and sat quietly while the others talked about Dollywood. Finally, Cassie called out that it was time to get back on the bus, and they all scraped back their chairs and followed her and the bus driver outside.

The rain had stopped, the streets already dry, and in the far distance they could see a blue haze in the sky where the mountains began. "See, I told you," Cassie called out with a look of pure bliss on her face. "The Lord did provide us with a sunny day. He looks after His own."

Looking up, Mavis felt her heart soar at the sight, and now the only shadow that clouded her mind was the memory of Eileen's frantic voice on the phone three nights before saying, "Mavis, I need you. Don't say no. When can you come?"

TWO

GOODNESS, HOW MANY YEARS had she known Eileen Hollowell? Too many to count. But however many there had been, Mavis could still remember as clear as if it had been yesterday her first sight of Eileen standing on the front porch of Mrs. Geneva Dalrymple's boarding house back in Willow Springs. With her crinkly gold hair crammed under a hat pulled halfway down to her ears, eager blue eyes peering through the screen door, and a smile as big as sunrise on her face, she could have been the answer to anyone's prayer. When she called out, "Anybody home?" Mavis thought to herself: She will be my friend.

"Come on in," she'd said. "Mrs. Dalrymple is down at the church at the Ladies Missionary Society meeting. But we've been expecting you. I'm Mavis Cole. I can show you your room. It's next to mine." She opened the door and Eileen thumped in two big leather suitcases and came inside.

"I swear," Eileen said, "they're heavy as lead, and I didn't bring half what I thought I'd need." She pulled off her hat and the golden curls sprang up like a jack-in-the-box. "You got a glass of cold water? I'm parched to the bone. I hope that's the last train ride I take for a long time to come."

"The kitchen's back here," Mavis said, pointing to

the doorway of the dining room where Mrs. Dalrymple's prized collection of potted plants sat in the bay window, dappled by the late-afternoon sunlight that shone through stiff, white lace curtains. "Come on," she said, and then touched Eileen lightly on the forearm to direct her, and the two of them walked through the silent house to the kitchen. Eileen chipped slivers from the big block of ice that sat in the icebox on the back porch and fixed them both a tall glass of water. "Welcome to Willow Springs," Mavis said and grinned.

"Thank you kindly," Eileen answered back with a wink.

And beginning that day, they had become the best of friends, and had remained so through all the intervening years no matter how much time went by between letters, however few the telephone calls. When one of them finally did call the other, or they met on one of their infrequent visits, they picked up where they had left off months or years ago, and anybody listening to them would have thought they were as close as neighbors gossiping across a backyard fence.

It was the first year of teaching for Mavis. Eileen, a few years older, had some previous experience, but for some reason, she had taken this job. She traveled all across the state on a day-long train trip, to teach in a country school with a wood stove they had to keep filled in winter and pale, undernourished children who stayed out of school in the spring when crops were planted and then again in the fall when they were brought in. They received little pay, but room and board was included, and Mrs. Dalrymple cooked heaping platters of food and urged second helpings, watching over them as if they had been her own. Her daughter had married and moved away, the way young people were already beginning to do, and her son was in the service. "I didn't see any need of wasting those rooms," she told them, "and Mr. Dalrymple agreed."

That year had been one of the happiest of Mavis's life. In spite of the conditions, she liked the school, and, a few times, she saw the pure joy of learning brighten a child's face for just a moment, enough reward to keep her going through those times when she felt she could do so little to change their lives. Even though the war was on and people sat glued to the radio to see what Mr. Hitler was up to, there were still ice cream suppers at the church (nobody doubted that Mavis and Eileen would attend) and Easter egg hunts and watermelon cuttings. In the black-paged album sitting now on Mavis's closet shelf at home, there were browning snapshots taken that year of her and Eileen and people she couldn't possibly remember posing around the countryside.

One photograph in particular seemed to capture those days. Taken on a spring day when Mavis's sister Florence came down for a visit, it showed the three of them standing like the figures on a vase in some museum amidst the snowy white blossoms of a pear tree. Eileen with the sun shining through her hair, Mavis with her dark curls cropped short, Florence grinning like a five-year-old. Their faces probably never looked as carefree again.

There were pictures of boys in the album, too, all shapes and sizes, the ones with flat feet and heart murmurs who hadn't gone off to war. It didn't matter. They never had a serious thought about a one of them, just out for a good time. They went riding around town in rented cars on rationed gas, and a few times traveled up to Markham to go to a picture show, all good friends and never more than a goodnight kiss between them.

They left nine months after Mavis had first seen Eileen standing bushy-haired on the front porch of Mrs. Dalrymple's house. Mavis got a job closer to home (her mother was ailing and she wanted to be near), and Eileen went back to the mountains. Each made promises to stay in touch forever. When they walked down the steps struggling with their suitcases, Mrs. Dalrymple stood on the porch with tears in her eyes telling them to write and at the station Mavis and Eileen both cried when they had to part. The one thing that Eileen never told Mavis during that joyous golden year was why in the world she had traipsed all across the state to come to teach in Willow Springs in the first place.

They kept their promises to keep in touch. Mavis wrote Eileen nearly every week, and Eileen's letters came back in reply. At special times—birthdays, holidays—they indulged in long distance phone calls, usually reserved for matters of life and death, chatting fanatically as the minutes clicked by. After the war, when Eileen's letters began to be filled with references to Vance Hollowell ("Vance did this, Vance did that"), Mavis felt a twinge of jealousy. But she quickly decided it was un-Christian to feel that way, and when Eileen finally wrote that she and Vance were getting married—a quiet ceremony, just family—Mavis went out to the fanciest jewelry store in town and bought a silver engraved bowl with the money she had been saving for a new winter coat and sent it off to the two of them.

The letters kept coming, though now with less frequency. Vance opened up a barbershop (he had learned hair cutting in the army), and they bought land way out in the country, "a farm, really," Eileen wrote. "Vance can have horses and cows and I'll have plenty of space for a garden." They were building their own home. Eileen continued to teach, kept on right up until three days before their son George was born. "I was scared every day that my water bag would burst with me standing up in front of the class." There were pictures of him, too, in Mavis's album, a fat, solemn child with Eileen's bright hair and a pair of pitch-dark eyes that Mavis saw later, when she finally met him, came from Vance.

Mavis and John went to visit Eileen and Vance on their wedding trip. "You come on up," Vance had ordered over the telephone. "We've got plenty of room, so you two lovebirds won't be disturbed. We'll have a real good time." And they enjoyed every minute of their visit. Vance welcomed them like old friends, and they took to him immediately, a short, wiry man with black eyes darker even than his son's, quick to anger though it disappeared a minute later like the passing of a summer storm.

More pictures recorded an afternoon they spent together on the grounds of a luxury hotel, high on a mountain just outside Monroeville. "They'll kick us out, sure as anything," John said. "They'll see in a minute that we're just poor folks."

"No such of a thing," Eileen said. "In your wedding finery you'll look just as good as anybody else. If anything, they'll throw the two of us out, though maybe I can get Vance in a tie for a change. I don't think he's worn one since *our* wedding."

"We'll see," Vance said, and the next afternoon when it was time to go, he showed up in a plaid suit, a Panama hat, and brown-and-white spectator shoes, dressed to beat the band. "Who says we can't be as spiffy as anybody else," he said, taking Mavis's arm. She blushed when he told her the delphinium blue of her going-away dress was the very same color as her eyes.

They piled into Vance's old Ford—new cars were still hard to get—and took off for the hotel. They stayed there till nearly dark, walking around the grounds, posing in front of artificial waterfalls, sitting on carved stone benches that looked like they might have come from a castle. Finally, getting up their courage, they walked into the main lobby ("Act like you own the place," Vance said.) filled with graceful wicker furniture and two huge stone fireplaces, big enough to walk into at either end. "Lord, you could get rid of a body in there," Vance said, and they all told him to hush, he really would get them kicked out, sure as anything. Later, reluctant, because they already knew they couldn't afford it, they walked to the entrance of the dining room and read the evening's menu, while expensively dressed couples passed them to be seated at snowy white tables. Giving Eileen a hug, Vance told her, "We'll come here one day, just you wait and see," in a nearly angry voice, and Mavis, hearing him, knew that he would keep that promise.

Real sadness entered their lives for the first time when Eileen's second child, Claude, was born. Mavis kept the letter, ragged now, folded in the back of the album, that Eileen wrote her after coming home from the hospital:

I'd had some spotting early on, nothing serious, but no other problems. Labor was long and hard, nearly two days, and they had to use for-

*ceps. The cord was around his neck. I guess we
nearly lost him. I knew the first time they brought
him to my room and put him in my arms that
something was wrong. That misshapen head, poor
little lips that had no strength to feed, body floppy
as a rag doll—I asked them, "What happened,
what did I do wrong?" And the nurses tried to
shush me, said these things just happen no matter
what, pray that he'll be all right. I did, but I got
no comfort. And Vance seemed to blame me for
what happened, wouldn't even hold the poor little
thing in his arms. I've cried my eyes out and feel
a little better now. What else could I do?*

Later, when Mavis and John went back for summer
visits, they saw Claude's body grow bigger and bigger
while his brain seemed to get stuck, never developing
beyond that of an eight-year-old. After a few years they
took him out of school (there weren't any special pro-
grams in those days) to work around the farm. "He
can do just about anything, long as you keep an eye
on him," Eileen said, and they watched him work the
garden and slop the hogs and water the horses down
in the pasture without complaint. When Vance spoke
to him, his voice was always sharp.

Eileen came back across the state on only two oc-
casions, both of them sad. But it was Eileen who had
provided Mavis the most comfort. When she saw Eileen walking towards her, arms wide open with a gesture that said, *You come right on in and rest,* it was
then that she could finally grieve. And those strong
arms held her through many dark and tearful hours in
which she lived over and over again that autumn when
her daughter Rose, leaving for school, still in sight of

Mavis, had been struck down by a silly young fool driving an old car too fast. John's death had been just as unexpected. He had eaten supper, walked into the living room, and turned on the radio and then sat down in his favorite chair. "You're not asleep *already,* are you?" Mavis had said to him jokingly, but he had not answered her and she discovered he was dead. Eileen had held her that time, too.

But Mavis was unable to give Eileen the same comfort when Vance died of a second stroke (the first one casually mentioned in a letter from Eileen that came shortly after he sold the barbershop and retired; they never saw him after). The words came three days later on the little paper strips of a telegram: VANCE PASSED ON. STROKE. BURIED 3/27. REMEMBER ME IN YOUR PRAYERS.

So, after all those years, when Eileen called and said, "Mavis, I need you. Don't say no. When can you come?" how could she refuse?

THREE

"WELL, MY GOODNESS, aren't you a sight for sore eyes!" Eileen opened her arms for Mavis as she stepped off the bus, and Mavis rushed into them, hugging her, and smelled the familiar scent of dry grass and sunshine that lingered in Eileen's hair.

"You, too," Mavis said and pulled back to look at her. "You haven't changed one bit."

And she hadn't, standing there, brown as a berry, in a pair of faded shorts, a man's shirt, and rubber thongs that revealed her toughened feet, the result of going barefoot all summer long, and that hair nothing could control, graying now but still with golden lights. Mavis could just imagine what the pants-suited ladies on the bus were saying, but she didn't care one jot. "Thank you kindly," she said to the driver when he got out her bag from beneath the bus, then picked it up, and, with one last wave at the blurry faces behind the windows, hurried after Eileen who was already halfway across the parking lot.

"Here, let's put your bag on the back seat," Eileen said, taking the suitcase from Mavis. She opened the door of the old dark green Chevrolet she had driven for years and flung the bag inside. Before going around to the driver's side, she squeezed Mavis's arm and said, "I *am* glad you're here," but said nothing at all about her urgent call three nights before.

Eileen drove through the old part of town that Mavis knew best. Monroeville had always been a popular summer resort. High in the mountains, it provided warm days and cool nights, and the town became a refuge for retirees from Florida when the summers got too hot down there. Year after year the same people filled the immaculately kept old houses on lower Main Street with tourist home signs out front signaling "No Vacancy" the entire season, rocking on wide front porches in the late afternoon, fine white hair gleaming in the fading light, the women in pastel summer dresses and the men in plaid golfing pants. They ate early in the cafeteria to get the senior citizen's special discount even though they could afford to go elsewhere.

"Well, I'm glad some things don't change," Mavis said, turning to Eileen. "I hardly know Markham any more, it's built up so."

"Don't let this fool you," Eileen said with a wave of her hand. "Downtown may look the same, but wait till you get out my way. The woods are full of condos and townhouses, and golf courses have replaced half the orchards. The animals are disappearing. All around me, subdivisions have sprung up, and they'd have my land, too, if they could. It's a shame. I reckon soon everything will just be houses and concrete, no more trees at all. I'm glad I won't live to see it."

They were near the edge of town now where the highway narrowed and began to dip up and down through a tunnel of dark fir trees that opened suddenly like a curtain onto a wide valley with low mountain ranges on either side. Mavis could see what Eileen meant about change. In the past, the mountains had

been a uniform green this time of year, with just a strip
of narrow roadway unwinding like a ribbon to the top.
But now the hills were dotted with bright rooftops and
you could see the wires of a ski lift stretching up to
the highest peak. Down below, where there used to be
farms, shopping malls had sprung up, along with garden centers and fancy looking restaurants. The roadway
was a tangle of signs.

But there was still one familiar landmark—the
church Eileen attended standing just off the road on a
little rise of ground beneath old trees, newly painted a
glistening white, with weathered gray stones neatly ordered in the graveyard at the side. Eileen's family plot
was there. On their first visit, Eileen had taken her and
John there on a day as bright and warm as this, when
there was hardly another house in sight, and pointed
out her grandparent's graves and the waiting space for
other family members. Over the years, Eileen's parents
and various relatives had filled up most of that ground,
and Vance, too, must be buried there. But when they
passed and Eileen didn't even look over at the church,
Mavis decided not to ask.

"Lord, what in the world is that?" Mavis asked as
Eileen slowed, ready to turn off onto a side road. She
pointed to a building at the junction that used to be a
supper club with a smiling hostess wearing a long skirt
and a strand of pearls who would seat you, and you
could order a nice steak or fried seafood dinner while
an organist in the background played songs you
couldn't quite remember the words of but enjoyed anyway. She and John and Eileen and Vance had gone
there a few times together to celebrate some special
occasion, and Mavis hadn't even been upset when

Vance ordered a bottle of wine and insisted she have a little in her glass.

Now, the building was painted a shiny black, with orange and red flames leaping up the sides and the picture of a grinning devil with a pitchfork over the front entrance. A sign there said THE PIT in big yellow hand-painted letters. Out in front three glistening motorcycles sat waiting, and a van and a dusty pickup truck were parked off to the side. The ground was littered with paper and cans. "If that isn't the trashiest thing," Mavis said and gripped her purse a little tighter.

"You can say that again." Eileen's voice sounded constricted, and when Mavis turned to look at her, she saw that her lips were pursed tightly together, accentuating the fine web of wrinkles that spread across her face. "The old place—you remember—it burned, and the building sat empty for a long time until some strangers took it over and turned it into *that*." She almost spat out the word. "It's been nothing but trouble ever since, drinking and worse, I hear, going on. Every Monday morning when you pick up the paper, you can read about some kind of fight there over the weekend, arrests. But they stay open despite all that, pay off, I guess—you never know."

She turned, and they were on what was once a graveled country road, smoothly paved now with entrances to subdivisions turning off through the trees. QUAIL HOLLOW, FOX GLEN, WILLOW BROOK said discreet signs, and you could see neat front yards where once wild flowers bloomed. Before, Eileen's neighbors had been country folks who lived in small cabins with dilapidated cars parked in the front yards and old tires painted white and filled with bright petunias by the door, somebody's attempt at prettiness. Now, they were probably all commuters, or retirees who played golf on the greens that ran across the hills. "See what I mean?" Eileen said. "Change. Everybody sold out but me. But what would I do if I gave up the place? Be lost, that's what, and Claude, too. He's never spent a night away from home in his entire life."

Just then, Mavis saw the white board fence covered in wild roses that marked the entrance to Eileen's farm, and she gave a little cry, so many memories of her and John's past visits there came rushing back. Before Mavis even realized, Eileen had turned off the road into the graveled drive down to the house, but then she stopped the car so abruptly that Mavis put her hand out on the dashboard to brace herself. "What in the world…" she started to say, but then she saw the large wooden sign next to the gate. MOUNTAIN VIEW BED & BREAKFAST, OPENING SOON, she read, and she looked at Eileen who had a smug little smile on her lips and said, "Well, I never. This *is* a surprise. And you never gave a hint. Tell me all about it."

Eileen started up the car again and pulled slowly through the gate. "In a minute," she said, looking pleased as punch. "Let's get down to the house first," and Mavis didn't question her more, but she did wonder to herself whether this was what Eileen's call was all about, this surprise, and if it was, why had she sounded so *serious* on the phone. Maybe she'd find out soon.

The road dipped down, and as soon as they were past the gateposts Mavis felt that this one spot, too, had not changed; it might have been thirty years ago when she and John came up for a visit. Ahead, lay the garage with the upstairs apartment that Vance had built, where she and John slept some summers when it wasn't rented. Before bed each night they would stand hand in hand on the little balcony out back and count the stars silvering the mountain until it would become too cold and Mavis would give a shiver and they would go inside to rest.

Over the years, Vance had built other outbuildings— a second kitchen for Eileen's canning and preserving, a playhouse for Claude, storage space—and now the complex blocked the view. But Mavis knew that if she looked just around the corner, she would see the wide green pasture where Vance had kept horses and sheep and (against Eileen's will—"The scent comes right into the house when the wind is up," she'd complain), pigs that rooted noisily at the trough when Claude carried them the slops. A small pond shimmered there, fed from the spring that provided water for the house, the home of the ducks that Claude raised as his own. On a quiet summer afternoon you could see him, a huge, slow, clumsy man, squatting at the edge of the pond, intent upon some bit of fluff he held gently in his hands. Just beyond began the woods that stretched up the mountainside like a coverlet, changing with each season, undisturbed since Indians roamed. Once, John had asked Vance, "How far does your property go?"

"To the top of the mountain," Vance had answered, and smiled.

Eileen parked in one side of the garage, pulled Mavis's bag from the back seat, and they started towards the house. Vance had built that, too, just a small cabin when Mavis had first visited—a living room, two bedrooms, a bath, and a basement kitchen that stayed cool all summer, constructed entirely of dark wormy chestnut boards Vance had collected after a blight. "You couldn't give that lumber away back then. Now it's worth a fortune," he had said proudly. Sometimes, just teasing, he'd tell Eileen he was going to tear down the house and sell the wood, and she'd say, "That's fine with me, we can sleep beneath the trees," and everyone would laugh.

But, like the garage, the house had grown, too (Vance's handiwork again), with the original cabin engulfed by new additions so that, now, as Mavis followed Eileen up the path towards the rear of the house and peered through the hedge of laurel that grew higher than their heads, the place looked enormous. A wide, glassed-in porch, with what would surely be a lovely view of the pasture and the pond, stretched across the back, and two new wings—bedrooms, Mavis assumed—stood on either side. Lord, no wonder Vance had a stroke, Mavis thought to herself. Who wouldn't after building all this? It was big as a barn.

Eileen must have guessed her thoughts. "What else could I do with all this space?" she said, turning to let Mavis catch up with her. She set the suitcase down. "With nobody here but me and Claude, we'd just rattle around. When somebody came up with the idea of a B&B, it seemed to make sense, something to keep me busy." She laughed. "I didn't know quite *how* busy it would keep me, though. We're supposed to open in a week, and there are still things to do."

She bent for the suitcase again, but just as she lifted it and started for the house there came a sound like hail from the driveway and a shower of gravel rattled the laurel leaves. Alarmed, Mavis turned and saw the flash of shiny chrome and black metal as a motorcycle roared past and stopped suddenly just at the edge of the garage. "That damn fool!" Eileen said. "I've told him a hundred times not to do that." And before Mavis had a chance even to ask who, Eileen thumped the bag back down and marched past her out to the drive.

"You're going to kill yourself one of these days," she called out, "and somebody else, too, driving like that. You must not have a lick of sense. And look at both of you without a helmet—you ought to be arrested."

Mavis followed Eileen down the path and looked at the man who sat on the motorcycle with a big grin on his face. Boy, really, skinny as a rail, pale, with stringy blond hair pulled back in a ponytail and a little goatee on his chin the cat could lick off. He had a tattoo on the back of his hand that Mavis couldn't make out, and he wore a black leather jacket even though the afternoon sun was warm. When he spoke there was a note in his voice that made you wonder if he was laughing at you all the while, but it gave not the slightest hint of where he came from. Looking down, Mavis shuddered at the sight of his snakeskin boots. "Aw, Miz Hollowell," he said. "We'll be all right. I ain't killed myself or anybody else yet. Come on, and I'll give you a ride."

Mavis thought Eileen would burst. "I may be old," she said back to him, "but I haven't completely lost my mind."

He laughed and looked at Mavis. "Well, what about that pretty lady? I bet she wouldn't mind."

Well, I never, Mavis thought. Freshest thing she'd ever seen. "No siree bobtail," she said. "You'll never catch me on a motorcycle. I've heard of too many folks getting broken up—or worse—riding one of those things."

Eileen moved slightly in front of Mavis, as if to protect her. "You hush up your foolishness," she said to the boy on the motorcycle. Then, pointing to the girl who sat behind him, silent till now, she turned to Mavis and said, "You remember Tara. You met her once when she was just a little bitty child visiting up here for the summer, my granddaughter, George's girl."

Lord have mercy, even if she remembered little Tara, how would she ever recognize her in this girl who sat on the back of the motorcycle in broad daylight like some haunt from Halloween? Hair bleached white as snow, enough makeup on to last a lifetime, half a dozen earrings running up one side of her ear, fingernails painted dark blue. Every stitch of clothes she had on (and it wasn't much) black as night. "Hello, honey," she said, wondering if Tara had escaped from one of those places where they put teenagers when they got on drugs. Tara smiled, and for just a moment Mavis could see some faint glimmer of past childhood in her eyes. "I remember," she said. "We went on a picnic. Maybe we could have another one."

Before Mavis could answer, the boy said, "Yeah," and nudged Tara in a familiar way. "Why don't you introduce us."

She looked at him and then said blankly, "This is Jordache. My boyfriend."

"It's just a nickname," he jumped in to say, "but everybody calls me that. Back when Jordache jeans were so popular, I had every style they made—that's how I got the name. It's stuck."

Eileen obviously wanted to change the subject. "Tara's here for the summer," she said, giving Mavis a look that said she'd tell her more later, "helping me get things ready for the opening of the B&B. She's got the garage apartment all to herself.''

"It's real neat," Tara said.

"Sure is." Jordache grinned and got off the bike and kicked down the stand.

Tara jumped off, too. "We'll see you later," she said, taking Jordache's hand and leading him towards the stairs that ran up the side of the garage. "We're going to listen to some music."

"Keep it down," Eileen said and then turned and walked back towards the house.

Mavis followed her, trying her best not to say something she'd regret later, but before she knew it the words just slipped out. "She's changed just a speck since I saw her last."

Eileen didn't look around but said, "For the worse, you mean." She bent down and picked up the suitcase that sat in the path and let out her breath. "I didn't know what I was getting myself into when George called and asked if Tara could come up here for a while to 'find herself.' She didn't want to go to college right yet, and she'd already had a baby (I didn't know about *that,* they'd never told me before), so I said yes even though I wondered right out loud how she could go off and leave her own child. 'Margie'll take care of it,' he said—that's George's wife—'it'll be all right,' and I didn't say more. The only thing she's 'found' so far is that Jordache who's always hanging around, and she hardly lifts a hand around the place. I guess I don't understand children any more. Even the near grown ones expect you to hand them everything on a platter."

Mavis's room was the same small bedroom that she and John had shared on other trips before, so familiar

that she almost turned, expecting to see him there beside her. This part of the house had changed very little;
Vance had built on all around it but left the sitting room
and bedrooms alone. A stone fireplace, blackened from
years of use, took up most of one wall, and the two
small high windows on either side were filled with the
brightly colored bottles Eileen had collected over the
years, sparkling like a kaleidoscope when the late-
afternoon sun shone through them. Eileen's chair sat
just by the hearth the same as always ("I swear, my
feet get cold when it's ninety degrees," she'd say,
stretching them to the fire on cool summer nights), and
a table beside it held the Bible she read each day, along
with a romance novel entitled *Passion's Fire.* Across
from it stood an old-fashioned loveseat with a pink and
blue and white afghan folded across the arm, crocheted
by Eileen's mother goodness knows how many years
before. "It's one of the few things of hers I still have,"
she'd say and get a faraway look in her eyes.

There never had been any real doors to the rooms,
and now, as Mavis stood holding the dark green piece
of cloth that hung in the doorway to give a little pri-
vacy, she remembered the nights long ago when she
and John and Eileen and Vance would talk back and
forth to each other across the small space that separated
their rooms, lying in semi-darkness with the moon just
outside the window. Gradually, they would drift off to
sleep one by one until the only sounds left in the night
were the swish of leaves against the screen and the
barking of a dog too far away to matter.

"You rest a while," Eileen had said when she
dropped Mavis's bag in the middle of the sitting room
floor. "Unpack, take a nap. It was a long bus ride.

We'll eat supper early. Claude'll have a conniption fit if it's late.''

Laying her purse on the loveseat, Mavis had said, "I won't do any such thing. Let me help you. I didn't come up here to be a guest."

Eileen had put her hands on her hips and tapped her foot on the floor. "I mean it. Mostly everything's done and you can give me some help tomorrow. Don't worry, I'll keep you busy. Take the chance to rest while you can." And then she had turned and walked out of the room, and Mavis knew better than to follow her.

"I guess I might as well get unpacked," she said aloud and lifted the suitcase onto the bed. The closet was small, but Eileen had cleared a space for her so there was plenty of room for the dresses she had brought. Almost as soon as she opened the door, she could smell the dry sweet scent of the potpourri Eileen made every year from the flowers in her garden. It would linger in her clothes long after she had gone home. Eileen had pointed out the new bathroom just off a hallway outside the sitting room door. So after she finished unpacking her clothes and putting them away, she gathered up her jar of cleansing cream, her hair brush, and the few cosmetics she used and placed them on a shelf there. Now, this *was* an improvement, she thought, looking around at the shiny new fixtures. The old bathroom was tiny, the lavatory rust-stained after so many years of use, with a shower that leaked water on the floor no matter how careful you were to wrap the curtain around you.

Then, with nothing else to do, Mavis removed her watch and put it on the nightstand beside the bed, removed her shoes, and pulled down the bedspread. My goodness, she thought as she lay down on top, wearing pants was kind of convenient after all. Before she knew it, she was sound asleep.

SHE AWOKE TO THE SOUND of pots and pans crashing somewhere off in another part of the house. Jumping up, she looked at her watch and saw that she had slept more than an hour. "Lord have mercy," she said aloud, "I'll never sleep a wink tonight." She made up the bed again, put on her shoes, and went to the bathroom to splash cold water on her eyelids. No need to change. Eileen would still be wearing shorts, her usual summer outfit, and no telling what Claude would show up in for supper.

She walked down the hallway to the entrance of the new glassed-in porch that stretched all across the back of the house. From the windows she could see the pasture, with the duck pond half in shadow and the woods rising up the mountain, golden in the reflected light of the setting sun. Now, isn't that the prettiest thing, she thought, just like a picture. Maybe when Dale came up she could get him to photograph the view so she could put it in her album along with all the old pictures she and John had taken years before.

The porch itself was like a picture, too, pretty as a page in one of those home magazines you saw on the newsstand, not real fancy, but a place where people might really *live*, with comfortable wicker sofas and chairs, magazines on low tables, vases of Eileen's flowers placed about. More of her bottles glittered in the windows, and bright rag rugs were scattered across the floor. At the far end, near the doorway to the kitchen, sat a long, old-fashioned dining table that, opened up, would seat a dozen or more. Mavis could close her eyes and see Eileen's B&B guests sitting there on a morning enjoying her good blueberry muffins as they watched the mists rise off the mountain.

"Well, you must have taken a little nap after all." Eileen poked her face around the doorframe and smiled at Mavis.

Mavis walked across the porch towards her. "More than I meant to. I reckon I was more tired than I thought. But you ought to let me help you. All I did was sit on a bus all day; you've worked more."

"No need. Come on in and sit down and talk to me." She pointed to a stool beside the counter. "I'll have supper done in a minute."

"Mercy, if this isn't fancy," Mavis said, as she walked into the kitchen. It was new, too, bright and shiny, with more windows framing the mountain-view.

"Better than that old kitchen in the basement. I wore out my legs walking up and down, I hate to think how many times in all these years." Eileen turned to the stove, picked up a fork and turned over something in the pan.

"Is that what I think it is?" Mavis asked.

"Country ham," Eileen said and laughed. "You've got a good smeller."

"You always did have the best ham. John used to look forward to it every time we came."

"My fresh vegetables, too. That's what we're having tonight, the ham and fried okra and corn, with some fresh sliced tomatoes and cucumbers. Claude's work— he does the garden all on his own."

"I can't wait," Mavis said. "All I get at home is shipped-in stuff unless Dale takes me out to the farmer's market, and then it's sky-high."

"I'm glad he's coming up," Eileen said. "Dale. I haven't seen him since I was there when John died."

She turned away, as if embarrassed, to stir a pot on the stove. There was an awkward silence, Mavis wasn't sure why. Though John had been gone a long time, he still lived in her heart, and there was no pain attached to that memory. Maybe it was because Eileen still hadn't said anything about Vance's death, and the silence hung between them like a curtain they pretended not to see.

"You got it ready yet?" Claude Hollowell bounded through a door at the far end of the room and pointed to the stove, as strange in this shiny new kitchen as a figure dropped from Mars. He wore bib overalls over a stained T-shirt, graying hair going every which way, the skin on his bare feet so thickened it would defeat a snake's tongue. Mavis remembered him as a boy who collected rocks and baseball cards and any piece of old machinery he could find, every item orderly displayed in the shed behind the garage that Vance had built for him. "You come look," he would tell Mavis each time he saw her. And she would follow him down to his playhouse, bending to keep from hitting her head on the low doorway, follow him inside and spend five minutes (Claude always wanted more), looking at his treasures in the half-light.

He was no longer a boy but a grown man now, almost middle-aged, with coarsened features, a week's worth of beard on his face, and intense, clear blue eyes. He would be frightening to anyone who didn't know him.

"Claude Hollowell! Haven't you got a bit of manners a-tall?" Eileen turned from the stove with an angry look on her face. "Say hello to Mavis. You've been asking all day when she'd be coming, and now that she's here, all you can think about is your stomach.''

Claude walked closer to Mavis, bent sideways, gave her a look, and then said, "You got white hair now."

Eileen rolled her eyes, but Mavis laughed and said, "I reckon I do. It's about time." She reached out and touched the fingers that he gingerly offered. "You still collecting things?"

"Sure am. You want to see?"

"Not now, Claude," Eileen said in a firm voice that Claude never disobeyed. "There'll be enough time for that foolishness later. You go on and wash up. We're about ready to eat."

Claude smiled once at Mavis, then turned and padded out of the room.

Eileen sighed and began dishing up the food. "Dear Lord, sometimes I do wonder what will become of him," she said, standing for a moment with the spoon in her hand, eyes turned towards the window. "He's good-hearted, strong as an ox, works like a horse—I don't know what I'd do without him around the place. But he hasn't got the sense of a child and can get in trouble before you can say Jack Rabbit."

She turned back to the food, and Mavis was silent. What could she say? She had lost her own child—what if she had had one that was afflicted? Which would cause the most pain? She was glad of an excuse to change the subject when she saw Eileen start out to the porch with two bowls in her hands. "Let me help," she said, getting up from her stool, and went over to the counter and picked up the platter of ham fried a deep red, lighter near the bone. "My, this looks good." She smiled at Eileen as they passed.

After Claude returned and they sat down at the table, Eileen asked Mavis to say the blessing. With a feeling of contentment as strong as any she'd known in recent years, she gave sincere thanks to the Lord for giving her a safe journey and the joy of loved ones around her. She thanked him, too, for the good food they were about to eat and the beauty of the world just outside the door. "Amen," Eileen said in a soft voice when she finished. Claude asked for a biscuit.

They ate without much talk in the fading light, no lamps lit, watching the purpling shadows climb up the mountainside. Claude ate fast, chewing loudly, and though Eileen told him once to mind his manners, he didn't seem to pay her any attention. When he finished the second helping he had served himself from the kitchen, he pushed his chair back and asked if he could have dessert. "I reckon so," Eileen said. "If you can't wait. Go get one of your ice cream bars out of the freezer on the porch."

Before the words were half out of her mouth, Claude jumped up and headed towards the back door. Eileen turned to Mavis and said, "I buy them by the box. That's all he'd eat if I'd let him."

Mavis smiled, then stood. "I think I'll have another mouthful of that okra," she said. "You always could cook it better than anybody I know."

"Why, thank you ma'am," Eileen said in a playful voice. "You help yourself."

Mavis went through the doorway to the kitchen, the bright white light nearly blinding her at first. She found a spoon and took two spoonfuls of okra, then added a slice of tomato from a plate on the counter. You couldn't beat that combination. She was still trying to decide if she'd have indigestion if she ate more cucumbers when the scream came.

High, wild, wordless, like that of an animal in pain, it spread over the pasture and echoed off the mountaintop. "What in the world?" said Mavis, and she dropped her plate, the little pieces of fried okra bouncing across the counter like marbles. She had probably broken it, but she couldn't take time to see as she rushed back into the other room where Eileen was already standing by the window.

"Is he all right?" Mavis asked when her eyes finally adjusted from the bright lights of the kitchen and she could see Claude halfway down the road that led through the pasture to the trees beyond, little more than a shadow now, his hands stretched out towards the pond.

Eileen didn't answer at first but made a choking sound, and Mavis looked closer. Then she saw it, too, the pond, its silvery sheen still reflecting enough light for her to clearly see the dark red stain that was beginning to spread across its surface.

"Somebody has killed Claude's ducks," Eileen said. "Whoever could have done such a hateful thing?"

FOUR

LATER, WHEN MAVIS TRIED to tell Dale what happened
that first night of her visit, it was like reliving a bad
dream.

At first, she and Eileen remained at the window, unable to move, watching Claude as he ran from the road
through the pasture over to the little pond, that awful
cry still echoing in the hills. When he reached the edge,
he knelt, bent forward, and picked up a small shadowy
body, which he held close to him, shoulders shaking.
The pool was black now, darkness coming down. "I'd
better go to him," Eileen said and turned.

Her voice startled Mavis. "You want me to go,
too?" she asked.

"No," Eileen answered. "You stay here. It's rough
down there and you've got on good clothes."

She stayed at the window, glad to be relieved of that
trip; the pasture might be snaky, and there was no telling what she might step on in the dark. Eileen crossed
the yard, moving fast on short legs, and Mavis watched
her as she ran on by the garage and other outbuildings
to the road that ran through the pasture and then was
lost in the woods on the other side. When she reached
Claude, who still knelt beside the pool, Eileen bent
down beside him, put her arm around his shoulders,

and gradually the shaking stopped. "Poor thing," Mavis said aloud and felt tears come to her eyes.

Eileen stood then, said something to Claude, and he got up, too. With an almost angry gesture, she pointed towards the house, and Claude, following her finger, hurried back up the road to a shed attached to the garage, disappeared for a minute inside, and then came out again with a shovel and a cardboard box. Back at the pond, with Eileen directing, he scooped up the dead ducks one by one, put them in the box, and carried it back into the woods where he must have buried the small bodies. When it was too dark to see any longer, Mavis sat down at the table, very tired, to wait.

Suddenly, as clear as day, she remembered a time when she was a child, surely no older than eight or nine. She and her sister and some neighborhood farmer's children, whose faces she couldn't recall, much less their names, had found four dead chicks in the hen house and decided to have a funeral for them. They made coffins from shoeboxes lined with scraps of fabric snitched from her mother's quilting bag and twined sprays of mock orange and marigolds together to make wreaths for the tops. In dress-up clothes they sang songs learned in Sunday school and then buried the boxes out behind the barn, wailing the way Mavis's aunts had done when her grandfather had died the year before. A week later, they dug up the boxes to see if the chicks had turned to dust, the way the preacher had said, or had disappeared completely, gone to heaven, the way their parents had told them. Neither had happened. As soon as they raised the lids, they had smelled the awful scent and seen the shrunken beaks, the hollow eyes, and, flinging the boxes aside, had run crying to the house, aware for the first time that death was no pretty thing. Perhaps that was what Claude was feeling now. Mavis wondered if he'd shed a tear at his daddy's death.

She shook herself, got up. At least she could wash the dishes. She found a light switch on the porch and turned it on; the kitchen was still brightly lit. Opening and closing cabinets until she found some small bowls, she took out several, scraped the leftovers into them, and searched some more until she found plastic wrap to cover the tops. Then she began to wash the dishes in the sink, afraid to try the dishwasher. This could have been such a pleasant time, she thought, her and Eileen there together laughing about old times while they cleaned up after supper. But now that one ugly act down by the pond had cast a pall over the entire day. Who would do such a mean thing? Did it have anything to do with Eileen's plea over the phone? What else might happen?

Eileen suddenly came in through the door leading out onto the back porch, startling Mavis. She almost dropped the dish she was drying. "Lordy," she said, "you scared me." Then, noticing the sweat on Eileen's forehead, the smudges of dirt on her feet and legs, she asked, "Are you all right?"

"Yes. Now." Eileen went to the sink and Mavis moved out of the way while she washed her hands. "I wanted to get that mess cleaned up."

"How about Claude?"

Eileen peeled off several sheets of paper towel, dried her hands and wiped her face. "Oh, he'll be all right. He went on to his room. Maybe he's luckier in some ways than we are, forgets things pretty easy. I'll buy him some more ducks and he'll be just fine."

"Should you do anything else? Call the police?"

"Pshaw!" Eileen laughed and waved her hand. "The sheriff's office would just laugh if we called and said what happened, say it was some animal got 'em. There *are* still wildcats in those hills." Her look sobered. "But I know that's not it. Somebody put out crumbs for the ducks just behind the trees and cut their heads off deliberately. It was meanness that did it, a two-legged animal, not four."

It was then that Eileen noticed that the dishes were washed. "My goodness, you shouldn't have done that," she said. "But thank you, anyway."

"There wasn't any reason for me to sit here and look at dirty dishes and wait for you when I could do them myself."

"You want anything else? There was ice cream and fresh peaches for dessert."

"No, I'm full. We can have the peaches tomorrow on cereal and do just fine without the ice cream."

Eileen looked relieved. "It's early," she said, "but what would you think of going ahead and getting ready for bed? I'm worn out."

"I'm not surprised, after all that's happened. At least I had my nap."

Eileen smiled, went to the door and out onto the porch. Mavis heard her lock the back door. "Never used to have to do that," she said, returning to the kitchen. "But now it's different. We've had robberies right next door in the development." She turned out the light, and the two of them went out into the hallway together. In her little bedroom in the old part of the house, Mavis changed into her gown behind the green curtain hanging in the doorway, aware of Eileen's movements just on the other side. She put on a robe— not the good silk one Dale had bought her recently, it was far too fancy—and then went into the bathroom. She washed her face, brushed her teeth, and smoothed the night cream she'd used for years on her face and neck. "You do have the nicest skin," Zeena would say, but Mavis never revealed her simple secret. (And what, she wondered, would Zeena and the others be doing right now over in Dollywood? Getting ready for bed in some anonymous hotel room, hoping they'd sleep through someone else's snores? Lord, was she glad not to be *there*.)

She went back into the sitting room and found Eileen curled up in her chair, feet tucked beneath her gown. There was no fire, and when Mavis sat down on the sofa opposite her, she could feel the coolness on her ankles. Eileen, apparently lost in thought, did not speak, and Mavis sat picking at a loose thread in the afghan until she could keep quiet no longer. "You want to tell me what's the matter?" she said. "We've never had many secrets from each other before."

Eileen gave a little start and looked at Mavis, the smile she had managed to keep on her face most of the day gone, her body slack, as if the wires that had held it taut had been loosened. She shook her head. "I put it off," she said. "It was so nice having you here. I think I hoped it would be like magic—the spell would be broken now that you'd come. But that didn't happen." She shifted her legs to one side, leaned on her elbow and propped her chin in her palm. Mavis, her feet already too cool, kicked off her bedroom slippers and put her feet up on the sofa with a corner of the afghan over them.

"The ducks aren't the first thing that's happened. We called them 'accidents,' the first one or two. A small fire that flared up down by the shed—we thought

it was set by one of the workmen careless with a cigarette. Claude put that out with a hose. Then the pipe
bringing water from the spring got broken. Still, we
didn't think much about it, didn't think it was done on
purpose. And when the blooms on all my flowers got
lopped off one night, I knew there weren't enough insects in the entire county to chew them off like that,
but even then, I thought it might be a gang of kids
from the development next door. They get into mis-
chief sometimes.

"It was the blood that finally did it."

"*Blood?*" Mavis sat straight up. The afghan tangled
around her feet. "Whatever do you mean?" she asked,
leaning towards Eileen.

"Animal blood," she said. "Chicken, cow—I hope
nothing worse—splattered all over my sign for the
B&B." She turned her head and looked past Mavis as
if she were seeing the scene all over again in her head.
"It was such a pretty morning, a week ago, no more,
one of those days when the sky looks too blue to be
real and the air as fresh as you ever smell it any more.
I'd gotten up early to do some work and decided I'd
take a little rest, drink another cup of coffee while I
read the mail, though I didn't expect anything to come
in it but trash. Claude was already out and gone.

"I took my time, no need to rush. Most everything
was done, ready for my first guests in the B&B, and I
thought I deserved a little enjoyment, hard as I had
worked. So I just strolled along, not expecting what
was waiting for me on the sign. I opened the gate, went
through, and was just reaching for the mail when I saw
it, the blood splattered all over. Even then, I suppose,
something in my head protected me from realizing
what it was for a minute or two. It's my red rambler

coming into a second bloom, I thought. How pretty. But then I realized that it was no red roses on the white fence but blood. I almost fainted dead away.''

"Oh, you poor thing!" Mavis said, untangled now from the afghan. She bent closer to Eileen, took her hand and squeezed it. "Whatever did you do?" she asked.

"Why, wash it off, what else?" Eileen broke from her faraway stare. "I didn't want Claude to see it, and no more neighbors than already had. So I got a big bucket full of hot water and detergent and scrubbed it off so that it was just the roses that were red again. But I still saw the blood in my eyes and knew for certain that somebody didn't want me to open up this place. One more proof came the next day.''

"What was that?"

"I'll show you."

Eileen got up, went through the green curtain to her room, and rummaged around. When she came back, she handed Mavis a wrinkled piece of paper. "That was in the mailbox," she said and then sat down again.

Mavis bent towards the light, smoothing out the paper on her knee. It was a ruled sheet torn from a cheap tablet; the letters were printed in pencil, and there were smudges on the page. It looked like the work of an eight-year-old. "Beware," she read aloud, aware that Eileen was watching her intently. "We don't need any B&B here on this mountain. We've left our signs. This is the last warning." Silent for a moment, she carefully folded the paper into a neat square. Then, hoping to make Eileen feel better, she said, "You're sure this isn't the work of those children you were talking about?"

Eileen shook her head. "Yes. They'd never kill the

ducks. Claude let them come over and feed them sometimes and they were as nice as could be. That was
going too far.''

"You didn't report *any* of this to the sheriff?''

"The blood on the sign. That was the last straw.''

"What did he say?''

"Just sorry, he didn't have the men to put on it what
with the festival coming up.''

"What festival?''

"The Mountain Apple Festival, happens every year
and brings in tourists from all over. It starts off with
the Miss Apple Contest next week, then an apple cook-
off with prizes for the best recipes, a street dance on
Friday night and a big parade on Saturday. I'm not
surprised the sheriff has his hands full. I was hoping
to have the B&B ready to open for all that, but now I
don't know.'' Tears came to her eyes. "Maybe I should
just call the whole thing off. Maybe it was a bad idea
to start with.''

Mavis almost jumped up and went over to her.
"Don't you talk that way!'' she said, and the loudness
of her voice in the small room startled her. "You've
put so much time and effort into this place, not to mention money, and it's something you want for *yourself.*
You can't let some darn fool make you give it all up.''

Eileen smiled, the tears still sparkling in her eyes.
"I really *do* want it,'' she said. "I was looking forward
to having company here, people to cook for that would
appreciate it. Give Claude a bowl of cereal and an ice
cream bar, and he would never ask for anything else.''
She looked down. "It's been lonely these past few
years, even before Vance died. Retirement isn't all it's
cracked up to be—I missed the school, even the kids
that drove me crazy in the classroom. Oh, I had

my friends, went to church, but that was about all. Vance wanted me at home.''

"Why was that?"

Eileen shrugged. "No reason. The stroke changed him. He couldn't get around as well, couldn't drive. And it affected his mind, too, made him suspicious of me even though I took care of him like a baby.''

"You poor thing," Mavis said, wondering if she wanted to hear more.

"That wasn't the worst of it," Eileen went on as if in a rush to get out the words. "You know Vance—he was always high tempered, easy to anger, but after the stroke he got just plain mean. Hit on Claude, though Claude could usually outrun him. I won't even repeat the things he called his own son. He turned against me, too. Sometimes even now, when I take a bath, I look for bruises before I remember he's gone and can't hurt me any more.''

The tears began again, and Mavis got up and went over and knelt beside Eileen's chair. Taking her hand, she said, "Oh, honey, why didn't you tell me?"

"I couldn't. I couldn't call you when he died. I was glad when he had the second stroke and was gone. He'd become a stranger to me and I was afraid of him all the time. I knew you'd see it in my eyes, and I wouldn't be able to pretend in front of all the others that I grieved. I wanted you so, you'll never know how much.''

Mavis squeezed Eileen's hand, her own eyes swimming. Eileen reached over the side of her chair with her other hand and pulled tissues from a box sitting there and handed one to Mavis. She blew her nose. "It wasn't too long after that I got the idea for the B&B," Eileen said. "Vance built on all these rooms—that was part of his craziness—and I thought it would be something to keep me busy, help me forget a lot of bad memories. Now, it seems like all my efforts have been for nothing.''

''You can't give up now,'' Mavis said, wiping her tears away. ''We're going to open this place and nobody is going to stop us. Come on. We'd both better get to bed. If there's work to do, we need our rest.'' Letting go of Eileen's hand, she pushed herself up. Her knees creaked. Her feet were ice cold.

With a laugh, Eileen got up, too, and threw her arms around Mavis. ''Thank you, honey. You always could cheer me up, no matter what was the matter. I'll thank the Lord tonight for the friend you've been to me all these years.''

And Mavis, standing there with her arms around Eileen's shoulders, ready to say goodnight, remembered a time long ago when she and Eileen first knew each other at Mrs. Dalrymple's boarding house and she had accidentally walked in on Eileen just as she was coming out of a bath. Eileen had covered herself quickly with a towel, but not before Mavis had seen the jagged red scars that crosscrossed her back like the scribbles of a child on a page. The incident was never mentioned, but Mavis wondered now as she had before, Who gave her those wounds? Who could be so mean? And when they finally said goodnight, lying there in the darkness with only the curtain between them, Mavis heard a note of worry in her voice she hadn't meant to put there.

IT MUST HAVE BEEN PAST two o'clock in the morning when Mavis awoke, thirsty as the dickens, her own fault, she knew, for eating so much of that salty country ham. Getting up quietly so that she wouldn't wake Eileen, she went out into the hallway and then to the kitchen, guided by starlight. She opened the refrigerator door, got out the water jar, and poured herself a tall glass. My, that's good, she thought as she walked back onto the porch to stand by the window.

The scene was peaceful now, the pond silvery, with the dark mountain behind it rising up into a luminous sky. Mist hung like gossamer scarves in the limbs of the laurel trees. "Let it all work out, dear Lord," she whispered in prayer. "Give poor Eileen some happiness after all that has befallen her." She was about to turn away when she caught the flicker of movement out of the corner of her eye.

It came from somewhere near the garage, just visible through the windows that opened onto the driveway at the opposite end of the room. Drawing back out of the light, she walked slowly toward it and stood very still in the shadows, looking out. No doubt about it now, someone was there. She leaned forward just slightly and saw a dark figure disappear around the side of the garage where the steps led up to Tara's apartment. Who could it be? she thought in alarm. Someone come to play another evil joke on Eileen? Then it occurred to her that it was probably Claude wandering around looking for treasures. Thank goodness she hadn't alarmed Eileen. Lord knows, she needed her rest.

She was about to turn, ready to take her glass back to the kitchen, when she thought she saw another movement in the darkness. But this time when she peered closer, she realized it was the flicker of stars reflected, bright light on chrome. A motorcycle, that's what it was, parked there in the shadows, the one Jordache had come roaring up on that afternoon. He must have rolled it down the drive in silence. It was his heels, not Claude's, that Mavis had just seen disappearing around the corner of the garage headed for Tara's stairs.

Well, I'll be doggone, she thought, frowning to herself. Those two were carrying on in the garage apartment right under Eileen's nose. She wondered if the poor thing knew.

FIVE

When Mavis awoke next morning, she wasn't sure at first where she was, confused by the bright sound of birds and the clear light coming through the undraped window. But then she raised up, saw the green curtain moving slightly in the doorway, and looked at her watch on the nightstand beside the bed. Lord have mercy, she'd slept half the day after promising Eileen she'd help her get ready to open the B&B! What would Eileen think?

Hurrying, she got dressed quickly in a nice print dress (she'd leave the pants suit hanging in the closet until she got ready to go home), put on her shoes and stockings, and washed her face in the bathroom. If her hair was a little mashed on one side, Eileen wouldn't care.

"Well, good *morning*," Eileen said, smiling, when Mavis walked into the kitchen. "You get a good rest?"

"Too good. You should have got me up long ago."

"No such thing. It's your first day of vacation, and I let you rest. There'll be plenty of work to do later. Sit down there at the counter and I'll have breakfast served up in a jiffy. Claude is already out and gone, no telling where. He's still mourning those ducks. I told him I'd buy him some more when we go to the Farmer's Market." Eileen bent down and checked the oven. "Blueberry muffins," she said and gave Mavis a smile. But when she stood back up again, she looked at her watch and frowned. "That girl," she said. "Where in the world could she be? If she doesn't show up soon, I'll have to buy berries for my cobbler at the Farmer's Market, too, and they'll cost an arm and a leg."

"Who?"

"Brenda Trull. She's been working for me this summer, helping to get the place ready. A high school girl, a freshman this coming year, usually as reliable as can be. She promised faithfully she'd come early this morning and pick me some blackberries so I could make you one of those old-fashioned cobblers you used to like so much. The woods are full of them this summer."

"Maybe she's just running late, slept half the morning, like me." Mavis laughed.

"No, I don't think so," Eileen said, the frown replaced by a worried look. "She's not the type. I've known her ever since she was in my class for first grade. Always was a smart little thing, a hard worker. As much as anything else, I hired her to help *her* out. She doesn't get much encouragement at home." Eileen suddenly snapped her fingers. "Maybe that's it," she said. "Maybe she got her feelings hurt."

"Why? What do you mean?"

"I was real busy when she was here yesterday morning, trying to get everything done before it was time to go pick you up from the bus. Brenda did everything I had for her to do, and when I asked her about the berries she said yes, ma'am, she didn't mind. But then she said, 'I've got something real important to talk to you about, Miz Hollowell, do you have time now?'

Well, I didn't and I told her so, but I said we could talk this morning after she came with the berries. I could see she was disappointed, but what else could I do?"

"Can you call her now?"

"No, the Trulls don't have a phone. In spite of all the developments, there are still some *backwards* folks in these hills." She shook her head. "Her family just scrapes by. Brenda's mama raises a few things to sell at the Farmer's Market, and her daddy does odd jobs around town when he's not at the church or out witnessing on street corners. He's so taken up with religion he hasn't got much time for anything else. Like I said, as much as anything else, I gave her a job so she'd have a little something for herself."

"Does she live far? Why don't you go check if it would make you feel better?"

"You don't think I'm crazy then?"

"No, of course not. I bet anything she just forgot. You know how flighty girls are at that age."

Eileen gave a big sigh. "Well, maybe I will," she said and bent over to take the pan of muffins out of the oven.

"Can I have one of them muffins?" It was Claude standing in the doorway to the back porch. His arms and hands were covered in dirt, burrs clung to his clothing.

"Where in the world have you been rooting?" Eileen said. "You're dirty as a pig."

"I've been looking for clues."

"Clues to what, pray tell?"

"Who killed my ducks."

"Well, did you *find* anything?" Eileen gave Mavis an exasperated look.

"There were some plants mashed down where who-ever did it stood. They must of come in the back way. I'm gonna see if I can follow their footsteps."

"It'll just be a waste of time."

"Won't neither."

"Claude Hollowell, don't you argue with me."

He hung his head, then looked at Mavis and changed the subject. "You want to come see my collections now?"

"Later, maybe, honey," she answered, not wanting to hurt his feelings. Sometimes, Eileen was real short with him.

"For the Lord's sake, let Mavis eat her breakfast in peace. Here." Eileen handed him a muffin, and he took it and went over to the coffeemaker and poured himself a cup.

"I bet I find something," he said, ducking out the door before Eileen could fuss at him again.

Setting a plate of muffins on the counter in front of Mavis, Eileen said, "That boy, he'll be the death of me yet." But something in her voice said she loved him more than anything else in the world and that if anything happened to Claude, it would be the end of her.

EILEEN CAREFULLY DROVE up the drive to the gate and then turned into the road, going in the opposite direction from town. As soon as they rounded the first curve, Mavis's favorite scene came into view: an old stone house sitting in the midst of a pasture surrounded by a split-rail fence. Flowers grew all across the front, and a neat garden lay behind. Nearly always, a pair of horses stood beneath a single graceful tree near a huge stone slab that looked as if someone had plunked them right down in the middle of the field to make a fine picture. Beyond, the land dipped down quite quickly, and you could see farms spread out across the valley, connected by ribbons of roads like an old-fashioned crazy quilt. Eventually they merged into a misty blur blue as a baby's eyes on the far horizon, and there was no way of telling where the mountains ended and the sky began.

"Well, at least that's one thing that hasn't changed," Mavis said with a sigh.

"What?" Eileen asked.

"That view." Mavis pointed. "I wish I had a painting of it to put over my mantel in the living room."

"Thank the Lord," Eileen said. "I hope I'm not around if somebody gets hold of that land and puts up a bunch of tacky houses to block the view."

The road narrowed after a mile or so, dipped down, and they were surrounded by overhanging trees. Sun shot through the leaves in bright patches, and they could see a last few rhododendron blossoms shining like ghostly lights in green shadow. The air was cool, smelling of damp, and every now and then they could hear the sound of water rushing over rocks. When Eileen suddenly slowed and turned off by a mailbox mounted on a pole, Mavis gave a little start, lulled by the ride. "My goodness," she said and sat up straighter.

There was no real road, just two dirt tracks cutting through the trees. In a cleared-off space up ahead the body of an old car sat on sawhorses, its wheels missing and its windshield smashed, weeds growing knee-high around it so that you knew no one had done a lick of work on it in years. A truck in not much better shape was parked beside it. Nearby stood the house, a cabin really, with a porch across the front, a swing, and a row of tin cans planted with coleus going to seed set at the edge. A four-legged washing machine with a wringer on the top was propped against the steps. "Lord, I don't know when I've seen one of those," Mavis said.

"Don't be surprised at anything," Eileen said and stopped the car. She honked the horn but did not get out, and when she got no answer, called, "Anybody home?" A dog came from beneath the house, a mongrel with burrs in its thin coat, stretched, wagged its tail as if glad of company, and then sat down. "Well, I guess we won't get bitten by that ferocious beast," Eileen said and opened her door. The dog didn't move, and she got out. Mavis followed.

"Looks like nobody's home," Mavis said as she followed Eileen up the dirt path to the steps. Old pieces of machinery lay in the yard like discarded bones.

"I'll just knock," Eileen said and started up the stairs.

Just then, the screen door opened and a girl came out, stood still holding the screen as if she might rush back inside, but didn't say anything. She couldn't have been more than ten or eleven, already developing, with small breasts that strained against the T-shirt she wore, no sign of a bra. A faded blue skirt drooped almost to her bare feet, and her pale hair fell lank around her face. "Why, hey there, Kristal," Eileen called out in a voice that Mavis knew she was trying to make sound friendly. "I came by to see if anything was wrong with Brenda. She didn't show up this morning the way she was supposed to."

The girl let go of the screen door and walked to the edge of the porch, looking down, her eyes still wary.

"She ain't here," she said and folded her arms across her breasts.

Eileen stayed where she was. "How about your mama and daddy, they home?"

Kristal jerked her head to the side. "Mama's gone to the Farmer's Market. My daddy's around yonder."

"Well, we'll go see him a minute," Eileen said, then turned away from the girl on the porch. "Come on," she said to Mavis and started across the yard. "There's one headed for trouble mighty sure and certain," she whispered as soon as they reached the corner of the house. "I had her in school, too, and she's not a bit like Brenda. And there are two more like her inside the house. Line 'em up and they'd look like stair steps. You can see the bad blood in their eyes."

The back yard was even more littered than the front, though there was a large flower garden, carefully tended, staked out in a sunny spot off to one side. Strangely, most of the blossoms had been cut. Near the back porch stood several flat wooden crates, and as Mavis and Eileen approached, they could hear the strains of a country music station, punctuated by the tapping of a hammer, coming from nearby. "Hey there," Eileen called out. The tapping stopped, and a head appeared around the side of the house, the eyes suspicious, the same look that Kristal had on her face when she first opened the screen door. "How're you, Mr. Trull," Eileen said and stopped, as if there was a line drawn in the dirt they shouldn't cross. The head disappeared for a moment; then Mr. Trull walked from behind the house towards them.

He was a thin man, wiry, the tendons in his neck stretched tight, as if he'd been pulled in opposite directions. He wore a baggy pair of dark gray pants that probably once had been part of a suit, a V-necked undershirt that needed washing, and a pair of work boots. On his head sat a felt hat with a greasy band, and when he stopped in front of them, he pulled it off with a dark-stained hand. "Good day, ladies," he said in a mournful voice, giving them a little nod. Mavis could smell his sweat.

"How are you, Alton," Eileen said. "This is my friend Mavis Lashley, visiting from Markham. I came to ask about Brenda. She didn't come this morning like she was supposed to, and that's not like her. Is she sick or something?"

Alton Trull put the hat back on his head. His eyes turned up as if he scanned the sky for rain clouds. "She's not here," he said after a moment.

"Well, where is she?"

"I don't rightly know. She won't in her bed this morning when little Kristal went in to wake her."

"Didn't you *worry?*"

Alton Trull gave Eileen a curious look. "No, ma'am. I believe in the Lord. She's in his hands. I gave up on her. It's not the first time she's strayed out, listening to godless music, dancing, nothing but boys on her mind. It wouldn't surprise me one bit if her and that one she's been seeing run off together."

"At fourteen? Mr. Trull, how could you imagine such a thing?"

"Her mama won't but fifteen when we got married," he said with a shrug.

"What about Mrs. Trull? What does she say?"

"She don't rightly know. I got up early to take her to the Farmer's Market. It won't till I come back that I found out Brenda was gone."

"Don't you think you should call the sheriff? What

if Brenda didn't run off on her own accord? Something could have happened to her. You can read about things like that in the paper every day.''

Mr. Trull shrugged again. "Like I said, I've left it up to the Lord. If it's his will, she'll be home again and accept her punishment. If she's run off to a life of sin, he will see her and punish her no matter where she goes. There's no escaping him.''

Have mercy, he looks like he's going to start up preaching right here in the middle of the yard, Mavis thought to herself. She looked at Eileen beside her and knew as good as anything Eileen was just about to burst with anger at this man who seemed to care so little about his child. "Maybe we should go," she said in a low voice, and Eileen nodded.

"Well, I thank you," Eileen managed to say. "If Brenda comes back, you tell her I'll be expecting her on Monday morning.''

"I'll do that," Mr. Trull said, tipping his hat again. He turned and loped away towards the rear of the house, and before Eileen and Mavis reached the front yard again they could hear his hammering.

"That turd!" Eileen said. "Any dog would care more about its puppies than that fool." She pointed to the animal still lying in the dirt that had first greeted them when they drove up, and it wagged its tail again. On the porch Kristal stood with two other younger children who watched Mavis and Eileen with careful eyes, scratching mosquito bites on their arms. "Bye, honey," Eileen said and waved, and Mavis could hear how hard she was trying to cover up the anger in her voice. The children did not respond. "Come on," she said to Mavis. "We've got someplace to go.''

They walked back across the yard, careful not to trip

over the scrap metal. Just before they reached the car, Eileen suddenly stopped and took hold of Mavis's arm. "Look," she said, pointing to a stand of trees at the edge of the road.

"What is it?" Mavis peered forward.

"Brenda's bicycle, lying there under the branches. That's how she gets around. If she's gone, why is it still here?" Eileen gripped Mavis's arm even tighter. "What if something bad really *has* happened to her?" she said. "Lord, if only I'd listened to her when she wanted to talk to me. What do you think she might have told?"

SIX

"WHERE ARE WE GOING?" Mavis asked when Eileen went whizzing right past her own gate, headed for the highway that led into town.

"To the Farmer's Market," Eileen answered her. "I want to talk to Wanda Faye Trull, Brenda's mama. I hope and pray *she's* got some human concern. I can't believe she'd just let her daughter roam without lifting one finger to find her."

When they got there, the parking lot was filled, and they had to circle around three times before they found a spot. Mavis remembered the market from before, when she and John had first started coming to Monroeville on their summer visits. Back then, it was a meeting place for local farmers to sell off any extra produce they might have and exchange a little gossip on Saturday morning. You could buy fresh fruits and vegetables for practically nothing, and jars of home-made jams and pickles that Mavis purchased as small gifts for friends back home.

Now, the place had become as much a tourist attraction as anything else. The white-painted wooden building, one block over from the main street, had been added onto two or three times, but even then, by eleven o'clock any summer morning you could hardly push your way through the crowds. There was no end of things for sale—vegetables gathered before dawn, still moist with dew, local peaches and apples just coming in, bouquets of old-fashioned flowers, Queen Anne's lace and wild pink summer roses, jars of jelly lined up on shelves in the windows as bright as stained glass when the sun shone through. Blue ribbons were proudly displayed. Out back, chickens and rabbits and ducks were for sale. Children played among the animals while their daddies, leaning against trees in the shade and talking baseball scores, watched them until their wives got back loaded down with bags and a treat for the kids—homemade lemonade, popcorn, or a penny whistle carved by some mountain man. To Mavis it was more fun than a county fair.

"Well, how're *you?*" Eileen greeted people in the stalls as they passed through the noisy aisles.

"I think you know every single soul here," Mavis shouted in her ear.

"Just about. I've been coming I don't know how many years. You get to know a lot of faces if not all the names." She suddenly stopped. "Now look here, aren't these the prettiest berries? Give me a quart," she said to the woman who stood behind the stand just beaming. "I'm going to make us that blackberry cobbler no matter what." They stood waiting while the woman carefully put the basket in a brown paper bag. "It's highway robbery," Eileen whispered to Mavis after she'd paid the woman and they were walking away. "But I can't get out to pick them and Brenda didn't show up the way she was supposed to."

Without warning, she stopped suddenly, and Mavis almost bumped into her. "Dear Jesus," she said. "I almost forgot why we'd come, too busy looking for my berries. Come on. Wanda Faye's stand is down this way.'' She started walking again and Mavis hurried to follow her, trying not to knock people aside.

Somehow, Mavis could tell which stall belonged to Wanda Faye Trull even before they got to it. Small and narrow, with just a little bit of stuff on display, it looked half empty, the jars of jelly watery looking and pale, the awkward printing on the little strips of adhesive tape to identify the flavor already beginning to fade. The snap beans put up in old-fashioned Mason jars looked gray, and the few tomatoes spread out on the counter were knotty, with bruised spots on the sides.

But, oh, the flowers, weren't they the prettiest things! Bunches of black-eyed Susans, tall shafts of red hot pokers, zinnias as wide across as a saucer, bright marigolds giving off a pungent scent. Mavis remembered the cut-off flower stems in the garden staked off in the debris of the Trull's backyard and realized that these flowers had bloomed there until just this morning when Wanda Faye, up before light, had cut them and brought them to the market. Did it hurt her to part with them, she wondered, that one gift of beauty in her life? Maybe the Lord, seeing the barrenness of Wanda Faye's days, had smiled down on that little plot of ground and blessed those plants. Certainly, it didn't seem like he'd done much else for Wanda Faye Trull.

"How do?" she said when Eileen introduced Mavis, briefly catching her eye, then looking down. She was a short woman with a moon-shaped face and a long plait of dull hair wound around her head. Her upper teeth were missing and the skin on her arms had reddish splotches from too much time spent in the sun. The pink polyester sweater she wore had a large stain at the waist. Poor thing, she's still *young!* Mavis thought to herself and almost put out her hand in comfort. What sort of life had she led?

"We were just over to the house," Eileen said.

Wanda Faye looked up. Mavis saw that her eyes were cornflower blue. "Is that right?" she said, waiting.

"Brenda didn't come over this morning. She was supposed to pick me some berries, and she was going to wash a whole bunch of new towels and sheets to get the sizing out. She's always been dependable before. Any idea where she's at?"

"No, ma'am." Wanda Faye looked down again and began to unravel a thread on her sweater.

"Did you see her this morning?"

"No, ma'am. I have to get up real early to get things ready to bring to the market. Alton drives me. The children don't get up till later."

"How about last night?"

Wanda Faye still didn't look up. "She ate supper with the rest of us, like usual, then went off to her room and shut the door. She's been real moody lately, changed. Her and her daddy get into these awful fusses about her not wanting to go to church. I tell Alton it's something she's going through, but he don't seem to understand."

"Mr. Trull said she might of run away."

"Why would she do a thing like that?"

"*I* don't know. You have any ideas?"

Wanda Faye shrugged her shoulders. "She's got nothing to be afraid of. I don't know why she'd be unhappy."

"Your husband said she'd been seeing some boy, sneaking off. Is that right?"

"Could be. Brenda never tells me a thing. Her daddy

said he seen her with some boy in town, he didn't know who.''

"Well, what will you *do* if she doesn't come home?'' Mavis could hear the exasperation in Eileen's voice. "Don't you think you should call the sheriff just in case?''

"In case of what?'' Wanda looked blank.

"In case something happened to her. You never know these days.''

"I'll have to ask her daddy. He don't have much truck with the law, not since they arrested him for witnessing on the street corner. We can take care of our own, thank you kindly, ma'am.''

Wanda Faye turned just slightly and began to rearrange the jars of jelly on the counter in front of her. It was obvious she wasn't going to say anything more. "Let's go,'' Eileen said and started to turn away.

"Wait,'' Mavis said, putting her hand on Eileen's arm. She got out her change purse. "I want to buy a few things. I always take back little gifts when I visit,'' she said to Wanda Faye. "Give me three of those jellies and a nice bunch of flowers. They'll be pretty on the supper table tonight. How much?''

For the first time, the woman smiled, then told Mavis the amount and pulled out a wrinkled paper bag, wrapped the jars in sheets of newspaper, and put them carefully inside. She shook the water from the stems of the flowers and rolled them, too, in newspaper. "Thank you kindly, ma'am,'' she said as she handed them to Mavis. "You come back again real soon.''

"What in the world did you do that for?'' Eileen said to Mavis as soon as they were out of earshot. "You saw the Trull place. There's no telling what's in those jars. You don't want to give them to any of your neighbors unless you plan to murder them.''

"I just felt so sorry for her, standing there like a whipped dog with that little bit of mess to sell and nobody going to touch it. But the flowers *are* pretty. I bought those for you.''

"Lordy, don't you have a soft heart, Mavis Lashley? Come on and let's get out of here before you find another charity case." Laughing, she led the way back to the car.

It wasn't until they were halfway home that Eileen suddenly said, "Oh, my goodness. I forgot to buy Claude some more ducks. I'll never hear the end of it. Well, he'll just have to wait until the next time I go to town.''

SEVEN

WHEN THEY GOT BACK to the house, a new black Cadillac, just washed and shiny, stood in the driveway. "Another damn fool," Eileen said beneath her breath and, hardly slowing, drove around it to the garage, scattering gravel in her wake.

"Looks like one of your guests arrived a week early," Mavis said, a little surprised by Eileen's remark.

"If it's who I think it is, he's going to have that big boxcar off my property in no time flat." She got out of the car, slammed the door and took off up the path to the house. Mavis had a hard time keeping up with her. They entered through the back door, then went into the kitchen where Eileen set the basket of berries she had bought at the market on the counter, and Mavis looked around for something to hold her flowers. By the time she found a metal bucket beneath the cabinet and was filling it at the sink, she could hear Eileen's loud voice in the next room saying, "I thought I told you not to come around pestering me any more. You got a hearing problem?"

Well, mercy, Mavis thought, who is that? She turned off the water before the bucket was full and walked through the doorway to the porch. Eileen didn't turn around but stood with her hands on her hips glaring at the man who sat at the dining table with Tara just across from him, two Coca Cola cans making dark wet stains on the wooden surface in front of them. Tara, dressed in high black boots and what passed these days for shorts but might have well been her underwear, was smiling like the cat that swallowed the canary, and the man, when he saw Mavis, jumped up so quickly that the cans trembled on the table. "Well, who's *this* pretty lady?" he said, grinning at Eileen.

"Nobody you need to know, Boyd Wilkinson. You just get yourself back in that car and drive out of here."

Mavis knew the type. She'd seen plenty like him in secondhand car commercials on TV. Beer belly, hair draped over his forehead the way he had worn it back in high school, dressed in powder blue pants and a patterned shirt to match. He thought he was a real hot shot, flashing his expensive watch whenever he had a chance and stretching up on tippy-toes in white patent leather half boots with extra-high heels, in an attempt to look taller. She wouldn't trust him a minute.

"Now is that any way to talk, Miz Hollowell? I just come by for a friendly little visit, and your granddaughter invited me in. Now, her and I are practically *strangers,* but she was real friendly. You and me, *we've* known each other for years and here you are ready to throw me out of the house." He waited, the grin still on his face. Tara crossed her legs, revealing even more skin, and Mavis thought to herself, I just bet she was friendly, but didn't say it.

"Come on, Boyd," Eileen said. "You wouldn't waste time on a social call. What is it?"

He winked at Mavis. "Isn't she a smart thing?" he said, then turned back to Eileen. "Well, you got me, Miz Hollowell. I came by to make you one more offer." He tapped a white envelope in his pocket. "It's one you can't refuse."

This time, Mavis couldn't keep quiet. "Offer for what?" she blurted out.

"This place," Eileen said, and Mavis could hear the exasperation in her voice. "He wants to buy my land and develop it. Put up some more of his trashy houses."

"Now, you know that's not true." He'd lost the grin and his face began to turn red. "They would be *executive* homes, top of the line, with restrictions so that not just everybody could buy them."

Eileen waved her hand as if she could brush his words away. "Whatever. It doesn't matter. You'd ruin the place, cut down the trees, drain the pond. The animals would disappear. I won't have it."

Boyd Wilkinson shook his head. "Sooner or later, it'll go. You can't stand in the way of progress." An earnest note crept into his voice. "Why not enjoy your later years? Instead of working yourself to death in this B&B you're planning to open up, you could be relaxing in Florida, travel, do whatever you wanted to, no money worries a-tall."

"I haven't lost a single thing down in Florida," Eileen said. "My son lives there, her daddy." She pointed to Tara who looked as if this was a surprise to her. "The one time I did visit it was as hot as the devil and I got eaten up by mosquitos. As for traveling, I like my own things around me and never saw any place else I liked better than home." She gave a little smirk and then said, "Anyway, the land's tied up. It can't be sold."

Boyd Wilkinson looked like somebody had pulled

his plug. His face went from red to pale. "What do you mean?" he finally got out.

"It's in trust," she said. "Fixed so that Claude can stay here the rest of his natural life, with somebody to look out for him. There's plenty in the bank for that—savings, my husband's insurance—and Claude won't want to leave. It's the only home he's ever known. No, he'll be sitting here happy as a jay bird after I'm gone." She laughed right out loud. "Why, I bet he'll outlive *you*, Boyd Wilkinson. He's got the constitution of a horse."

Boyd took two steps forward, then stopped. He threw the white envelope down on the table and he didn't smile. "That's my last offer," he said. "Better take it. There are ways, legal ways, to get you out of here, or at least close up your silly B&B. I'm not finished, not by a long shot." Turning, he bent down and said to Tara in a loud whisper, "Thank you, honey, for your hospitality," then without a word to Eileen or Mavis, opened the porch door and marched outside.

"Well, the hateful thing," Mavis said, as the car started up and then went roaring up the driveway. "Somebody ought to take a horsewhip to that man."

Eileen shuddered and gave Mavis a stricken look. "Don''t say that," she said. "He's just a fool…"

"You're the fool," said Tara, taking out a cigarette and lighting it. She threw the match stem in the Coke can so that it sizzled.

And somebody ought to mash *that* little hussy's mouth, Mavis thought; but Eileen said, "Why? What do you mean?"

"He's right. You ought to sell the place while you can get a good price. It's downright *selfish* to keep hanging on to the place. My daddy could use some

money, so could I. It's unfair to give it all to Claude.
We all should have a share.''

Mavis thought Eileen would surely burst. ''Why
should I do a single thing for either one of you?'' she
asked. ''I hardly even get a Christmas card once a year
from your dear daddy. He never calls. And all he ever
did for Claude was be ashamed of him as soon as he
realized he was afflicted, never wanted to be around
him when he was a child, then moved as far away from
him as he could after he grew up.

''As for you, my darling granddaughter,'' Eileen
said, walking towards Tara who still sat at the table
with a wreath of smoke around her head, a look of fear
rising in her eyes, ''I've done more for you than I ever
got any thanks for. Paid your way to come up here on
vacations, sent you presents on your birthday and at
Christmas time with never a note of thanks in return,
took you in this summer not asking a single question
about what you might be running from. And what do
you do? Call me a fool and lie around the house without lifting a finger to help me—when you're not running off with that trashy Jordache no telling where. It's
a wonder both of you haven't been broken to bits. Just
by the way,'' she said as an afterthought, ''put out that
cigarette. You know I don't allow smoking in the
house.''

Tara jumped up, jabbing the cigarette into the Coke
can. She slammed it down, and it turned over and clat-
tered to the floor. ''You're just hoping!'' she screamed,
her mouth twisting like some small animal in pain.
''Well, it won't be me that gets broken up. You'd better watch your step. You're not so smart after all!''
With that, she turned and headed for the outside
door, dark red, angry looking indentations from

her chair marking the backs of her legs. After the slam of the screen, the house seemed very quiet.

Eileen reached over and took Mavis's hand. She looked tired enough to have done a day's work. "Lord, honey," she said, "I never meant you to come up here to witness all this."

Mavis clasped her other hand over Eileen's. "Now you just hush. You needed me and I came. That's what a friend is for."

Eileen suddenly dropped her hands. "A fine friend I am," she said, her face brightening. "In all this uproar, I forgot we didn't eat lunch. Come on. I'm going to fix us something right now."

WHILE EILEEN FRIED BACON for bacon, lettuce, and tomato sandwiches, Mavis arranged the flowers she had bought at the market in a pretty, cut-glass vase Eileen had taken from the top shelf of the china cabinet on the porch. "It belonged to my mama," she said, "one of the few things of hers I still have, besides the afghan. Everything else just sort of disappeared after she died. Nobody cared anything a-tall about such things back then."

"I know," Mavis said. "I go to some antique shops with Dale—he's a nut about old stuff—and I think: Why didn't I hold on to this or that, it'd be worth a *fortune* now. I guess you're really getting old when they start selling the plates you used to eat out of as antiques."

Eileen laughed and turned from the stove with the spatula still in her hand. "My goodness, aren't they pretty," she said as Mavis stood back to admire her arrangement. "Me, I'd just stick them in there any old jack-leg way and they'd come out looking like weeds."

"I try," Mavis said. "Used to have a nice little garden in the back yard. But it got to be too much work, all that bending and watering. Now, I have a cape jasmine bush that's full of blooms every year, and a rose or two, but that's about all. Except, of course, when Dale comes over with a big bouquet just as a surprise, not even my birthday. He's sweet that way."

Mavis took the vase of flowers to the porch and Eileen followed her carrying the sandwiches. "My, they do look good, I haven't had a decent tomato all summer," Mavis said. Eileen went back to the kitchen for a pitcher of iced tea, and when she came back again, they sat down to eat. "Where's Claude?" Mavis asked, about to bow her head for the blessing.

"Who knows?" said Eileen. "He's probably fixed himself something already. I can't keep up with him." She closed her eyes and said in a sing-song voice, "Thank you for this food, dear Lord, and bless it to the nourishment of our bodies. In Jesus' name, amen."

Looking up, she unfolded the paper napkin Mavis had placed by her plate and said with a laugh, "Well, we finally got a chance to eat something. I bet you're about starved."

"Honey, don't *fret* so. Half the time at home, I forget to eat anything a-tall, or just have me a piece of fruit and a glass of milk. With all you've had to put up with today, I'm surprised you can even think straight."

"That Boyd Wilkinson..." Eileen shook her head. "He'll be the death of me yet."

"Don't say such a thing," Mavis said, "even as a joke."

"I didn't mean it that way. He's just so aggravating."

"How long has he been at you about selling?"

"Since right after Vance died. He must have seen the estate listed in the paper. Naturally, I was polite at first, told him no thank you as nice as could be when he made an offer. It was the first time I'd realized what the land might be worth, and it almost took my breath away.

"But then he started pestering me, always with that smile, but you can see it's not one-inch deep. Sometimes, he'd be a little threatening, say I was violating some ordinance or another keeping livestock, did I know the water was pure, things like that. I still said no. Now I've got Tara putting her two cents in, like they were in it together. Maybe I ought to get out the shot gun and drop some lead around his feet." She laughed. "That'd make him dance a new step or two."

"You said it was all tied up?"

"Yes. I never let that slip out before. Didn't think it was any of his business, and certainly none of Tara's. But I don't suppose it matters now. It's all arranged at the bank. Claude will stay on here as long as he lives, and if he needs anyone to take care of him, that's all arranged, too. Everything around here is going to stay the same if I have anything to do with it."

Eileen balled up her fist and gave the table a slight smack, then wiped her mouth with her nǎpkin. "Well," she said, holding up a finger, "not quite everything. I take it back."

"What? What do you mean?"

"I've been giving a few things away, here and there, to friends. I want to see the expressions on their faces before I'm six feet under. Come on, I'll show you. You can pick *yours* out.'' Eileen stood.

''Where?'' asked Mavis, still puzzled.

''The bottle house,'' Eileen said, already at the door at the end of the porch. ''You know.''

Actually, Mavis had forgotten all about it until now. One day, years ago, on one of her and John's first visits, Eileen had shown them her bottle house. An outbuilding attached to the garage, it was used mainly for storage, for farm implements, and the overflow of canned goods Eileen put up every year in the hot little canning kitchen on the other side. It was dusty, dirty, but all across the back windows, facing the mountains, sat Eileen''s collection of bottles on the wooden shelves Vance had built for her there. All of them were lined up according to size, shape, and color, hundreds of them shining bright as a cathedral window when the sun shone through. Eileen had taken a few into the house, just for decoration, but most of her collection was still here in the bottle house, some of them quite valuable now, Mavis thought. She herself had contributed a few bottles to the display over the years, pretty little ones she'd found real cheap at yard sales on her neighbor's lawns.

''You don't want to give your *bottles* away,'' Mavis said as they entered the unlocked door. She was about out of breath, chasing Eileen down the road that led to the pasture.

''Why not? I've given away some already. If I leave them, they'll just disappear, like all my mama's things. I want people to have one to remember me by.''

The light was murky inside, the sun already hidden by the trees across the drive. Mavis stumbled on the doorsill. Then, when her eyes adjusted, she could see the discards of a lifetime piled up there. Broken garden tools, a torn mattress with a rusty set of springs, bundles of old magazines tied up with cord, a bicycle with one wheel missing, and goodness knows what else packed away in cardboard boxes—there was hardly room to walk. She smelled a damp, musty scent and had to try hard not to sneeze. Maybe Eileen ought to get Claude in here to clean the place out.

She walked slowly. Ahead of her, the rear windows gave a little more light, and dust motes floated in the air. For a moment, she lost sight of Eileen, her view blocked by the elaborate fringed shade of an old floor lamp, and when she heard Eileen suck in her breath as if in pain, her first thought was that she had stepped on something and hurt herself. "What is it, honey?" she called out. "Are you all *right?*" She pushed aside the fringe and caught sight of Eileen's stricken face.

"Oh, Mavis, *look!*" Eileen pointed towards the windows. Tears glistened in her eyes.

Mavis followed her pointing finger and peered through the gloom. "I don't see…" she started to say, but then she realized that the shelves where Eileen's bottles had once stood were all empty, the bottles shattered into a thousand fragments like pieces of a broken rainbow on the floor. Someone had walked up and down the shelves sweeping the bottles off until nearly every last one of them was smashed.

"This is just too much," Eileen said, the tears running down her cheeks. "The ducks, all the other things. Now this. I don't know that I can stand anything more."

Mavis couldn't think of any words of comfort. The bottles could never be replaced. There was no reason on earth for anybody to be so hateful. She wondered if Boyd Wilkinson could have done it, hoping Eileen would change her mind. But how would he have known about the bottle house, and when would he have had a chance, anyway?

Mavis put her arm around Eileen's trembling body. "Come on," she said in a soft voice, tugging just a little, as if Eileen were a sorrowing child who needed comfort. "Let's go back to the house. I'll fix us some tea, put some honey in it. That always makes me feel better, no matter what."

EIGHT

MAVIS AWOKE ON SUNDAY morning and knew it was late by the sun. Still, she did not get up right away but lay staring at the strip of blue sky visible through the window and listening to the whispery sounds of insects in the leaves outside. The house was silent, empty, with Eileen at church and Claude wandering around somewhere, no doubt, in the woods. Nobody had seen hide nor hair of Tara since she'd stomped out of the house yesterday after her argument with Eileen, and if she and Jordache had gone riding off on that motorcycle of his, they'd kept down the racket.

Yesterday. Lord, how painful it was to remember Eileen's tears after the two of them had discovered the broken bottles. They had stood there in silence, arms around each other until Eileen stopped shaking; then she said, "I'll get Claude to come down here and clean up the mess." With the offer of tea, Mavis had gently begun to lead her towards the door, but suddenly Eileen had pulled back and said, "We came out here to get you a bottle. Maybe there's one or two left that's not broken. Let's look." And with that, she had gone over to the pile of broken glass and had begun to brush through it with the tip of her shoe.

"You be careful!" Mavis called out. "And if you

find any bottle that's not smashed, you keep it for yourself.''

"I'll not do it," Eileen said, suddenly crouching down to retrieve an intact bottle. "I made you a promise and I intend to keep it." In no time at all she had found two more, and then, crunching over the broken glass, she led Mavis back outside, a triumphant look on her face, the newfound treasures carefully nestled against her breast.

Mavis raised up in bed on one arm and looked across the room to the small pine chest where the bottles sat catching the morning sunlight. Weren't they pretty! A cherry-red one shaped like a violin, an old medicine bottle with a faded label, and, best of all, a perfume bottle, square cut with a crystal stopper, that reminded her of the ads she read in movie magazines when she was a girl. Mercy, she hadn't been inside a movie theater in years, but back then she'd gone every week and spent any extra money she had on the fan magazines that fed her dreams. In the bottom drawer of her dresser, where she hoped her mother wouldn't look, buried deep beneath some Bible story books she'd had as a child, she kept a box full of powder and lipstick samples. Endorsed by the stars, she'd sent away for them in secret and, feeling quite sinful, used them to paint her face when no one else was home.

She really should get up. Last night, when they were just finishing up supper (Mavis had fixed the meal, insisting after they had returned from the bottle house that Eileen go take a nice bath and relax with her tea), Eileen asked her if she wanted to go to church this morning. Mavis said, "I don't think so, I'll just stay here." If she were at home, she would have been at church bright and early, ready for Sunday school, but attending another church was different, like sleeping in a strange bed. You didn't know the people, the preacher; they sang songs you've never heard from the hymnal, and the choir robes were the wrong color. You just got *used* to things and wanted them to stay the same. "No, you go on by yourself," she'd told Eileen. "Maybe it'll do you good to get this place off your mind for a little while."

She turned back the covers, got out of bed and made it, then went to the bathroom. She liked the quiet of the house, the small sounds and whispers it made; it would be different when Eileen's B&B guests arrived. Returning to her room, she decided not to dress just yet, no need, and put on her robe and walked down the hallway to the porch and the kitchen. The coffeemaker was on—Claude drank endless cups between his wanderings and Eileen always kept a pot full on the counter—so she poured herself a cup, then looked in the refrigerator and took out a piece of cantaloupe and a container of juice and set them on the counter. All she could get on the radio was the high thin voice of some country preacher whining on about sin, or a rap song with lyrics she knew she didn't want to understand, so she turned it off and took her food out onto the porch and sat down at the table with the view of the pasture and mountain spread out before her like a picture to enjoy.

Claude was probably out there in the woods somewhere. So far, she hadn't seen him go in his old playhouse; maybe he'd outgrown it. She wondered if Eileen had told him to go and clean up the mess in the bottle house. Then she had an idea—*she* could clean up the broken glass, throw it away so that Eileen wouldn't have to give it another moment's thought.

Quickly finishing her breakfast, she washed up her plate and cup and went back to her room to dress. She put on the pants suit from her trip (she'd change later, she'd be embarrassed if anybody caught her wearing pants on a Sunday), and then went outside.

The day was warm, the light bright against the tree leaves. She looked up, and there wasn't a cloud in sight. Eileen's flowers would need watering if it didn't rain soon. Far away, she heard church bells ring, and for just a moment a small feeling of guilt quivered in her chest. Now that's foolishness, she told herself. She went to church every other Sunday during the year— surely the Lord could give her one day off.

Nothing had changed in the bottle house, except that it was brighter, the sun shining through the windows on the back side of the building. Claude hadn't cleaned. Looking around, she found a broom and an empty cardboard box, even a pair of old gardening gloves, Eileen's no doubt, that she put on, and then she began to sweep. She enjoyed the activity—she'd been sitting around long enough—and she began to hum the tune of an old hymn under her breath while she worked. The only other sounds were the scrape of the broom against the floor and the clatter of broken glass when she swept it up into a piece of newspaper and dumped it in the box.

It was then that she heard the roar of the motorcycle flying down the drive, nearly obscene on a Sunday morning. She wouldn't go out. She was still upset about the way Tara had talked to Eileen and had no desire to see Tara's smirking, painted face. Have mercy, she thought, what if she and that Jordache were planning to come to Sunday dinner? She couldn't imagine sitting with the two of them around Eileen's damask-covered dining table set with her good china and silver. Whatever would they talk about?

The noise died down and she went back to sweeping. The job took longer than she expected, and when she had finished getting up the last tiny pieces of glass and putting them in the box, she stood up straight, a sudden sharp pain in her side, and rested for a moment. Goodness knows she didn't want to get down in her back way up here away from home. Maybe she'd have a long soak in the tub. After taking off the gloves and propping the broom against the wall, she went outside again and walked back to the house, careful to stay near the walls of the garage so that if Tara was looking out the window, she wouldn't see her. Parked beneath the trees, the motorcycle seemed to glare at her like an animal.

Goodness, she *was* dirty, dust coating her arms, a dark streak across one pants leg. She had to get that bath. Hurrying, she crossed the porch to the hallway, walked through the shadows to the little sitting room, and then pulled open the curtain in the doorway. "Have mercy!" she said and jumped back, startled. There was Jordache, half-sitting, half-lying, legs spread out, on Eileen's mama's afghan, as pretty as you please.

He looked just as surprised as he raised up and said, "What are *you* doing here?"

Before Mavis had a chance to tell him she certainly had more of a reason to be there than he ever would, she heard a sound from Eileen's bedroom, and hurried over to the doorway and pulled back the curtain before Jordache could get up to stop her. "Well, look who's here," she said.

Tara, trying to poke a bunch of papers back inside

Eileen's bottom dresser drawer, didn't answer her at first. Then, when she was finally able to slam the drawer shut, she stood up and said, "Why aren't you in church?" as innocent as could be.

"Why aren't *you?*" Mavis said right back. "Seems to me you just might need a little help from the Lord."

Tara ignored her remarks. Her eyes narrowed. "Why did you come here, anyway, snooping around. You don't belong."

Well, if that wasn't the pot calling the kettle black! "*I'm* not the one who's doing the snooping," she said, pointing to the dresser. "I suppose you've been through my stuff, too."

Tara smiled. "Whatever," she said. "I like to know what's going on."

"There's not a thing going on except what you're responsible for."

"What do you mean?"

Before Mavis could answer, Jordache got up from the loveseat and came over and stood behind her in the doorway, dark as a shadow. She could smell sweat and a sweet, almost medicinal scent coming from him. For a moment she was frightened, caught there between the two of them with no one else in the house—what might they do to her? But then she half turned, looked up, and saw a gleam of laughter in Jordache's red-rimmed eyes. He was enjoying this, Mavis and Tara arguing like children struggling over a toy. "Why don't you two ladies cool it?" he said in a slow voice. "No need to work up a sweat."

Tara glared at him and said, "Are you taking her side?"

Jordache just laughed at her and rubbed his splayed fingers over his chest. Tara ducked under his other arm propped against the doorway and went flouncing out of the room. "Fuck you!" she called back over her shoulder, and the green curtain fluttered out behind her like a banner.

Hateful thing! Mavis thought. Jordache turned, gave Mavis a wink, and then slowly followed Tara out of the room. "Have a good day," he said, his voice as teasing as his eyes.

Mavis's knees were weak. She sat down on the edge of Eileen's chair by the fireplace. What in the world! Tara going through Eileen's papers while Jordache sat watching—whatever did they hope to find? Eileen's will? The papers guaranteeing that Claude could stay on at the farm after her death? Surely Eileen would keep such things in a safety deposit box at the bank.

Mavis got up and went into Eileen's bedroom. She'd just check the drawer to be sure Tara had left it neat. No need for Eileen to know that her own flesh and blood was snooping through her things. She'd had enough upon her shoulders this summer—getting the B&B in shape, watching over Claude, putting up with that Boyd Wilkinson trying to buy the place out from under her, and now Tara—it was too much for any one person to bear. No, she would not tell Eileen what she had seen.

Bending down in front of the dresser, Mavis had to tug on the drawer to get it open. It was just as she had expected—Tara had left it stirred up like a rat's nest, papers turned every which way. Mavis began to straighten them, trying not to read a single word, but right on top, the very first thing she picked up, was a bundle of letters addressed in a spidery hand she couldn't fail to recognize—Eileen's mother's writing, she'd know it anywhere. Once a week, as regular as clockwork, back when they were young and living in Mrs. Dalrymple's boarding house, Eileen would come back from the post office with a letter from her mother and read it in the cool shadows of the front parlor, later telling Mavis the news from home. Over that year, Mavis had watched the letters pile up on Eileen's side of the dresser, and she would never forget that writing.

She straightened the letters, retied the faded ribbon around them, and started to put them back in the drawer. Beneath the spot where they had sat were a pile of loose envelopes and scraps of paper—valentines, birthday cards (from Vance in happier days, she would guess), a poem cut from the newspaper, a sweet note perhaps from some child Eileen had taught years ago. Mavis put these in order, too, before setting the letters back on top. She was about to close the drawer when she saw the yellowed edge of a folded newspaper at the bottom. "I'm not a bit better than that Tara," she told herself, but she couldn't help but pull it out and read the headline: LOCAL WOMAN CONVICTED IN BEATING. The date above was in the spring before the fall Mavis first met Eileen, and the picture below was of Eileen young and pretty at what must have been her graduation. Next to it was the grainy photograph of a big-boned woman with a stony face being led down what looked like courthouse steps by a man with a gun at his waist. Mavis shuddered and read the story:

This morning at the county courthouse in Monroeville, Mrs. Mamie Spence was convicted of the beating of Miss Eileen Coates earlier this year. Judge Henry Potts deferred sentencing till tomorrow morning.

Miss Coates, a teacher at Six Forks School, had Mrs. Spence's daughter, Tula Spence, in her class this year. According to Miss Coates, the girl had been a problem, and she had talked with Mrs. Spence a number of times about this, to no avail. After one particularly difficult time, Miss Coates said, she resorted to corporal punishment, no more than tapping Tula's hand with a ruler and then standing her in the corner. She thought no more of it at the time.

Mrs. Spence, as was brought out in the trial, was greatly upset and decided to take revenge on Miss Coates. Waiting for her one morning before school (Miss Coates walked from the house nearby where she roomed), Mrs. Spence confronted her on a deserted road. After an argument, during which, Miss Coates testified, she apologized and tried to reason with Mrs. Spence, Mrs. Spence began to beat Miss Coates with a horsewhip, inflicting serious bodily harm. Dr. Walt Pearson, who attended Miss Coates after the beating, indicated that Miss Coates could have been killed if a neighbor had not happened by and stopped the beating.

Mrs. Spence has been held in the Monroeville County Jail since her arrest shortly after the beating since she could not make bail. Her daughter is being cared for by relatives. Mr. Spence disappeared before his wife's trial.

Miss Coates did not wish to be interviewed after the end of the trial, but a family member said that she would probably not be teaching in this area next year, hoping to secure a position somewhere

else since this has been such a traumatic time for
her. Mrs. Spence has not made available any
statement.

Mavis sat very still, the house quiet about her, as if
a pall had fallen over it despite the bright sunlight that
streamed through the windows. Poor, poor Eileen—she
had had so much sadness in her life. This awful event
(no wonder she had wanted to get away and had come
all across the state to Willow Springs to teach, a time
Mavis had thought, until now, was one of such happiness), Claude's twisted birth, Vance's meanness in
the years before he died. Suddenly, Mavis remembered
the criss-crossed scars she'd glimpsed on Eileen's back
in Mrs. Dalrymple's steamy bathroom that morning
long ago. Of course—they were from the beating ad-
ministered by Mamie Spence on the lonely mountain
road. Had Vance added others? She didn't want to
think of it. And, now that Eileen had a chance, finally,
for peace and happiness, somebody was trying to ruin
it by keeping her from opening the B&B.

The sound was like a shot, the car door closing. Mavis jerked her head around but knew without having to
go to the window that Eileen had returned from church.
Hurrying, she carefully folded the newspaper into its
original creases, slipped it into the bottom of the
drawer, and placed the envelopes and papers on top.
Maybe Eileen wouldn't notice.

She got up, her knees stiff from having stooped so
long, and went outside to the hallway and then into the
bathroom, closing the door firmly behind her. Lord,
what a morning it had been! She looked in the mirror
and saw bright tears in her eyes. I'm just a mess, she
thought, dirty as a pig and eyes blood red from crying.

I haven't been of any use at all to Eileen. Well, maybe a bath would help.

She ran the water halfway to the top of the tub and dumped in a handful of the bath crystals she found in the medicine chest and pulled off her clothes. Then, carefully holding onto the rail at the side, she slid into the tub, leaned back, and let the steaming water reach up to her chin. My, the scent was nice. She closed her eyes and let the painful thoughts slowly drift away.

NINE

CLAUDE ARRIVED LIKE CLOCKWORK five minutes before Eileen and Mavis got Sunday dinner on the table. Taking rolls out of the oven, Eileen put them on the counter and said, "I swear, he can smell fried chicken a mile away. It's his favorite. Go on and get washed up," she told him. "It'll be ready by the time you get back." Mavis poured the iced tea while Eileen dished up the chicken and vegetables, and they sat down together when Claude returned from the bathroom, his hands, Mavis couldn't help but observe, not noticeably cleaner.

Claude was quieter than usual during the meal, but he piled his plate high with mashed potatoes and gravy and Eileen's good home-cooked vegetables, and ate three chicken legs and one thigh before he finished. Eileen laughed and said she hoped somebody would invent a four-legged chicken one of these days, it would save her from having to cook up two so that Claude could have all the legs he wanted. "Go get an ice cream bar," she told him as he pushed away from the table, and he got up and went out to the back porch, never answering when she said, "Don't you wander too far. I may need you around here later for a little job or two."

For their dessert Mavis and Eileen had the blackberry cobbler, still a little warm, that Eileen had gotten up before church to make. "You shouldn't have done that, honey," Mavis told her. "You need your rest."

"Shoot," Eileen answered. "I wake up before light most days and can't go back to sleep. I might as well accomplish something instead of just lying there and watching the sun come up. Anyway, I wanted you to have a berry cobbler. It's one of the things you always loved so when you and John used to come up for a visit. Him, too. And it's no trouble. I could make it with one arm tied behind my back. The only thing was, I expected Brenda Trull to pick the berries for me. I'm glad we found some at the market."

When she mentioned Brenda's name, Eileen's smiling face suddenly clouded. She had been in such a good mood after she had come home at noontime, chatting about church business or whatnot while the two of them warmed up the food; it might have been the old days. Now, it seemed as if all her worries had returned. Before Mavis could think of something to cheer her up again, Eileen said, "I do wonder what's happened to that poor girl. I've got a good mind to drive over to the Trulls' place again to see if they've heard from her."

"I'm sure she's just fine," Mavis said, trying to sound hopeful. "She'll probably come riding up on her bicycle tomorrow morning as pretty as you please, wondering what all the fuss is about. Maybe she decided to stay over with a girl friend and forgot to call."

"That's not like her," Eileen said, eating her last bite of cobbler. "And anyway, she couldn't call. Like I said, the Trulls don't have a phone." She shook her head. "I suppose it would be a waste of time, going over to the Trulls' now. They'd never be home on a Sunday afternoon.''

"Why not? They visit kinfolks?''

"No, not that I know of. They're at church.''

"All day?''

"Practically. They belong to one of those old-time churches these mountains are still full of. Strict. Women can't wear makeup or pants, and drinking's out, though I expect a lot of the men cheat on that score. They'd take the kids out of school to shield them from sinful ways if there wasn't a law against it. Alton Trull is one of the founding fathers of the church, so he's there every time the door is open and makes Wanda Faye and the kids go along, too. Maybe it's a chance for Wanda to get a little rest, though I don't know how. You can hear them singing and praising Jesus in unknown tongues a mile away. It would give me a headache.''

They sat quietly for a while after that. Eileen poured them another glass of tea, and they drank slowly, cracking small bits of ice with their teeth. There were no other sounds in the room. My, my, Mavis thought, Tara and Jordache must have made up after their little spat in Eileen's sitting room and gone off together while she was taking her bath. She could see through the window that the motorcycle was gone. Whatever did those two eat? Mavis hadn't seen either one of them set foot under Eileen's table since she'd been there. Probably ruining their health on junk food—no great loss, though that probably was an un-Christian thought, particularly on a Sunday afternoon.

"Well, this ain't buying the baby no shoes, as my grandaddy used to say. I guess we can't sit here all the afternoon.'' Eileen got up and began to stack the plates.

"Here, you let me do that," Mavis said, pushing back her chair and standing. "You haven't let me do diddley squat since I've been here. I'm not a guest in your B&B. I'm going to help with these dishes no matter what you say."

Eileen laughed. "Well come on, then," she said. "I won't refuse. The time *is* creeping up if I'm going to open before the festival. I don't know what I'll do if Brenda really has disappeared."

Mavis felt like suggesting she put that lazy Tara to work, but she couldn't. Eileen had enough to worry about without Mavis bringing up the subject of Tara. Instead, she said, "I've got two hands and feet, and I'm not so old that I can't do a decent day's work. I can help out if you tell me what to do."

"Bless your heart," Eileen said. "I appreciate the offer, and I'll take you up on it. But right now I'm going to follow in the Lord's footsteps."

"What do you mean?"

"He rested on the seventh day, and I'm going to do the same as soon as we get these dishes done. Maybe a little nap will perk me up. I slept even worse than usual last night, after all that happened." Eileen turned and started towards the kitchen with a stack of plates, and Mavis followed along behind her. Then, all of a sudden, Eileen stopped right in the middle of the floor so that Mavis almost bumped into her. "Darn!" Eileen said. "I forgot. Maybe I won't get that nap after all."

"Why?" Mavis asked.

Eileen put the plates on the counter and reached for her apron. "The mess in the bottle house," she said.

"All that broken glass. I meant to tell Claude to clean it up, but I forgot. I'm afraid to just leave it—somebody might go in there by accident and get hurt. Then I *would* be in trouble. I'll go do it as soon as we get the dishes done."

"No you won't." Mavis knew she was giving Eileen a smug little smile.

"Why not?"

"I did it this morning while you were at church."

"Why, what in the world!"

"I told you I'm not helpless. I wanted to do something useful, and maybe I felt a little guilty about not going to church. Anyway, the glass is all swept up. All you need to do is tell Claude where to dump it."

"Well, thank *you*. I guess I *will* get my nap. You want to lie down, too?"

"Goodness no! I laid in bed half the morning. You go on. I'll finish up here and then read a while. Don't worry about me."

Eileen untied her apron. "I'll take you up on that kind offer," she said, laughing, and then started out of the room. "If you don't hear me in a half hour or so, call. If I sleep too long, I won't get a wink tonight."

Mavis finished putting the dishes in the dishwasher, but didn't turn it on. She washed the pots and pans by hand, wiped off the counter, and hung up the dishcloths on the back porch. It didn't take her five minutes. From now on, she'd insist on helping Eileen more. Poor thing, she'd worked herself half to death. Now that she was here, Mavis could at least do what she could to help.

She went out onto the porch and sat down in one of the easy chairs. On a table beside her lay a copy of *Southern Living,* and she picked it up. Leafing through

the pages, she read all the recipes, but she knew she'd
never make such fancy dishes even if she asked Eileen
if she could cut out the pages. When John was alive,
he had liked plain cooking, and though she knew that
Dale went out to some of the fancy restaurants that had
opened in Markham in the past few years, when he
came to her house for a meal, he'd always tell her
beforehand, "Keep it simple. I don't get much home
cooking. And if there are any leftovers, I'll gladly take
them with me."

Feeling a little restless, she put down the magazine.
"Maybe I'll take a walk," she said aloud and then got
up from her chair. She could stroll down the road to
the pasture. So far, she hadn't gone any further than
the bottle house, and the exercise would do her good.
She still felt a little stiff from the long bus ride. Turning, she started towards the door, but suddenly she
caught sight of the pond and remembered its darkening
surface the night the ducks were killed. She shuddered.
Maybe it wouldn't be safe to go down there alone.
Then she told herself she was being silly. It was broad
daylight on the Lord's day, and she'd just have to trust
in him to protect her.

Outside, the sun shone brightly, a few scattered
clouds making dark shadows on the mountain top, not
enough to promise rain. The flowers along the road
were beginning to droop, but when Mavis passed the
bottle house and stopped at the edge of Claude's garden, she saw that the earth there was damp from a
recent watering. She laughed. Wasn't that just like
him? He wouldn't take notice of the flowers at all but
he'd keep his garden watered as regular as clockwork.

She reached the gate to the pasture, pushed it open.
With no animals there any longer it was never kept

locked. Walking carefully so as not to snag her hose on the weeds that grew between the tracks, she started down the road. A Sunday afternoon quiet prevailed, though once she heard the slam of a car door and a child's cry coming from just beyond the trees at the edge of Eileen's property. It was easy to forget the development was there. She hoped Eileen could hold out against the pressures to sell her land, though she supposed it was only a matter of time. When she and John first started coming here, it was a real wilderness, with deer coming every morning down to the little pond to drink and the sharp cry of wildcats interrupting the night.

Now, there was another kind of animal, two-legged, lurking there, one that killed ducks and no telling what else. She shook herself and walked further down the road.

The pond was placid now, the surface a mirror reflecting the clouds. She'd cross the pasture except that there was no clear path and the weeds grew high there. Instead, she walked over to the other side of the pasture where the road disappeared into the trees. She and John had walked through the dappled leaves with no fear, listening to birdsong and looking for wildflowers; the road seemed to have no end. Once Eileen had told them, "Vance has cleared him off a place way on down that road in the middle of nowhere and says he's going to build us a house there. 'You do, and you'll live in it by yourself,' I said. 'I'm perfectly happy right here and don't aim to become a hillbilly.'" Mavis wondered if the spot had all grown up again.

She did not enter the woods. Lord knows, there was nothing foreboding about them on this quiet Sunday, the pale green shade inviting, but, somehow, she didn't want to wander there alone. Turning, she stood for a moment before retracing her steps back along the road, looking at the view. It was like a picture seen from a different angle—the house with Vance's additions, the garage and the apartment on top where Tara entertained that trashy Jordache, the bottle house with its empty windows—so placid, until you remembered all that had happened there. She breathed a little prayer that Eileen could find some happiness with her B&B in her remaining days.

The dog seemed to come out of nowhere, its spotted head suddenly appearing through the leaves. Oh, dear Jesus! she thought. All I need is some wild dog chasing after me. She bent down and picked up a rock, but the dog pushed on through the undergrowth, eyes bright, shaggy tail wagging, just waiting for a kind word from her to break into a friendly grin. "You silly thing," she said to it. "You're just out looking for squirrels, aren't you?" And, throwing down the rock, she asked herself, "What in the world is wrong with you, scared of your shadow? Get on back to the house while you've still got some sense." The dog barked once, as if to answer her, then bounded away, and she walked down the road back up to the gate again and let herself out. When she passed Claude's garden, its neat, well-watered rows of vegetables were a welcome sight.

No one was about, Eileen still napping and Tara, no doubt, flying down some country road on the back of Jordache's motorcycle. Where Claude might be roaming was anybody's guess. Mavis looked over at the garage, with Eileen's tacked-on canning room and Claude's playhouse beyond it on the other side, and smiled. KEEP OUT ON PAIN OF DEATH! was printed in big childish letters on the playhouse door.

Poor Claude and all his treasures. How proud he'd always been to show them to her and John. Maybe she'd take a look at them again now. After all, he'd invited her, hadn't he?

She walked past the garage and the canning room to the playhouse and tried the door. It wasn't locked. Pushing it open, she stepped carefully on the clean-swept piece of linoleum covering the dirt floor, bent down, and went inside. How in the world did Claude, big as he was, move around in here? The passageway was narrow—she could hardly stand—and the walls were lined with all the things he'd collected through the years: old license plates, baseball cards, outdated calendars, funeral home fans with pictures of Jesus welcoming the little children on the front, magazines, a few colored bottles that Eileen must have given him from her collection. Everything was stacked as neat as the rows in his garden, and Mavis thought to herself that some of his castoffs might be quite valuable now though she knew Claude would never part with them.

She moved a little farther on, walking carefully so as not to trip. The light coming from the doorway behind her thinned, and she smelled a dank, unpleasant odor that she could almost feel clinging to her skin. A good airing out would help this place, but she didn't suppose Claude would care. Ahead of her lay a slightly larger room, and it, too, was filled with more of his possessions. She looked around and wondered if he had ever played the board games piled there. And where did he get the white-sprayed artificial Christmas tree? Had he won the Kewpie doll and teddy bear at the county fair? Poor thing, they were probably his only friends.

Suddenly, she felt saddened by Claude's hoard of

simple treasures. She was an intruder; she should have waited until he brought her there, let him have that simple joy. If he asked her again, she would come willingly and show more interest than she had ever done before. She turned, ready to go out, but just before she bent down to go through the narrow passage, she glimpsed something out of the corner of her eye. What was it? She moved closer and saw pale limbs, the gleam of hair. Where in the world would Claude get a mannequin to hide here in his secret room? Perhaps he had taken it from the trash behind a store in town.

But then, in horror, she realized that what she saw was no mannequin. It was a real body, a girl, dressed in blue jeans and a bright pullover, dead for sure, a snakebite on her outstretched arm. Now she knew the source of the scent she'd smelled when she pushed open the door with Claude's warning, DO NOT ENTER ON PAIN OF DEATH!

She had to get out. She turned, banged her head, could not see for a moment. The room had become suddenly darker. But that was because Claude was standing in the entranceway blocking out the sunlight, a look of dismay on his face.

It was at that moment Mavis began to scream.

TEN

THANK THE LORD SHE didn't faint. As soon as she began to scream, Claude backed out of the playhouse, turned, and went loping across the pasture faster than a buck and disappeared into the trees on the other side. She'd probably scared him as much as he'd scared her. But even though he was no longer a threat to her, her heart was pounding loud enough to hear in the afternoon stillness, and once she was out the door of the playhouse, she began to run towards the house yelling Eileen's name. When she finally reached the steps to the porch, she felt as if she'd run a long race.

"What in the world is the matter?" Eileen said, opening the screen door. She looked as scared as Mavis felt, standing there in her stocking feet, the press of the pillow still wrinkling the side of her face. "I thought I was having a bad dream, but then I woke up and recognized your voice."

Mavis had to wait a minute to get her breath. If she didn't have a heart attack right then and there, she'd probably be good for another twenty years. "I'm okay," she said between deep breaths. "But somebody else isn't." She pointed over her shoulder in the direction of the garage.

Eileen's cheeks went white. "It's not Claude, is it? Nothing's happened to him?"

"I reckon not. But it's in his playhouse. A dead body. Somebody I haven't seen before."

Eileen's mouth moved, as if she were trying to find the right words, but nothing came out at first. Finally, she simply said, "What? How?"

Mavis shook her head. "I'm not sure. Maybe a snakebite. And I have a guess who it is."

"Who?" Eileen said but there was something in her voice that told Mavis she guessed the same thing.

"Brenda. Brenda Trull. Whoever it is, she's the right age, young."

"Oh, the poor thing. Let me go see about her." Eileen started down the steps towards Mavis.

Mavis reached out and touched her on the arm. "Why don't you wait, honey? You can't do a thing. She's been dead a while, that's for sure. What we've got to do now is call the police. They'll probably ask you to identify the body, and there's no need to put yourself through that twice if you don't have to."

Eileen nodded, started back up the stairs; Mavis followed her. Once they were inside, Eileen stopped, and when she faced Mavis again, Mavis could see tears in her eyes. "Maybe it's all my fault."

"Why? What do you mean?"

"I'd asked Brenda to pick me some berries—to make you a cobbler—maybe that's how she got bitten."

Mavis shook her head. "You're no more to blame than I am," she said. "And anyway, I didn't see any berries. I expect somebody put her there after she died."

Eileen still wasn't comforted. "Do you think it had anything to do with what she wanted to talk to me about?"

"What was that?"

"You know. I told you. On Friday, Brenda said she had something she wanted to talk about, but I was too busy and told her to wait, we'd discuss it when she came on Saturday. She never showed up." Tears welled up in Eileen's eyes again. "Maybe she was already dead by that time."

"It's not your fault a-tall," Mavis said, putting her arm around Eileen. "Now you go on and call the police. If you don't want to, just show me the number and I'll call. Then I'm going to make us both a nice cup of tea."

THEY SAT ON THE PORCH in silence drinking from paper-thin cups Mavis found on the upper shelf of the cabinet next to the teapot. Eileen had calmed down enough to make the call after all. When she came back she told Mavis that the sheriff wasn't in the office that morning, was taking the day off, but they'd call him and he'd be right there since he lived halfway between Eileen's place and town.

When the car pulled up, there was no way in the world you'd ever know it belonged to a public official. Old, a mustard-colored compact covered in dust, it might have belonged to some joy-riding teenager, not the tall gangly man who unfolded himself and climbed out like a clown in the circus. He was well over six feet, younger than Mavis would have expected, out of uniform and wearing a T-shirt with a big splash of color across the front, faded jeans. His hair was bright red, rivaling Eileen's zinnias that grew along the drive, and he had more freckles on his face than you could ever count in a million years. His blue eyes gleamed. "How're you, Miz Hollowell?" he asked Eileen who had gone to the door to greet him. "How's my favorite teacher?"

"I've been better," she said, opening the screen door for him, but Mavis could see that her face had brightened with a smile.

"I guess I know why," he said, starting up the steps. "They said something about a body when they called me."

"Yes, there's one in the shed out by the garage. Mavis here found it."

"How do, ma'am," the man said, his hand going to his head as if he had a cap to tip. He walked past Eileen into the room.

"Lord," she said, "where are my manners. I didn't even introduce you. Mavis, honey, this is Sheriff Lee Rhodes. I taught him in first grade, meanest thing I ever did see." She winked. "Now look at him, wearing a sheriff's badge—at least, when he remembers to pin it on. Lee, this is my friend Miz Mavis Lashley visiting from over in Markham. We've known each other since before you were born."

Mavis offered her hand, and Lee Rhodes held it gently for a moment in his big paw, smiling at her with those pretty blue eyes. Mercy, she thought, if I was forty years younger, I'd set my cap for that one. He was the sweetest looking thing she'd seen since canned peaches.

"Reckon you could tell us what happened?" he said. He looked around, and Eileen made a motion for them to sit down. He perched on the edge of a wicker chair as if he'd break it. His eyes were no longer shining. Mavis sank back into the cushions of her chair, suddenly remembering the darkened playhouse, the figure in the corner with its pale arms and silky hair. Her heart beat faster again. She wished she could make what happened go away so that the three of them could sit there on the porch and drink tea and talk of other things.

"I went out for a walk this afternoon," she said with a sigh. "Down the road past the garden to the pasture. Eileen was asleep and nobody else was around, and I thought I'd just get me a little exercise. It was pretty down there, quiet. I opened the gate and walked down to the pond and up the other side again to the trees." She stopped a moment. She didn't want to tell him of her sense of foreboding, her fright of the dog. Maybe he'd think she was just a foolish old woman imagining things. She shifted in her seat and began again.

"I stood there a minute, enjoying the view, then walked on back towards the house. I would have gone on, but I spied the door to Claude's playhouse and decided to go inside. He'd asked me to come out and look at his things—I'd been there before."

Lee Rhodes had a puzzled look on his face. Eileen came in at that point. "You know Claude," she said, lowering her eyes. "Since he was a little boy, we've let him have the shed out behind the garage where he can keep his mess. Collects everything—you name it and he's got one—and he'll show it off any chance he gets. I told him not to bother Mavis, but it went in one ear and right out the other."

"The door wasn't locked," Mavis continued. "I pushed it open and went inside. Nothing much had changed—just the scent was different, like some animal had died. Then something caught my eye. At first, I thought it was some dummy Claude had picked up, but then I realized it was a real body, a girl, with a snakebite on her arm. I got out as quick as I could and went yelling my head off to Eileen."

Mavis stopped then, and the three of them sat without speaking for a minute. The only sound was the tick of a clock in the hallway and the buzz of insects outside in the trees. Mavis closed her eyes and tried to blot out the scene in Claude's playhouse, not quite sure why she hadn't told Lee Rhodes that Claude had found her there and then, frightened, had run away.

Finally, Lee asked, "Do you know her? The girl, I mean?"

"Not for sure," Mavis answered. "I have a guess."

"Guess?"

Eileen explained again. "She doesn't know her, but we've been talking about her all weekend. Brenda Trull, the girl that's been working for me this summer. She didn't show up Saturday morning the way she was supposed to, and I haven't heard a word from her since. That's not like her. Mavis and I talked to Mr. Trull over at the house and his wife at the Farmer's Market, and they didn't know where she was, either. I tried to get them to report her missing, but they think she's run away with some boy and there's no need. Stubbornest things I've ever seen."

The sheriff raised his eyebrows so that the freckles almost merged. "Alton Trull's girl?"

"Yes. You know him?"

"Better than I'd like to. We have a little trouble with him every now and then over in town. Brother Trull and some of the other members of the congregation preach on street corners, and sometimes they get carried away."

"Well, that's not the worst thing…" Mavis said.

"I know, but they get wound up and start in on passersby, calling out to ladies in shorts and halters 'harlot' and 'strumpet' and such." He looked at Mavis as if to beg her pardon for the words. "It doesn't help the tourist trade a whole lot. Some of the merchants have complained, but we can't do much about their preaching, just tell them to keep it down. I guess if his girl's run away, he's already consigned her to the devil and thinks it's too late to do anything." Lee Rhodes shook his head as if to change the subject. Then he looked up and said to Mavis, "Do you mind showing us what you found?"

"No, sir," she said and stood up. All three of them went outside. Eileen led the way, the sheriff and Mavis following along behind. Now isn't this strange, Mavis thought to herself, walking through bright shade amidst Sunday calm to look at a dead body. It seemed almost a dream. By the time they reached the edge of the garage, she could smell the scent (stronger now, the day had grown warmer), and she thought the others must smell it, too. Eileen stopped at the door with Claude's pathetic warning. "I guess I should go inside. I'm the one that knows Brenda. No need to make Mavis go through it again."

Lee Rhodes pushed open the door, bent down, tall as Claude, and slowly crept through the opening. Eileen followed. Mavis stood outside trying not to breathe, her eyes fixed on the silvery pond where the ducks had been killed.

Then she heard a sob. "Oh, sweet Jesus!" It was Eileen's voice. "It's her," she said. "I was hoping it wouldn't be, but I guess I knew all along it was Brenda. Poor, poor girl. I wonder what happened to her."

Mavis turned away from the pond and looked back at the entrance of the playhouse. Eileen and Lee Rhodes emerged, Eileen leaning heavily on his arm as if he were the only thing in the world that could keep her upright. Tears streamed down her cheeks. Lee pulled out a neatly folded white handkerchief and gave it to her and she blew her nose. "I still feel like I'm to blame," she said, returning the handkerchief to him.

"What do you mean?" he asked her.

"I asked Brenda to pick some blackberries for me to make a cobbler. Maybe that's how she got bit."

"I doubt it. I don't think there's any snakes wandering around your garage. Somebody had to have put her there." Lee patted Eileen's arm. "Come on. Let's get you back to the house. I've got some calls to make. You just take it easy."

"Yes." Mavis took Eileen's arm. "You go on ahead," she said to Lee. "We'll be just fine." He gave her a smile and hurried back up the path towards the house. "Come on," she said to Eileen. "We can't do anything else here. It'll be up to somebody else from now on."

Lee Rhodes was just finishing up a call to the medical examiner's office when they got back to the house. "He'll be out shortly," he said, "along with some people that do the laboratory work. You shouldn't have to answer any more questions." He gave his radiant smile again, but then his face darkened, as if a cloud had passed over the sun. When he spoke, his voice was low and halting. "I hate to ask, Miz Hollowell, but I do have one last question."

"What's that?" Eileen sank down into a chair, and Mavis saw the weary lines on her face.

"Do you know where Claude is? We'll need to talk to him."

Mavis thought Eileen might faint. She went over and stood by her chair.

"Oh, Lord, you don't think he had anything to do with this?" she said.

"It's hard to know. It *was* his place where the body was found. But, of course, anybody could have put it there, not just him."

Mavis almost told him that Claude had found her in the playhouse and then had gone running off to the woods when she screamed, but she caught herself and remained silent. No need to add to Eileen's worries; they'd find Claude sooner or later without her help.

"I can ring the bell," Eileen said, trying to stand. Mavis helped her up.

"Bell?"

"Yes. Vance, my husband, put it up years ago out by the garage. If he wanted Claude for something, he'd bang on it and you could bet Claude would come running, wouldn't want to make his daddy mad. It'll probably still work."

"You sit still," Lee said. "Tell me where, and I'll go ring it."

"Thank you," Eileen said. "I don't think I'd have the strength. It's just past the garage, next to the bottle house. You can't miss it."

Lee hurried out the door, and Mavis and Eileen sat down again. If he didn't know where the bottle house was, he didn't say. Mavis wondered if they should tell him about the broken bottles. So many strange things were happening. Maybe they were all connected in some way. Would somebody kill to keep Eileen from opening her B&B?

The bell rang out then, the sound reverberating in waves over the pasture to the trees and beyond, echoes extending it. Dogs barked in the development next door, and out on the road a few passing cards honked their horns. "That's enough to wake the dead," Mavis said and immediately regretted her words.

Eileen didn't seem to notice. "That'll get him, if anything will. Vance would wear him out even after he was grown if he didn't come running."

They waited on the porch until Lee came back. No one said a word, waiting for Claude to appear. But the clock ticked on in the hallway and there was no sign of him, and when two cars and a van crunched down the driveway and stopped, it gave them a feeling of relief, no one having to ask finally: Where in the world could he be?

"It's the medical examiner and the guys from the lab," Lee said and walked towards the door. "You ladies don't need to come. We'll make it as short as we possibly can."

Well, thank goodness for that! Mavis thought to herself. At least, Eileen wouldn't have to go identify the body all over again. But, as she sat there and watched the sheriff walk down the path to greet the three men standing there ("Hey, old buddies, thought you were going to have a Sunday off, didn't you?") and give them a little pat on the back, she had to admit she was curious. And instead of picking up a magazine and flipping through it, like Eileen, trying to take her mind off of what was happening, she watched the men closely as they unloaded their equipment and headed for the garage. "Well, have *mercy!*" she said, almost without thinking, and Eileen looked up and asked, "What?"

"A video camera," Mavis said, pointing out the window. "They're going to put it all on video. Dale says they do that now instead of taking a lot of photographs at the scene of a crime." She shook her head.

"Somehow, it doesn't seem right, though, so *personal* to video someone that's just died."

Eileen threw down the magazine she had been holding and stared out the window with Mavis. The men had reached the door to Claude's playhouse and had begun to film it, letting the camera swing around past the door to the pasture. Mavis half expected to see the pond turn blood red again, but its surface remained flat as a mirror, silver, reflecting. When Lee Rhodes opened the door and bent down and went inside, she could see all over again, as if she stood there beside him, Claude's small treasures, the teddy bear and Kewpie doll and the shiny Christmas tree. And over in the corner, Brenda's body that the camera would track up and down, revealing all its secrets. "Oh, that poor thing," she said almost in a whisper.

"What?" Eileen asked and her voice, too, was low.

"Brenda. I hate to think of those men looking at her."

"I know. I wish there was something I could do. I've got half a mind to get in the car right now and go over to the Trulls' and tell them what's happened, but I guess I better wait on Lee. It may be his duty." She brushed the crinkly hair from her forehead. "Maybe it's just the mean part of me that wants to see their faces when they find out she's dead after they've claimed all along she'd run away with some boy and didn't seem to care."

"You haven't got a mean bone in your body," Mavis told her. "I guess it's hard *not* to be mad with them. But let them live in peace a little longer. Their lives will never be the same again once they find out she's gone."

Eileen got a stricken look on her face. "Oh, Mavis,

honey, I didn't think. Rose, your daughter, she would have been just a little younger than Brenda when the accident happened. You've been through the same thing, lost a child.''

"Yes," she said, "but maybe one thing was different.''

"What?''

"I knew how it happened, saw it right in front of my eyes. The Trulls may never know how Brenda died. I'd think that would be even worse.''

Eileen didn't answer, and she and Mavis sat on the porch in silence watching the door of the playhouse for what seemed like a very long time. Finally, Lee Rhodes pushed it open and came out again, the two men who had gone inside with him following behind. The one with the camera carefully placed it back in its case, and then motioned to the other one to go back inside the building with him. "Oh, dear," Eileen said, "I don't know that I can watch," but she did not turn away.

They brought Brenda's body out, head lolling, the bright curve of her hair falling over her face, and lowered it gently to the ground. Her skin was very pale, and when her arms flipped up as they laid her on a plastic sheet, one of the men grabbed them and held them in the air for a moment like two white, unstained lilies to be placed upon her bier. Remembering the pink roses on her own daughter's casket, Mavis felt tears come into her eyes.

The men worked quickly after that, filming Brenda's body, the medical examiner bending close to examine her. Lee stood just a little ways away watching, but then moved closer and stooped down beside the medical examiner when the other man motioned to him. To Mavis it seemed as if she and Eileen were watching a movie without the sound, except that they already knew the story and could guess the words. Death needed little explanation.

Finally, the men seemed to be finished, stood up, faces solemn, hearty greetings and Sunday afternoon plans forgotten now, and stared down at the body, blocking the view from the porch. Lee must have said something because the little group split apart and the men began packing up their equipment, and Lee started towards the house. Before he was halfway there, they could see that his head hung down, his pace was slow, looking for all the world as if he carried a burden too heavy to bear.

Suddenly, Eileen jumped up. "Oh, dear Lord," she said, "I hope there isn't some worse news." Mavis got up and stood just behind her but didn't answer, and the two of them stayed there on the porch while Lee made his reluctant way, like some messenger with no good news, down the path and up the steps to the porch.

"That poor little girl," he said, looking up so that they could see his wounded eyes.

"What?" Eileen asked and waited.

He came on in and let the screen door slam shut behind him, and the sharp sound seemed to release them. "She didn't die from any snakebite," he said as he leaned against the wall, body relaxed, his freckled arms crossed over his chest. "Soon as we pulled her out in the daylight, you could see the marks on her neck, bruises, made by somebody's fingers. She's been dead at least a day—killed somewhere else and then brought here."

Mavis put her arm around Eileen's shoulder. "Who could have done such a thing?" Mavis asked.

Lee shook his head. "That's what we've got to find out," he said. He looked down again, silent for a moment, and when he spoke, he might have been the little boy Eileen once taught, apologizing for some misbehavior. "Do you have any idea where Claude might be?" he asked her. "You understand, we *do* have to talk to him."

Mavis felt Eileen's body begin to shake, but whatever words she might have spoken were drowned out by the sudden roar of Jordache's motorcycle racing down the driveway, and they heard instead, in the silence that followed, the raspy sound of Tara's voice saying, "What the hell's going on? The place looks like a goddamn used car lot!"

ELEVEN

"YA'LL EXPECTING COMPANY?" Lee asked Eileen and Mavis. His look had changed. Mavis could see anger in those blue eyes. Go on out there and snatch that Tara baldheaded, she'd like to tell him. Swearing like that in public—and on the Lord's day—it was disgraceful. But she felt Eileen's body stiffen and move just slightly away from her arms, and she remained silent.

"It's my granddaughter and her...uh, boyfriend," Eileen said, and Mavis knew how embarrassed she must feel.

"She lives here," Mavis said to Lee and tried to tell him with her eyes that this wasn't the whole story, not by a long shot.

Maybe he understood her. Turning around, he hitched up his blue jeans and with that little swagger men have sometimes, he walked over to the door, opened it, and went down the steps. Mavis and Eileen followed close on his heels.

"I've told them a hundred times they ought to wear helmets," Eileen said in a nervous voice. Mavis wondered if she thought Lee might arrest them then and there.

"Yes, ma'am," he said, still strutting. "We'll see."

Just as he'd been the first time Mavis had seen him, Jordache was lounging against his motorcycle, with Tara standing close beside. When Lee walked up to him, Jordache looked just about as big as a bug you could squash under your foot, and even though he stood up straighter then in his high-heeled boots, he didn't look much taller. Tara, of course, was all wide eyes and pouty lips, about ready to bust a gut, Mavis thought. Most anything wearing pants could get her going, and, no doubt about it, Mr. Lee Rhodes was something *special*.

"Ya'll seem to be in a mighty big hurry," Lee said. Jordache, standing with his eyes down, didn't answer at first, but then mumbled a few words.

"What was that?" Lee said. "Can you speak up a bit?" He looked just like a cop on a TV police show, Mavis thought.

"I was just trying to get Tara home," Jordache said, taking a little swipe at his goatee.

Eileen moved up beside Lee. "Well, I'm glad she's in one piece," she said. "I keep expecting to get a call saying you're both spread all over the highway somewhere."

"There *is* a law about helmets," Lee said.

Tara twitched up and said, "They mess up my *hair*. You wouldn't want that to happen, now would you?" She gave what she must have thought was a dazzling smile, and said, "We haven't been introduced. I'm Tara Hollowell. I'm staying here this summer with my grandmother. Who're you?"

"Sheriff Lee Rhodes," he said and just stood there, hands in the back pockets of his jeans.

Well, that sure took the wind out of their sails, Mavis thought. Jordache looked like he'd like to melt and run away, and Tara's face turned paler than her makeup.

"Who're you?" Lee asked Jordache.

"He's my boyfriend," Tara said before Jordache could answer, her lips less full now and not smiling. "Jordache."

"Jordache?" Lee had taken a little note pad out of his pocket and had begun to write in it.

"That's just a nickname," Jordache said with his hairy chin stuck out. "Real name is Dennis Spence." Lee wrote it down.

"What's happened?" Tara asked.

Recovered now, Eileen said in an angry voice, "If you ever stayed around here more than one minute, maybe you'd know. There's been a murder. Brenda Trull, poor thing, strangled somewhere else and then put in Claude's playhouse. You know anything about it?"

Tara's eyes widened again, this time with a look of fear. Mavis thought it was real. About the only acting Tara was capable of was her flirty act with men, and right at that moment she looked just plain frightened. But she ignored Eileen's question and asked instead, "Did Claude do it? I bet he did. It would be just like him." Right away, the fear began to fade, and Tara glared at Eileen.

"You see," she went on without giving Eileen a chance to answer, though her face looked stricken. "I told you he shouldn't be running around loose. Now, you'll have to sell the place. Claude can't stay here by himself. He'd be too dangerous."

"What do you mean?" Eileen''s words were quite distinct, said one at a time over what seemed like

minutes. When she took a step forward towards Tara, Lee touched her arm.

"Rape." Tara didn't step back. "Did he rape her, Brenda, I mean? I wouldn't be surprised at all." She thrust out her breasts. "He looked at me funny. I told him I'd tell Jordache if he tried to mess around with me. But I felt a little bit sorry for him, though. How could he have a normal sex life stuck out here all the time?"

Well, my goodness, Mavis thought, it was just like watching one of those talk shows on TV, standing around in the broad daylight discussing people's sex lives and such. Any minute, she expected to see Miss Oprah Winfrey come walking around the side of the garage. Then, catching sight of the tears in Eileen's eyes, she felt ashamed of such thoughts, and she put her arm around Eileen's shoulders again.

"That's an awful thing to say," Eileen said, "blaming Claude. Almost anybody could have killed Brenda and put her in the playhouse. It's not locked. Whoever it was could certainly find a time when nobody was around. And if Claude doesn't have a sex life, maybe that's not the worst thing in the world. Better than flaunting it in other people's faces."

"What do you mean?" Tara put her hands on her hips.

"You two." Eileen pointed to Tara and Jordache. "Do you think I don't know what you're doing up there over the garage?"

Smirking, Tara said, "You been peeping?"

"I don't have to. I can hear all the way up to the house."

"Ladies!" Lee Rhodes said. Mavis looked at him and smiled when she saw that the skin between his freckles had flushed bright red. "This isn't the time and place for that kind of argument. A girl's lying out yonder dead, and I've got to call an ambulance to take the body away." He pointed to the three men down by the garage who had been mutely watching. "And they may have a few more things to do on the scene. Can I use your phone again, Miz Hollowell?" He'd already turned and started up the path.

"Of course you can," Eileen called after him and smiled, as if relieved.

Suddenly, Lee turned back around. "Don't you two disappear," he said to Jordache and Tara. "I may want to talk to you some more later on."

Jordache frowned, but Tara had a smile on her bright red lips. If Lee saw it, he gave no sign as he moved off towards the house.

Well, bless him, Mavis thought to herself. At least there's one man that hasn't fallen for Tara's charms. Thank the Lord for *that!*

MAVIS AND EILEEN FOLLOWED Lee back into the house and sat on the porch in silence while he made his call. He kept his voice low, and they couldn't hear his words. When he finished, he walked past them with a smile and a "Thank you, ma'am," aimed at Eileen, and then went back down the path towards the driveway where the others were still standing. Taking out his little pad again, he went up to Jordache and Tara and began to write down the answers to the questions he asked them. By the looks on their faces, Mavis could tell they weren't enjoying that little conversation one bit, and when the ambulance drove slowly down the drive, they looked even more unhappy, as if they realized for the first time that there was an actual body to be carried away.

The two attendants got out of the ambulance, went around to the rear doors, opened them up, and took out a black plastic bag. Lee Rhodes led them down past the garage to the playhouse. Tara and Jordache stayed put, but the men from the lab and the medical examiner joined in behind the others so that they looked to Mavis like a small funeral procession moving out towards the pasture.

"Oh, Lord, I don't want to look," Eileen said, turning aside, but Mavis stood and went to the window and watched the men as they made their slow way.

Working quickly, they unzipped the black bag and spread it on the ground so that they could lay Brenda's body inside. Mavis saw one brief flash of pale skin, but then, with a single quick movement, one of the attendants zipped the bag all the way up again and Brenda was gone. Mavis half expected to hear the sharp sound rend the afternoon quiet. For just a moment, the men stood around the bag, heads bowed as if in silent prayer, but then the two attendants bent down and picked it up. When they began to move back up the driveway, the bag seemed no heavier with Brenda's body inside. The others followed, leaving one of the lab men behind to seal up the door with an official-looking sign.

"Have they finished?" Eileen asked, her head still turned away from the scene.

"Just about," Mavis answered her. "They're putting Brenda's body in the ambulance. That should be about all."

"I certainly hope so," Eileen said, taking a quick look. "I don't think I can stand much more."

"You poor thing." Mavis shook her head. "Sometimes I just don't understand what goes on in the Lord's head to let things like this happen. That poor girl dead, you with what you've been through—let's hope there's some purpose in it all."

Before Eileen could answer, the doors to the ambulance slammed shut, the engine turned over, and the driver began to slowly back up the driveway. The others got into their cars, waiting until the ambulance was through the gate, and then began to move out, too. For a minute Lee Rhodes stood with his arm raised in goodbye, a forlorn gesture that almost brought tears to Mavis's eyes. Jordache and Tara still stood silently by, huddled close to the motorcycle as if they might need to make a quick getaway. Lee ignored them as he walked past and headed for the house.

"Well, that's done," he said, coming onto the porch. Mavis thought she heard him sigh. He smiled at Eileen. "I hope we won't have to bother you much more. The lab people may want to come back again so we've sealed the playhouse for now. But I don't think it'll tell us much more than it already has."

"Did you find anything?" Mavis hoped her voice didn't sound too eager.

Lee brushed back his hair. "Not a lot," he said. "Grass stains on the back of her shirt and jeans, which means she was dragged on the ground somewhere. The snakebite on her arm, though it's not likely that those two little marks killed her. The bruises on her throat. The medical examiner's report is the important thing. We'll just have to wait."

They were silent then. Outside, the birds began to twitter in the trees as the sun sank down. Lee Rhodes stood in the middle of the floor with a worried look on his face, and when he spoke again, his voice was very soft.

"I guess we still haven't heard anything from Claude," he said.

"No sir," Eileen answered him very quickly. "But he might have come up in the woods and seen all the commotion out by the garage and got scared. He'll be back. He's never stayed away from home one night in his life."

"I certainly hope so. But I had to put out a search for him. There was nothing else I could do."

"Oh, no!" Eileen said, her arm thrust out in the air as if she might push back Lee's words from her hearing. Mavis looked sharply at her, not sure what she might do, but Eileen just stood there with an awful look on her face. Maybe it was the first time she'd let sink in how serious all this might be for Claude.

"It doesn't mean we think he did it," Lee tried to reassure her. "But if he put Brenda's body in his playhouse, we need to know where he found her. And he may have other clues. Nobody's going to hurt him. I'll see to it."

"I won't worry about that," Eileen said and sounded as if she meant it. "I just wonder what all this might put into his poor head. He's like a child, never grew up. That foolish Tara, talking about him and sex—why, he'd never think of such a thing. Oh, one time he attended a workshop for a while and started to brag about his 'girlfriend' there, but it was all talk, nothing serious. He wouldn't know what to do even if he got the urge."

Lee didn't answer, and Mavis knew he wasn't convinced. She didn't know whether she was, either. While she wanted to believe Eileen—well, good Lord, you could read all sorts of things in the paper—Claude had a grown man's body, and there were some things you didn't have to learn or be too bright to figure out.

Lee changed the subject. "I'd like to ask you a favor, Miz Hollowell," he said with a question in his voice.

"What's that?"

"I've got one more sad deed—going out to the Trulls' to tell them about their daughter. Would you go along? I'm not even sure I know the way. And it might be easier for them if a neighbor was there with them."

"Why, of course I would, though I'm not sure the Trulls will see me as much of a neighbor. Can Mavis come along? It's been a long day and *I* need a friend there with *me*."

"Sure thing," Lee said, and gave Mavis the biggest smile.

TWELVE

WHEN THEY WALKED OUT to Lee's car, there was no sign of Tara or Jordache. I hope Lee Rhodes put the fear of God into both of them, Mavis thought. They'd probably snuck back over to that dark roadhouse at the junction like two bugs seeking shelter under a rock. The others had gone, too, and a Sunday afternoon stillness prevailed. Any other time it would be a chance to catch a little nap or visit quietly with a friend. But here was Mavis, climbing into the back seat of a sheriff's car ready to go off with Eileen and Lee to tell of murder—what in the world would Zeena and the others at Dollywood think if they could only see her!

There were no other cars on the road when they turned out of Eileen's gate. Around the bend the familiar valley view came in sight again, the mountains a smoky blue now, fading in the light, and flashes of gold were here and there where the sun was reflected for a few brief moments in scattered windows. Mavis, sitting alone in the back seat, almost forgot their destination. In front, Lee and Eileen were silent the whole time, except when Eileen told him where to turn off at the Trulls' mailbox and he said back quietly, "Thank you, ma'am."

At first, it looked as if no one was at home. The rattletrap old truck was gone, and the house looked deserted, the dark windows like empty eyes. The dog, if he was around, didn't bother to come from beneath the porch to greet them.

"Honk," Eileen said when Lee stopped the car at the edge of the yard, and he blew the horn three times, then waited. Nothing happened, so he blew once again, and then they saw the screen door move just slightly. "Well, somebody's home," Eileen said. Mavis, leaning forward to peer through the windshield, thought she didn't sound too happy about it.

Two little boys slipped out the front door, followed by the older girl, Kristal. "Hey, how're you?" Lee called out to them in a hearty voice as he got out of the car, but the children didn't answer, just stood there staring. Careful not to snag her hose, Mavis stepped out onto the grass and then followed Eileen and Lee across the littered yard up to the front steps. "Your mama and daddy home?" Lee asked in a softer voice, and they waited in silence while doves cooed somewhere off in the trees.

Well, at least somebody tried to get them up in better clothes for Sunday, Mavis thought as she looked at the children. Even though they were barefoot, the two boys had on clean shirts and pants, and Kristal wore a nice print dress with a lace-trimmed collar and black patent leather shoes. Mavis would bet anything the dress was a hand-me-down from Brenda and wondered if Eileen had bought the dress for the other girl—it was too nice to have come from the Goodwill store. Kristal pushed back her pale hair and said, "My mama," but no more, and then stood studying the chipped polish on her bitten-off fingernails like a TV movie queen. Sure as anything, Mavis thought, she'd be in trouble before she was fifteen.

"You want to call her then?" Lee said. "We've got business."

Shrugging her shoulders, Kristal started to turn back inside, but at that moment Wanda Faye pushed open the screen door and came out onto the porch. She, too, was dressed in Sunday clothes, navy blue dress, thick, hot-looking hose. Reaching inside her dress to adjust her bra straps, she said, "Well, how're y'all?" in a voice that held no other question and with a look that indicated bad news would be no surprise.

"Is Mr. Trull here?" Lee asked. Mavis looked around the side of the house, half expecting to see him working there, but the yard was empty except for bright new blossoms in Wanda Faye's garden. The crates he had been working on were gone.

"No sir, he's at the church." She gave a vague wave of her hand. "Being one of the deacons, he has a lot of responsibility. They have meetings on Sunday afternoon." She was silent a moment, a vague frown spreading across her face, then asked, "He ain't in no trouble, is he?"

She's recognized him, Mavis thought, Lee Rhodes, the sheriff. But, of course, she would have been the one who would have to go into town to get Alton Trull out of jail when he'd been arrested for disturbing the peace with his street corner preaching. "No, ma'am," Lee told her. He nodded to Kristal and the two little boys. "Maybe you'd like to tell the children to go inside."

Wanda Faye turned to Kristal and said in a sharper voice than she'd used before, "Kristal, take those young'uns inside and read 'em a Bible story," then turned back to Lee and Eileen and Mavis and said sweetly, "Ya'll come on up and sit on the porch. It'll be cooler there.'' Kristal jerked one of the little boys around so hard he almost fell and pushed him and the other one inside. Mavis knew that she'd be standing just behind the screen door listening to every word they said.

Eileen, Mavis, and Lee sat down in rust-eaten metal chairs that Mavis would have wiped off with her handkerchief if she'd had the chance. Crossing over in front of them, Wanda Faye sat down in a slatted swing that looked like it might break at any moment, her feet crossed at the ankles above the floor. Why, she looks exactly like a little girl, Mavis thought. Poor thing, the news they had for her would age her beyond her years.

Lee Rhodes bent forward, as if closeness could somehow soften the blow. ''I'm afraid I've got some bad news,'' he said. ''It's your daughter. Brenda. We've found her—dead. Somebody killed her and left her body over on Miz Hollowell's property.''

Wanda Faye said nothing and her expression didn't change, but tears as big as raindrops began to run down her cheeks. Then she began to make little moans, her body shaking so that the swing began to move back and forth. Her feet dangled. Mavis wanted to bend over and touch her, but she knew the gesture would be unwelcome—nothing could assuage Wanda Faye's pain—so she reached in her purse and brought out a flower-embroidered handkerchief and pressed it into Wanda Faye's hands. Wanda Faye let it lie there as if she didn't know what it was for.

They let her cry, sitting there on the dilapidated front porch while shadows crept across the front yard towards the house. Finally, Wanda Faye seemed to have used up all her tears, and she raised Mavis's handkerchief to her eyes, wiped them, and said in a hoarse voice, "Who done it?"

Lee shook his head. "We don't know. If you feel like it, I'd like to ask you a few questions that might help us find out who it was."

"That's all right," she said, not looking at him. "You go ahead."

Lee sat back again and took out his pad. "Do *you* have any idea who might of done it?" he asked.

"No sir," she said. "Brenda was a good girl, worked hard, made good grades in school. Far as I could tell, everybody liked her. Of course, we couldn't give her all the things the others had—nice clothes, a radio to carry around—but she didn't complain." Wanda smiled at Eileen. "Miz Hollowell was nice enough to help out sometimes. I do appreciate it."

"She give you any trouble at home?"

Wanda Faye was silent for a moment, twisting the handkerchief with her fingers. Then she said, "Her and her daddy got into arguments sometimes. Our church don't believe in wearing makeup, dancing and such, but Brenda was like most girls her age, wanting to try out things. Her daddy didn't like that. And she wanted to go with this boy when we both thought she wasn't ready."

"Who was that?" Lee looked up from his pad.

"Kevin Norris, lives over in town."

"*Kevin Norris?*" It was Eileen. "Why, I know him, taught him way back. He's a nice boy. His mama, too. His daddy got killed in an automobile accident a while ago."

"It didn't matter," Wanda Faye said. "Her daddy didn't approve."

"When did you last see her?" Lee continued.

"Friday night. She went to her room early, said she had to get up early next morning and go pick some berries for Miz Hollowell. I didn't see her after that. I got up at dawn to go to the Farmer's Market. Mr. Trull said that after he got home from taking me she was gone."

"You didn't report her missing?"

Wanda Faye looked down. "We weren't sure she was. She didn't take a thing with her—I checked her room. And Mr. Trull said if she'd run away with that Kevin, it wouldn't make any difference anyway. She'd already be ruint, if you know what I mean. We just hoped they'd go somewhere and get married. Me and Mr. Trull wasn't much older when we did. It's worked out."

Well, you poor thing! Mavis thought. Standing by that fool of a husband, no more concern about her daughter than if she'd been another dog beneath the porch. Hadn't she hoped for Brenda a better life than had been her lot? If she lived to be a hundred, Mavis would never understand how some people's minds worked.

Lee Rhodes seemed to be stumped, too. "That's about all now," he said, standing up. "You get in touch if you think of anything else. Somebody'll be back to talk to Mr. Trull, too."

Struggling towards the edge of the swing, Wanda Faye said, "What about the body?"

"Body?"

"Brenda's."

"Oh, I almost forgot." Lee blushed again beneath the freckles. "There'll be an autopsy. Then we can release the body to whichever undertaker you choose. We'll let you know when it's ready."

"Thank you kindly," Wanda Faye said as she stood up. The swing shot out behind her. Mavis and Eileen pushed back their chairs, walked across the porch, and followed Lee down the steps to the ground. "Y'all come back," Wanda called to them as they started across the yard, no more concern in her voice than if they had dropped by on a Sunday afternoon call to talk about the weather.

And when they got to the car, turned, and looked back at the porch, they could see Wanda Faye still standing there in the same spot, unchanged, except that now Kristal and the two little tow-headed boys were leaning hard against her, like plants needing support. Poor things, Mavis thought to herself. Brenda's death was only one more sad event in their lives. How many more were to come?

THIRTEEN

MAVIS AND EILEEN SPENT what was left of the afternoon puttering around the house. At first, feeling a little guilty that she hadn't gone to church that morning, Mavis tried to read an inspirational tract she had brought along with her Bible, but she couldn't keep her mind on it. And Eileen was off upstairs somewhere doing goodness-knows-what, readying the B&B.

"Can't I help you?" Mavis called out, but Eileen answered back, "No, not really. I've folded these towels forty times already and polished the windows so much I've probably worn them right through. There's not much else to do."

Finally, Eileen came down the stairs, turned on the TV, and the two of them sat watching a ball game with the sound too low to hear until Eileen jumped up when the local news came on and turned up the volume.

"You think they'll have anything on about the murder?" she asked Mavis as she sat down again.

"Lord, I hadn't even thought of that."

"What'll we do if a TV van pulls down the drive and stops right over yonder?" Eileen pointed towards the drive.

"Just tell them to back right out to where they came from and close the gate after them. We aren't obliged to tell them anything."

But there was nothing on the news about Brenda's death, just a lot of baseball scores and warnings about a hurricane forming off the coast and a tune or two from some music festival back in the mountains. "Maybe we'll have one more night of peace," Eileen said, and Mavis could see her relief.

They warmed up what was left from dinner for supper. Neither one expected to be hungry, and when Eileen said the blessing, including a special little prayer for Claude's safety, her voice was shaky with tears. But they both ate a plateful of food, with seconds of iced tea, as if they needed that sustenance to get them through the rest of the evening. There was little cleaning up to do, just a few plates, and they finished washing them quickly. Then they went to sit on the porch, wondering how they would occupy their time.

They were both waiting for the same thing, of course, the call to come from Lee—or someone else—that Claude had been found. Poor thing, Mavis thought, was he alone and hungry in the woods somewhere watching the night come down, the cries of animals in his ears? Was he hiding in someone's barn? Or, maybe even worse, was he locked up with a bunch of hardened criminals behind bars? She wouldn't dare mention a word of what she was thinking to Eileen, but she could tell by the worried frown on Eileen's face that her thoughts were the same.

Still, when the call did come, it startled them so that they both jumped, as if a gun had gone off outside. Half running, Eileen hurried towards the hallway, and when she said, "Hello?" into the phone, her voice was almost a shout.

Mavis couldn't hear most of the conversation, just Eileen saying, "Unhuh, unhuh," in a calmer voice now to whoever it was on the other end of the line. But then she said, "Oh, my God!" and Mavis jumped up, unsure whether some even more dreadful thing had happened and she needed to run to Eileen's aid. The conversation continued, and she heard Eileen say, "Should I come tonight?" There was a pause, and then finally, with some relief, the words, "You're sure now?... Well, if you think it's okay... We'll see you bright and early in the morning."

When Eileen came back onto the porch, her face looked very tired. "What is it, honey?" Mavis asked.

Eileen shook herself, almost as if she might be about to fall asleep. "They've got Claude. Down at the jail. They found him walking along the highway like some lost dog. A couple of people reported him to the sheriff's office, thought he was just another homeless person and were afraid. No wonder. His clothes were all muddy and he was barefoot, of course."

"Are they going to hold him?"

Eileen shook her head, and a look of relief flooded her face. "Just overnight. They aren't going to charge him with anything, at least not yet. They want to question him, but he's too tired right now." A sad little smile tilted the corners of her mouth. "Lee said they brought him supper from the all-night diner across the street. Lord, won't Claude be tickled! He'll eat hamburgers until he busts. Already, Lee said, he's more interested in the officer's badges and guns than anything else. The silly fool probably thinks he's on some outing like the ones he went on while he was at the workshop."

Eileen suddenly looked serious again. "You *will* go with me down to see him tomorrow, won't you?" she asked Mavis. "I don't think I could bear it alone."

Mavis walked over and put her arm around her and gave her a hug. "Of course I will," she said. "You don't even have to ask. But come on now, we both need to get some sleep. Think you'll rest easy?"

"I'll try. At least Claude's been found, but I'll still worry about him. It'll be the first night he's spent away from this place since I brought him home from the hospital. But Lee says he'll be okay, and I have to believe him. I don't have any other choice, do I?"

Leading Eileen out into the hallway again, Mavis turned off the light on the porch. "I'll say a prayer for him," she said. "The Lord will keep him safe."

NEITHER OF THEM SLEPT very well. Mavis kept waking up at the slightest sound—the backfire of a car out on the road, the wind rattling the leaves outside her window—and she could hear Eileen tossing and turning in the next room. And though she would have liked to call out some words of comfort, she couldn't think of anything to say, so she lay quietly, trying to make her mind a blank, in the attempt to go back to sleep again.

Now, as they turned out of the gate into the road, Mavis maintained her silence. Reassuring words for Eileen would just be a waste of time. She drove with her eyes straight ahead, chin thrust out and a determined look on her face, and Mavis knew that her heart wouldn't rest until she had seen Claude and knew that he was all right. What if they *did* charge him with murder? It happened all the time, things like that. Somebody retarded, a drifter—they could trip him up so easily, make him say things he didn't mean. She could only hope that Lee Rhodes was as good a man as he seemed. They'd soon find out.

The jail was in the country courthouse, a red brick

building with white columns and a wide expanse of steps located one block off main street just up from the Farmer's Market. "You mind a little walk?" Eileen asked Mavis. "There's no market today, and we can probably find a place to park there." Mavis told her no, so Eileen turned into the lot, found a spot beneath a tree, and they got out of the car and headed back towards the jail.

The entrance was on the side, a doorway at ground level with no sign that led into a dark hallway filled with smells Mavis wasn't sure she'd want to identify. They walked slowly, half blinded after the early morning brightness, then saw a sign that said VISITORS with an arrow pointing left. Turning, they came to a large room with wooden benches, all empty this time of day, and a single person on duty at the desk there, a woman with bleached blonde hair in a uniform reading the paper. "Can I help you?" she asked without looking up.

Eileen stepped close to the desk and said, "I'm Miz Eileen Hollowell," and waited for just a moment. Mavis remembered that steely voice. Back when she and Eileen were teaching together, Eileen would use it on some fresh boy in her class, a head taller than she was, and it would stop him dead in his tracks.

"Yes, ma'am?" Laying down the paper, the woman looked up and smiled.

"My son's here. Claude Hollowell. Sheriff Rhodes knows me. You care to call him?"

The woman reached for the phone, dialed, then said, "Miz Hollowell out here to see you," and then hung up. "He'll be right out," she said and gave Eileen another smile.

"This *is* bright and early," Lee said, looking at his

watch as he came through the doorway. "You want some coffee?" he asked, looking first at Eileen, then at Mavis.

Eileen said, "No, thank you, we had some at home." Hardly a sip, Mavis would have told him, Eileen was so anxious to get out of the house and come here to see Claude. Mavis barely had time to eat a piece a toast.

"Probably wise," he said. "It's all from a machine. Come on, I'll take you to Claude. He's having his breakfast right now."

They walked through another room with dark paneled walls and waist-high partitions, with desks so close together that you could hardly pass. Behind a Coke machine, another hallway opened, barred this time, and Lee took out a big ring of keys, selected one, and unlocked the door. "After you, ladies," he said, standing aside until they passed, then locked the door behind them. Mavis heard Eileen give a little gasp.

Claude was in the last cell. Walking past the others, Mavis tried not to look at the sleeping bodies curled up inside on metal cots, afraid of what she might see. But she couldn't shut her ears to the snores and coughs that filled the air, and the scent of urine and sweat almost overwhelmed her. What some people sank to, she thought (because, sure as anything, every other person there had been booked as drunk and disorderly). She'd never understand.

"Hey there," Claude called out in a bright voice even before Lee unlocked his cell. When they went in, he was holding a fork full of pancake halfway to his mouth, and he gave them a big smile and then shoveled the food inside. "They let me have all the syrup I wanted," he said, his mouth still full. He pointed to half a dozen little foil cups sitting on his tray. "Butter, too." Had he been home, Eileen would surely have told him not to talk while he chewed.

This time, though, she didn't scold him. Her face showed all her feelings—surprise, pain, anger at him sitting there like a five-year-old with no awareness of what was going on—but the most important thing was that he was *found, safe,* and relief shone in her eyes like diamonds.

"Ya'll have a little visit," Lee said, opening the cell door and then closing it behind him. "Just bang when you finish and I'll come get you." He walked away.

"Sit down, Mavis," Eileen said, as if they were on the porch back home.

Mavis looked dubiously at the rumpled cot in the corner. Eileen followed her eyes. "You get up and let Mavis have your chair," she said to Claude. "You and me can sit on the bed." While she held his tray, Claude went over to the bed and sat down. Then Eileen placed the tray on his knees again and sat beside him. You could see she wanted to put her arms around that big body. "Tell us what happened, honey," she said in a low voice.

Claude took another bite and got a puzzled look on his face. "About what?"

"About the girl in the playhouse. Brenda. You know."

"Oh, her." Claude might have been talking about the counter girl at McDonald's. "I just wanted her to be my friend. I didn't do nothing wrong. She was always nice to me, didn't tease me like the others. And sometimes she gave me a candy bar, Bit-O-Honey, my favorite. When I found her, I decided to put her in my special place with all my other things.''

"Found her?"

"Yeah, way back in the woods."

"When was that?"

"Saturday, early. I was playing police." Claude gave a great big smile.

A look of irritation flashed across Eileen's face, and her voice was sharper when she asked, "What in the world do you mean?"

"Looking for clues. I wanted to see if I could find out who killed my ducks."

"And?"

Claude shrugged his shoulders. "Didn't find no clues, but I did find her." He stopped chewing, looked up. "At first, I thought it was just an old piece of cloth caught on the bushes. Then I saw there was arms and legs, and when I went closer, I saw it was Brenda. Looked like she'd been picking berries and a snake got her, had a bite on her arm."

"Lord, I'd have run," Mavis said, picturing the scene.

"The snake was gone," Claude said. "I looked around."

"What did you do then?" Eileen removed the tray from Claude's knees and set it on the floor, then bent a little closer to him.

"Just picked her up—she was light as anything— and took her down to where the woods end and the pasture starts and waited around in the trees until you and Mavis had gone off. Then I put her in my playhouse."

"So you knew you were doing wrong then," Eileen

said. "You wouldn't have hidden the body away like that if you didn't."

Claude looked down at his hands, then clasped them between his knees. "Yes, ma'am. I just wanted her to be my secret for a little while. I checked on her to be sure she was okay. Then, when I opened up the door and saw Mavis there, I got scared and ran away."

If Eileen realized Mavis hadn't told her about that encounter, her face didn't show it. "Is that why you didn't come back when we rang the bell?"

Claude bobbed his head up and down. "I knew I'd done something real bad then," he said, "so I stayed in the woods till dark. Then I thought about when I used to go to the workshop and decided to walk there. Maybe they'd help me. That's when the police came and picked me up on the road."

"Dear Lord, what am I going to do with you?" Eileen said. She shook her head, not expecting an answer, then stood up. "Well, I reckon the first thing is to get you out of here." Walking over to the bars, she called, "Can somebody come let us out?" and in no time at all Lee Rhodes came down the hallway and unlocked the door. "You through with Claude?" she asked. "I'd like to get him home. He's had enough adventure to last him till next year at least."

"Well, not just yet."

"Why?"

Taking Eileen's arm, Lee led her outside the cell, waited for Mavis, then locked the door again behind her. If Claude was upset about their departure, he didn't say a word. "We have a few more questions to ask him," Lee said. "Come on and I'll explain."

Gently, he guided Eileen down the hallway through the door of the partitioned room to a desk in the corner.

Mavis followed right behind. "Y'all sit," Lee said, sweeping paper off two straight back chairs. Mavis could see the dust flying up into the air. When they were comfortable, he sat down in a scuffed-up wooden desk chair that squawked every time he moved. "You find Claude okay?" he asked Eileen, leaning back with his hands behind his head.

"Yes," she said. "I didn't see any signs of police brutality. The poor fool would move in here if he thought you'd feed him pancakes every morning."

"Yes, ma'am," he said. "He's a nice man." Mavis noticed he didn't smile.

"Why can't I take him home then?" Lowering his arms slowly, Lee sat forward in his chair. It seemed a long time before he spoke.

"We just got the medical examiner's report," he said. "Brenda was strangled all right, like we thought, but there was something else."

"What? Is that what you want to ask Claude about?"

"Yes, ma'am," he said in a soft voice. "Brenda was pregnant. About two months. Do you think Claude could have had anything to do with that?"

Eileen turned white as plaster. "Oh, dear Jesus!" she said, but it almost sounded as if she was laughing. Mavis wondered if she might become hysterical. "Claude? What in the world would she want with an old man? And him the way he is—for all his talk about the girls in the workshop, he's never had one bit of experience with them. Even if you drew him a picture, he wouldn't know what to do."

"Maybe," Lee said, "but we've got to ask him."

Eileen shook her head. "Go ahead," she said. "But it's just a waste of time." She started to get up, but then sat down again hard on the wooden chair. Her face paled even more. To Mavis, she looked like she'd seen a ghost. "So that was it," she said, her body shaking just slightly. "And I didn't listen."

"What?" Mavis asked in a gentle voice. Lee's forehead was wrinkled with a puzzled look.

"Brenda. She said she had something to tell me that Friday and I put her off, told her I didn't have time and we'd talk next day. But by then, it was too late, she was already dead. Sure as anything, she'd have told me about the pregnancy. Who else did she have to go to? Her mama and daddy would probably have thrown her out, and whoever was the father may not have wanted anything to do with her once she told him about the baby. No, Brenda wanted my help, and I turned her away. Maybe even caused her death. I'll have to bear that guilt the rest of my days." Her eyes filled with tears.

Mavis wanted to provide some words of comfort, but what Eileen said probably was true—without a doubt Brenda *had* wanted to tell Eileen about her trouble, hoping she'd help her find a way out—and Mavis couldn't lie. Reaching out, she clasped Eileen's trembling fingers and said, "You had no way of knowing, honey. You did the best you could and it won't help to blame yourself. What we've got to do now is try to find out who murdered her."

"That's right," Lee Rhodes said quickly. You could tell he was embarrassed by Eileen's tears. He gave Mavis a thankful smile for giving him a way to end the interview. "We want to take Claude out to your place, Miz Hollowell. He says he can show us where he found the body. We've lost a lot of time already, and what clues that might have been there may already be gone. You mind? We could leave right away if that's all right with you.''

Mavis gave Eileen a tissue from her purse, and Eileen blew her nose. "I reckon so," she said. "I just want to get this over with so Claude can come home."

"Yes, ma'am," Lee said but made no promises. "You and Miz Mavis go on home, and we'll come along with Claude. He'll be just fine."

"No doubt," Eileen said and tried to smile. "He'll be tickled to death riding in a police car. For the Lord's sake, don't turn on the siren. We'll never hear the end of it."

Eileen got up then, took Mavis's arm, and they walked through the visitor's area to the hallway that led outside. "I hope that's the last time I ever set foot through that door again," Eileen said as she stopped for a moment for her eyes to adjust to the bright sunlight. "I'll pray to Jesus every night this is my first and last visit." She blinked one last time, then started to walk quickly out to the street with Mavis just behind her.

"Well, look a-here," came a booming voice from the steps going up to the main entrance of the courthouse. A figure stood there, just a silhouette at first with the sunlight behind him. But then he bent forward, swept off his hat, and they recognized his shiny face— Boyd Wilkinson, big-mouth thing, who wanted to buy up all of Eileen's land and turn it into houses. He tapped down two steps in his high-heeled boots but still managed to stay a little above them. With a big wink at Mavis he said to Eileen, "I hope you haven't been in there signing away your property to somebody else. I told you I'd give you the best price going."

"No, sirree," Eileen said right back to him. "But I

reckon *you* were in there swindling somebody else out of *their* property.''

Boyd laughed, throwing back his head so far that they could see the gold in his upper teeth. ''Now isn't that the funniest joke?'' he said, but then his smile quickly faded and he added, ''I bet things aren't so funny out at your place right now,'' and stood with his hands on his protruding stomach as if he held some treasure.

''What do you mean?'' Eileen walked up a step or two so that she was even with Boyd.

''Murder,'' he said. ''Aren't many folks going to be attracted to a B&B with a murderer running around.''

''How did you know?''

''The paper. It was on the front page this morning. You didn't see it? Why, they had a real nice photo of your gate and the B&B sign.''

Oh, Lord, Mavis wondered, was that the backfire she'd heard in the night, some photographer taking a picture in the darkness?

''I won't ever sell to you,'' Eileen said, her head stretched out towards Boyd so that the tendons in her neck were taut as rubber bands. ''Do what you will.''

''What do you mean by that?''

This time, Eileen smiled. ''Oh, little things to try to discourage me from opening the B&B. We've had some accidents around the place, some damage— maybe that was all your work. And now murder. Did you have something to do with that, too?''

Boyd Wilkinson suddenly looked like somebody had knocked the breath out of him. Making little puffing sounds, he turned first to Eileen, then to Mavis, but he didn't say anything. Mavis thought, maybe he'll have sunstroke right here on the courthouse steps. He deserved it, however un-Christian such a thought might be.

"Come on," Eileen said to Mavis as she turned around. "We've got to get home."

Without even glancing at Boyd who still stood there breathing hard, she walked down the steps to where Mavis stood, took her arm again, and headed for the parking lot at the Farmer's Market. "That *jackass!*" she said, more than loud enough for Boyd Wilkinson to hear.

FOURTEEN

MAVIS AND EILEEN ARRIVED home no more than ten minutes before Sheriff Rhodes drove up with two other officers and Claude in the backseat of his car. As soon as Mavis slammed the car door, she spotted Jordache's motorcycle parked beneath the trees, but she saw no sign of him or Tara, and she thought to herself that they were probably upstairs over the garage peeking out the window at what was going on. Jordache wouldn't dare show his face with Lee around.

Claude looked happy as a jaybird when he got out of the sheriff's car. Maybe it was better he didn't know what was going on. Would they put someone that innocent in the electric chair? Mavis smiled at Eileen in hopes she wouldn't guess what was going on inside her head.

"We'll just ask Claude to take us over in the woods a few minutes and show us where he found the body," Lee said as he walked up to Mavis and Eileen, with Claude just a little behind him between the other two men. His voice sounded casual, as if he'd just announced that the four of them were going off to a baseball game. Maybe he, too, was trying to tell Eileen not to worry.

"Well, I'm going with you," Eileen said right away. "Mavis, too. Don't say no."

"I wouldn't dare," Lee said and gave a little laugh.
"But you ladies be careful. It's mighty rough down
there. You don't want to ruin your shoes. And there
may be a rattler or two sunning himself so watch where
you step."

"Lord, don't you worry," Eileen said. "I've been
running up and down these hills for Lord knows how
many years, and I haven't been bitten yet."

Mavis gave a shudder, remembering from her childhood warnings about snakes, and thought to herself that
she'd still be careful where she set her feet.

Turning, Lee walked a few steps backwards and took
hold of Claude's arm, and they began to walk down
the drive towards the pasture. His touch was gentle, as
if he was the parent and Claude some big hulking child
who'd gone astray, and when Eileen began to walk
very fast, as if to catch up with them, Mavis put her
hand on her arm and said, "You let them go on ahead.
I don't know that you need to worry." Eileen gave her
a thankful smile.

It was as if they were a little parade that wended its
way down the road through the pasture and up to the
other side where the woods began. Lee with Claude
chattering away in front followed by the two burly officers, both of them wearing mirror-like sunglasses, not
far behind, with Mavis and Eileen bringing up the rear.
Lord, if only this were some other day, Mavis thought,
with no more purpose than an afternoon walk in the
woods. When she was a girl and relatives congregated
at the home place for Sunday dinner, later, after the
dishes were washed and the men had begun to nap in
the living room, someone (a child, perhaps, bored with
the stillness) would say, "Let's go take a walk." And
although there would be grumbling, the men would

rouse, stretch, and walk out to the porch and light cigarettes while the women would repair their makeup and
put a handkerchief under their watch bands in case they
needed one to wave away flies, and join the others
outside.

Then, with the children running up ahead, released,
ignoring calls of, *"Be careful!"* they would all set out
along the road that led past cotton fields dry-brown
with last year's stalks into the sudden coolness of the
woods. There, conversation would become hushed,
steps slower, and they would draw closer together, a
little band where hands would reach out if someone
stumbled, even the children, dipping down to pick wild
flowers from thick moss, calmed. Later, when they all
returned to the house, they would gather up Sunday
hats, pocketbooks, quarrelsome babies, leftovers that
would provide supper later that night carefully packed
in paper bags, and pile into cars parked under trees with
some hope of coolness. Then they'd head homeward
with loud goodbyes: *"See you next Sunday. Have a
good week!"* Mavis remembered no happier time.

They were far down the road into the woods now,
further than Mavis had ever gone. No sounds pene-
trated from the housing development just on the other
side of Eileen's property line, and the trees seemed
thicker, the light a watery green. Claude and Lee were
still up in front, Claude talking with wide gestures;
he'd probably never had so much attention before. Silent, the other two men followed them closely, while
Eileen and Mavis fell further behind, slowed by the
weeds that filled the tracks. But when Claude suddenly
stopped up ahead, pointed, and then stood back while
Lee stooped slightly to peer beneath the leaves, they
hurried their pace and caught up with the others.

"What is it?" Eileen asked, her voice loud in the silence of the woods.

"There," Lee said and pointed. They followed his finger and there was no mystery at all about what they saw—broken stems, leaves already yellowing, where Brenda's body must have lain. A wooden basket overturned with rotting blackberries spilled out on the ground provided a feast for the two yellow jackets that buzzed above the sodden mess. Mavis expected to hear a snake's rattle wiggling off into the trees.

"She'd come to pick my blackberries," Eileen said in a soft voice, and for a minute or two nobody answered her; even Claude was silent, standing with the rest of them around what was intended to be Brenda's last resting place. Was she bitten by a snake and then strangled, Mavis wondered to herself, or killed and a snake came along right after. Either way, it was too awful to think about, such a sad ending for anybody to have.

"You're sure where you found her?" Lee asked Claude, though there didn't seem to be any doubt in anyone's mind.

"Yessir," Claude said, his talkativeness gone. He looked sheepishly at Eileen, then back at Lee.

"Say how."

Claude shrugged his shoulders. "Just lying there on her back with her arms spread out. The basket had fallen over."

"Did you touch it?"

"Nossir."

"But you moved her?"

"Yessir."

"Carried her back to the playhouse?"

"Yessir. Not at first, though. I left her in the edge of the woods until Mama and Miz Mavis was gone."

Lee shook his head. "Did you see anything else around here?" he asked. "See any sign of a snake?"

"Oh, no. I'd have killed it if I had."

Lee turned from Claude to the other two men. "I reckon that's all we're going to find out right now," he said. "We'll go back to the house, and I'll call the lab and have them come out and see what they come up with. You two stay here till they do. You can take a look around to see if you find anything else, but don't disturb that basket. If we're real lucky, the killer may have left fingerprints on it."

They shook their heads but didn't respond and began to move out beneath the trees, scanning the ground through their sunglasses. Mavis wondered how they would see a thing with them on. With a wave of his hand at Claude to follow him, Lee smiled at Eileen and Mavis and said, "Come on," and began to move off down the road.

But then he suddenly stopped. "Where does this road go?" he asked Eileen.

"Halfway up the mountain. Vance had it cut through when we bought the place."

"Anything there?"

"Not really. Maybe a cleared-off space where Vance once had an idea of building a house, but that was years ago and it's probably all grown up now."

"Is there any other way to get back there?"

"Off the county road." Eileen pointed vaguely through the trees. "But that's all grown up, too. I doubt anybody could get through."

"Which way would Brenda come?"

Eileen's voice sounded surprised when she answered.

"Why, I never thought of that. The easiest way would have been through my place though there wasn't any sign. And her bicycle was at home—Mavis and I saw it there when we went over to ask the Trulls where she'd gone to. She might have come through the housing development, but that would seem strange when she didn't have any reason."

"Maybe," said Lee, "but we'll check anyway, ask if anybody saw her that morning. Any chance she'd come in through the back?"

"Not that I know of. I doubt she even knew about the old road."

Lee didn't ask any more questions, though when he turned and began to walk back down the road, he still had a quizzical look on his face. Taking one last look at the spot where Brenda had died before she followed the others, Mavis wondered if Lee Rhodes had the same feeling she had—that the answer to Brenda's death was right there in front of them if they could only see it. Something bothered her about the scene, and about the sudden vision that came before her eyes of Brenda's pale body when it was taken from the playhouse and laid upon the ground by the sheriff's men. But she couldn't put it all together, and she hurried after the others who were already disappearing down the road, suddenly afraid she might be left alone there in the woods.

When they came out of the trees into the sunlight at the top of the hill where the road dipped down through the pasture, they paused a moment, as if they had arrived from a long dark journey. A breeze ruffled the surface of the pond and dried the sweat on their foreheads. The sight of the house across the way, the garage and outbuildings, the last remnants of laurel blooms with Eileen's flowers beneath, provided a kind of comfort, as if the everyday order of their lives had been established again, thoughts of murder momentarily gone. "Well, I'm glad *that's* over!" Eileen said and began to walk faster towards the house.

Following her, Mavis would have agreed, but then, when she looked up at the garage, the sudden pleasure she had felt was spoiled by a reminder of Tara's and Jordache's cavorting there. On the porch railing, like bright little flags, waved Tara's underwear, and although Mavis thought, well, at least she washes her own underclothes and doesn't pile it on Eileen to do, she wondered if it was necessary for her to put it out on display on the little balcony for all the world to see.

Eileen must have noticed it, too. "You go on and make your call," she said to Lee when they were near the house. "Claude, you take a bath and get cleaned up and stay in your room till I tell you to come out. I hope you won't be going back to any jail cell today." She gave Lee a sharp look and he nodded his head. Then she turned to Mavis. "Come on," she said as she started climbing up the steps to the garage apartment. "We have a little errand to do."

"Sure thing," Mavis said and followed right behind her.

The steps slanted slightly, and Mavis held tightly to the rail. A wasp's nest, dry as tissue paper, hung beneath the eaves, and though she could tell it was long abandoned, she leaned away from it when they passed. At the top, Eileen knocked on the screen door, and Mavis waited with her for an answer, eyeing Tara's brief bikinis, slightly embarrassed, wondering if that was what they wore in the porno movies she'd heard you could get just about anywhere these days.

"Well, my goodness, we've got visitors!" Tara's sarcastic voice came from behind the silvery screen door. When she pushed it open, Mavis could see that she wasn't wearing much more than the skimpy underwear—cut-off blue jean shorts and a black halter top that didn't halt much of anything from jiggling around. "Come on in," Tara said and held open the door. Eileen went inside and Mavis followed her, but they both suddenly stopped when they saw Jordache sprawled out on a beanbag chair. Legs spread wide, barefoot, shirt off so that you could count the few dark hairs on his narrow white chest, a red tattooed heart over his left breast. The ugly snakeskin boots stood in the corner, and clothes were scattered across the floor. A sweet smell hung in the air.

Well, you've certainly made a mess of this place, Mavis thought, remembering the times she and John had stayed here in the apartment. She almost said her thoughts aloud. Back then, the apartment was neat as a pin, the kitchen with bright new fixtures and tieback curtains at the windows, the pine-paneled walls warm and cozy, reflecting the heat from a black wood stove in the corner on a chilly night. It was like a honeymoon cottage raised above the ground, the place where she and John had looked at stars before going to sleep beneath sheets that smelled of sunlight.

Tara didn't ask them to sit down, and Mavis wasn't sure she'd want to even if she had. "I've got something serious I want to talk to you two about," Eileen said. "It won't take a minute." Tara didn't answer, standing by the bar that separated the kitchen from the living room with a smirk on her face. Jordache looked bored, eyelids drooping. "It's about Brenda."

That seemed to perk them up a bit. Tara's smile

faded, and Jordache sat up straighter. "What about her?" Tara finally answered.

"Did you ever have anything to do with her?"

"What do you mean?" Tara said sharply.

Eileen didn't answer her right away, her eyes turned away, embarrassed. Finally, she said, "She was pregnant. Did you know?"

"Well, ain't that a surprise." The nasty tone in Tara's voice returned. "That stuck-up little bitch with her holier-than-thou attitude got herself pregnant."

"That's no way to speak of the dead," Eileen said, eyes flashing, but before Tara could say anything else, she turned to Jordache. "What I want to know," she said to his widening eyes, "is did you have anything to do with it, Brenda getting pregnant, I mean?"

"Me?" he said. "Did I mess around with her?" Laughing, he looked over at Tara. "This lady here keeps me plenty busy. I wouldn't have the energy to do it with anybody else."

Well, the nasty things, Mavis thought, flaunting themselves. Her heart went out to Eileen having to hear such things about her own granddaughter. She wanted to tell her, Come on, let's go before they come out with something worse, but Tara butted in. "He didn't have anything to do with Brenda's little secret, but maybe her boyfriend did."

"How would you know?" Eileen asked.

Tara shrugged. "We saw them in town, her and that nerdy looking thing she was going with. At the mall. At the pool a couple of times. And I heard her talking to her girlfriends about him. Get a makeover, I wanted to tell her. You can find somebody a lot cooler than that. But I didn't bother. She'd never listen. Maybe her boyfriend *did* do it. Why don't you tell that cute sheriff?''

Eileen gave Tara a look that said she'd better watch her tongue or she wouldn't be spreading her underwear out on the porch rail much longer and said, ''You just worry about yourselves and don't go off telling anybody about anything else. Not if you know what's good for you. I brought you here, and I can send you packing again, even if you are my own flesh and blood. A person can only take so much.'' With that, she said, ''Come on, Mavis, we've got things to do,'' and she opened the screen door and marched out to the balcony. Following along behind, Mavis, just for meanness, called out in a loud voice. ''Better not leave that underwear out in the hot sun too long or it'll shrink. Lord knows, if it gets much smaller, it won't be of much use a-tall.''

Eileen turned and gave Mavis a big smile, but when she turned back around again and started down the stairs, she suddenly said, ''Oh, my goodness, who's that?'' pointing to a car coming down the drive in a cloud of dust. ''I can't stand it if it's more bad news.''

''It's not bad news a-tall,'' Mavis said, her heart pounding. ''I'd recognize that little red car anywhere. It's Dale. He's finally made it. With him here, maybe we can find out what's going on!''

FIFTEEN

"LORD HAVE MERCY, I don't know when I've had such a welcome!" Dale stepped back, holding Mavis at arm's length so that he could look at her. When he'd first driven up, Mavis was so glad to see him she had grabbed him and hugged him before he was halfway out of the car.

Eileen came up behind them, smiling for the first time that day. "You'd never know she cared anything about you a-tall, now would you?" She laughed and stuck out her hand. "*I'm* glad you're here, too," she said to Dale. "It's been a long time—you were just a boy the last time I saw you." Then she looked at Mavis and said, "He's still as pretty as ever. Aren't you the lucky one!"

Rolling his eyes, Dale slipped out of Mavis's embrace, grabbed Eileen's hand, and gave her a hug, too. "It just keeps getting better," he said, "though not a word of it's true. I'm getting O-L-D, hair falling out and gaining weight in all the wrong places. Blonds may have more fun but they fade quicker."

"Shoot, you look just fine to me. I don't see a spare ounce anywhere on that body. But come on, let's go on up to the house. We don't need to stand out here gossiping."

Dale let her go and Eileen took off up the path, her

step lighter now, it seemed to Mavis. Dale was just like a tonic. Grabbing his arm, she reached up and whispered in his ear, "Wait till you hear what I've got to tell you!" But she didn't have a chance to say more because just at that moment Tara's voice, sweet as sugar, floated down from the garage apartment, saying, "Well, have we got some *more* company?" and she followed right behind it, switching down the steps with a few more clothes on than she'd had before, but not much. Mercy, Mavis thought to herself, that girl could smell a man a mile away.

Mavis stepped in front of Dale. "This is my nephew, Dale Sumner," she said. "He's just the sweetest thing, always doing something for me." She hoped Tara would get the message. Turning around to Dale, she said, "This is Eileen's granddaughter, Tara. She's here for just a *short* visit."

Just then, Jordache slunk up behind Tara. She ignored him, but Mavis said, "And this is her boyfriend—what's your name, honey, I've never heard anything but that nickname?"

If looks could kill, Mavis thought, she'd be spread out on the ground. "Dennis Spence," he mumbled, and then walked away to look at Dale's car.

Pulling on Dale's arm, Mavis said, "We've got to go now," and before Tara could say another word, she turned and tugged him after her as if he'd been six years old and she was helping him cross the street. He *was* her good luck charm! Already, with him there no more than five minutes, she'd come up with what might be a clue. Dennis Spence—Jordache—she knew she'd heard the name before when he'd given it to the sheriff—now she knew where. When the motorcycle started up with an angry sound, she didn't even

look back. "You're going to have one of my brand
new guest rooms upstairs," Eileen said to Dale when
they went into the house. "You can have your
choice—the Dolly Madison Room, the Marie Antoi-
nette Room, or the Florence Nightingale Room."

"Darn, if I'd only known," Dale said, pointing to
the small leather bag he'd carried in from the car, "I
could have brought a hoop skirt along with me. About
all I've got is another pair of jeans and some clean
underwear."

"Don't be silly. They're just names. The information
I got from the bed-and-breakfast association suggested
giving the rooms some character by having a theme. I
decided on Women in History. Come on."

Eileen led them out into the hallway and upstairs to
the new addition. When she threw open the door to the
Dolly Madison Room and Dale saw the big four poster
bed with a canopy on the top set against the far wall,
he said, "Honey, it's *fabulous!*" and gave Eileen another hug. Mavis, standing in the doorway, thought to
herself, If Eileen's face beams any brighter, she'll light
up like a Christmas tree.

"Now, you stop acting silly," Eileen said to Dale.
"Take your time, unpack, wash up—you've got your
own bath, the door's over there—and then come on
down when you're ready. Mavis and I are going to fix
us a little lunch."

Grinning, Dale let her go, then went over to the bathroom and opened the door. "I won't be long," he said.
Mavis and Eileen went out.

"I can see why you love him so," Eileen said as
they walked down the stairs. "He's about the sweetest
thing I've ever come across."

Mavis just said, "Yes, he sure is," afraid to say

more, wondering if Eileen was comparing him to Tara. But she thought to herself, How grateful I am for his love, too. Just those few days away from him and she'd missed him something terrible.

DALE ATE LIKE HE'D JUST BEEN released from a prison camp. Half a bowl of cucumbers in vinegar and sugar, three ears of corn, goodness knows how many servings of squash, not counting the country biscuits he sopped up with chicken gravy. "I'm about to pop," he said, loosening the top button of his jeans. "For sure, I've undone a week's worth of work at the gym in just one sitting."

"Shoot," Eileen said. "You're on vacation. And, anyway, you've got a figure most folks would give their eyeteeth for. I'll be insulted if you don't have some of my deep-dish peach pie."

Dale moaned but said, "With a little ice cream on top?" and they all laughed till their sides nearly split. Dale had seconds on the pie, too, along with Claude who had sat through the entire meal without saying a word. Well, at least he's cleaned up a bit, Mavis thought, looking at the nicks in his neck from shaving and the freshly ironed shirt he had put on. After he finished, he asked Eileen if he could go outside and she told him yes but not to go off too far. He slid back his chair and bounded away, still barefoot.

"What's the matter with him?" Dale asked when Claude was out of earshot. "He hasn't said two words to me the whole time I've been here. Before, when I came up, you couldn't shut him up, made me look at every rock and baseball card he'd ever collected in that playhouse of his. Is he sick?"

Clearing her throat, Mavis said, "He's been having

a few little problems,'' and gave Dale a look she hoped would say, *Hush up for now, I'll tell you later.* Eileen didn't say a word.

Mavis insisted that she was going to clean up the dishes, and Dale jumped up to help her. ''You go right in yonder and take a nap,'' she told Eileen. ''You've been through a lot today and need some rest.''

Eileen gave one feeble protest—''I hate to think of Dale down here doing dishes when he's just arrived'' —but then she said, ''Well, I *am* a little tired…'' and Mavis hurried her out the door.

She'd hardly disappeared down the hallway when Dale said, ''Okay, Miz Mavis, what's going on? Something is, don't you deny it.''

Giving him a dishtowel, Mavis carefully washed a bowl and handed it to him. ''Murder,'' she said, ''that's what's going on. Thank goodness you're here to help solve it.''

He almost dropped the bowl. ''Not again!'' he almost shouted, and Mavis shushed him with her finger, hoping Eileen hadn't heard. ''You find a dead body everywhere you go.''

''That's not true and you know it.'' She waited a minute, then added, ''I *did* find this one, but it was practically dropped in my lap.''

''Where?''

''Down in Claude's playhouse. You've been there.''

''You mean he did it?''

''Of course not, though he got brought in and questioned by the sheriff and spent a night in jail.''

''No wonder he looked so down at the mouth at dinner.''

Mavis waved her wet hand vaguely in the direction

Claude had gone. "Aw, that's not the reason. I expect he already realizes Eileen's going to keep tabs on him for a while and he won't be able to run all over the place the way he usually does. Claude wasn't upset by jail at all—just the opposite—he couldn't keep his eyes off the badges and guns down there, happy as I don't know what with all the attention."

"Then who could have committed the murder and left the body there?"

"Oh, she wasn't killed *there*. Claude just put her there in the playhouse. I guess he was actually the person who found the body, out yonder in the woods." She pointed again, this time through the window towards the pasture.

"I'm confused."

"Well, you just keep on drying and I'll try to tell you what happened." And while they stood there doing dishes together the way they'd done so many times before, Mavis told Dale all about the problems Eileen had been having getting the B&B ready to open, stuck the whole summer long with Tara and that boyfriend of hers, neither one worth the powder and shot it would take to blow their heads off, and pestered by Boyd Wilkinson who wanted to buy up her land. Then she told him about Brenda, sweet as anything, no thanks to her parents, and how she'd been supposed to come help Eileen but then seemed to have disappeared until Mavis found her body in Claude's playhouse and he'd shown them in the woods where the body had lain, strangled, a snake bite on her arm.

Dale finished drying the last pot and Mavis reached up and put it into the cabinet. "Whew!" he said. "That's a lot. How is Eileen taking it?"

"She's had her down times, but she's still set on

opening the B&B this weekend in time for the Fall Apple Festival they're having, no matter what. But with Brenda gone and Tara sorry as dirt, it's going to be hard. Claude's good help, but you have to stand right over him to be sure he does a decent job. I'll do what I can, but that's not a lot.''

''Well, you've got me now. I'd better do some work or I won't be able to fit in my car by the time I leave here, much less my clothes, eating this way.''

Not even drying her hands, Mavis hugged him and left wet spots on his shirt. ''I *am* glad you're here,'' she said. ''I'm sure Eileen is, too. I just bet we can find out what's going on.''

Mavis decided to take a nap, too, and Dale said he'd go for a walk. ''Don't poke around too much, or you might discover another body,'' she told him. With a big laugh, he said he wouldn't and walked out the door. Removing her apron, Mavis went to her room.

BUT SHE COULDN'T SLEEP. After removing her shoes, careful not to disturb Eileen behind the curtain in the other room, she got into bed and lay perfectly still and tried to make her mind a blank, but it didn't work. She was too excited about Dale's arrival, too anxious to confirm her suspicions about Jordache, ever to drift off. So when she heard Eileen stirring, she lay with her eyes closed in case Eileen peeped in until she heard her get up and go out into the hallway. Then, after waiting a few minutes longer she got out of bed and, still in her stocking feet, walked quickly through the curtain to the other room.

It wasn't really snooping—looking once more at the newspaper at the bottom of Eileen's dresser drawer, the one that Tara had stirred up when she was going through it—she needed to check a clue. So, quickly laying aside the letters Eileen had received from her mama all those years ago, the birthday cards and the thank-you notes, Mavis found the newspaper again. It didn't take long. She scanned the article, there was the name. That's all she needed to know. After carefully putting the drawer back in order again, she closed it and went out into the sitting room to see if she could find a telephone book for Monroeville. It was on a shelf right next to the fireplace. Bending close, heart pounding, she began to flip through the pages: "Si... So... Sp..." Ah, it was there! She and Dale would be taking a little trip as soon as she could find a way.

After she put on her shoes and fluffed up the curls surrounding her head, she walked to the porch, expecting to find Dale there with Eileen. But the room was empty, the whole house quiet, and for just a moment, she felt panic rush through her as strong as an ocean wave so that she was all ready to call out, *Anybody here? Where are you?* when she heard the voices outside. Turning, she looked out the door through the laurel to the driveway and saw Eileen and Dale there talking with some other person, a stranger, and she wondered if it meant more bad news.

But then, after she'd opened the screen door and let it slam behind her and started down the steps, she saw that the face suddenly turned towards her could never intentionally be responsible for one bad moment in anybody's life. Gawky, not all the parts of him fitting together comfortably yet, a beginning fuzz on his upper lip, the boy standing there couldn't have been more than fifteen. He had big dark eyes and still darker lashes that would make the girl in the Maybelline ad give up and go away. He should have smiled, but his mouth was turned down in a frown that said he'd already learned too much about this world. Though his bicycle was turned over in Eileen's flowerbed, you could tell he wasn't there on a paper route.

"Hey there," Mavis said, coming up to the little group. She stuck her hand out at the boy and said, "I'm Mavis Lashley, who're you?" and gave him a smile.

"Kevin Phillips," he said in a soft voice. "I was Brenda's friend."

"I'm just as sorry as I can be about what happened," she told him.

Before he could answer Eileen jumped in, as if to protect him, and said, "He just heard about Brenda and rode over here to see if we knew anything more than what was in the paper. I said, 'Not a lot,'" and filled him in on a few details." She gave Mavis a look that said, *No need to make him hurt more than he does already,* then turned back to Kevin. "The sheriff is making an investigation."

But then a look of pain passed across Eileen's face, and she blurted out, "Had she seemed different to you in the past few days? Brenda? Had she said anything?"

Mavis knew why Eileen was asking. Brenda had come to her, told her that she needed to talk, no doubt about the baby on the way, but Eileen had put her off. She was still trying to deal with that guilt. (And maybe, it suddenly occurred to Mavis, she was also asking, *Did you do it? Are you the daddy of that dead baby that will go with her to her grave?*)

Kevin lowered those pretty eyelashes, then looked back up at Eileen, still with his frown. "She didn't *say* anything, but she did seem quieter, like she was off in her own world sometimes." For a moment he was silent, then burst out, "That family of hers, they're enough to make anybody feel down."

"What do you mean?"

"Always at her, her daddy especially, fussing about everything. Brenda was like any other girl, wanted to wear lipstick and do up her hair, but *he* said it was the Devil's work. She did, anyway, in spite of him—or maybe *to* spite him. Her mama mainly just stayed silent. They didn't like me, either, told Brenda to stay away from me, so we had to sneak around. I told her I'd stand up to her daddy any day of the week, but she said no, it wouldn't be a good idea."

"How long you two been going together?" It was Dale, speaking for the first time, with a note in his voice that Mavis hadn't heard before, of caring and concern, yet something more, almost like that of a father talking to a son. And then it dawned on her—these two were alike, both had lost their daddies at an early age and had grown up without a big brother around to help. Dale would understand how much Brenda had meant to Kevin, how great a loss her death had been. And when Kevin smiled up at him—the first time his expression had changed the whole time they'd been standing there—Mavis wanted to give Dale a hug.

"We went all through grammar school together," Kevin said. "Mrs. Hollowell here taught both of us." He blushed and looked down at the ground. "I'm not real sure when things got more serious between us—a few months ago maybe—I don't know."

Eileen started to say something, but Dale put his hand on Kevin's shoulder and said, "Let's me and you walk down to the pasture. I want to ask you a thing or two," that fatherly note still in his voice. Smiling at Eileen and Mavis, he told them, "You ladies go and rest, we won't be long,'' and turned, and the two of them walked off down the road.

"Well, my goodness,'' Eileen said. "I wonder what Dale wants to ask him about.''

Mavis thought she might have a guess, but she said, "I don't know. I expect we'll just have to wait to find out. Why don't we go sit on the porch the way Dale said.'' Shrugging her shoulders, Eileen went off along the way and Mavis followed close behind.

But Eileen couldn't sit still once they got inside. "I'm just too antsy,'' she said. "You rest. I'll put away what's in the dishwasher. You do so much by hand it's hardly a chore.''

Mavis didn't sit either. Standing by the window, she watched Dale and Kevin walk down the drive to the pasture, one bright head, one dark head, bent close in conversation. Just at the gate, they stopped, talked a minute more, and then Kevin raised one arm as if to ward off a blow, his body shaking. Very slowly Dale put his arm around his shoulders. They stayed that way for what seemed a long time, no indication that they spoke, until Dale finally pulled his handkerchief from his pocket and gave it to Kevin to wipe his eyes. When he finished, they trudged back up the drive again, a little apart now with fewer words between them, till they reached the spot where Kevin's bike lay turned over in the flowerbed. He picked it up, shook hands with Dale, then rode off. Dale stood there by himself before he turned and came into the house.

"Well, what in the world was all that about?'' Mavis asked before he was through the door. Eileen poked her head in from the kitchen.

Dale had a solemn look on his face. "I told him Brenda was pregnant, asked him about the baby, was it his? He was real upset. He said he didn't know a thing about it, and him and Brenda never did anything like that.''

"Do you believe him?'' Eileen's voice trembled, and she looked like she might break in half the plate that she was holding.

"Yes. I never saw him before, but you can tell there's good in that boy. And why would he come riding over here today if he had something to hide? No, I don't think he was the father of Brenda's child.''

"Then who is?'' Mavis asked.

Dale gave her a wink. "That's what we're going to find out. But not right this minute—I need a shower to perk me up. I didn't get a nap like you two ladies.'' Turning, he started towards the door to the hallway, but before Mavis had a chance to tell him she hadn't slept a wink that afternoon, he turned back and said to Eileen, "Kevin asked would you call him if you get any news about Brenda's funeral. He'd like to go along if you go, said he'd feel more comfortable if he didn't have to sit in the church alone. Apparently, it's kind of weird.''

"My heavens,'' Eileen said, still clutching the plate she held to her breast. "I hadn't even thought ahead that far. Whenever I think of Brenda, all I see is her poor body spread out on a table somewhere, covered by a sheet. Of course Kevin can go. You'll go, too, won't you?'' she asked, looking first at Mavis and then at Dale.

"Why sure I will,'' Mavis said. "You couldn't keep me away.''

Dale just smiled and disappeared through the doorway to the hall.

SIXTEEN

EVERYTHING WORKED OUT perfectly. Later that afternoon, when Eileen announced that she had to go to a meeting at church that night to help get ready for the Ladies Missionary Society's booth at the apple festival and they'd just have a pick-up supper, Dale had said right quick, "Don't you worry about us. You go on. I'll take Miss Mavis out somewhere, and we'll go for a little ride."

Mavis winked at him and said, "I don't *need* anything else to eat, but it would be nice just to ride around. It'll still be light at nine o'clock."

"You'll be hungry by then," Dale said to her, then asked Eileen, "Where's a good place to eat? Not some tourist trap out on the highway—I've seen enough salad bars to last me forever—a place where folks around here would go."

Eileen recommended a place out near the state park simply called The Fish House. "It's cheap, clean," she added. "The food's fresh, and those summer people in their leisure suits who stay over in town wouldn't be caught dead there."

"That sounds good to me," Mavis said. "I accept!" She grabbed Dale's arm and gave it a little squeeze. And before she caught herself she almost said, I know exactly where we'll go for a ride, too. We've got another little trip to make.

Eileen was right about the restaurant. It was plain, a long low wooden building next to a dusty parking lot, with tartar sauce in plastic squeeze bottles set on the oil-cloth covered tables inside and coffee mugs chipped from years of use. But the fish was so fresh you'd swear it had just come from the stream that spilled over the rocks outside the door if you didn't know the water was polluted and that the fish were raised on a farm. Dale ate so many hushpuppies that it became a joke, the waitress coming back and forth through the swinging doors to the kitchen with a new basket every few minutes while the other customers, all locals, looked on, stony-eyed at first, then with smiles. "Just bring me the check," he said when the woman asked him if he wanted some pie to finish off, and she shook her head so hard that her piled-up hair wobbled from side to side and she said, "Honey, I can't charge you for all them hushpuppies you ate. You never in this world could afford it. They'll just be a little gift."

"Well, thank you kindly, ma'am," he said and gave a little bow. "I'm real obliged."

"Come on," Mavis said to him, then smiled at the other woman. "He'll carry on his foolishness all night," she said. "He doesn't need a bit of encouragement."

"I can see," she said, starting to clear the table. "Y'all come back, you hear?" They said they would and Dale took Mavis's arm and they went outside.

"Now what's this about a little trip?" he asked as he helped her into the car.

"It's a long story," she said as he got in on the other side. "But to make it short, Eileen had some trouble a long time ago before we met over a child she had in her class. The mama attacked her, eventually went to jail for it, a woman by the name of Mamie Spence. That's Jordache's name, Spence, *Dennis* Spence—Jordache is just a nickname. I heard him when he told the sheriff. Now, that may be just a coincidence, but I wonder. Maybe it figures in somewhere in all that's been going on. Anyway, I want to make a call on Mamie Spence. She's still alive—I looked her up in the phone book—at least, if it's the same one. You going to take me?''

''Why sure,'' Dale said, starting up the car. ''But what makes you think she'll talk to us?''

''Not one thing. But what have we got to lose? If nothing else, we'll have us that ride we told Eileen about and won't even have to tell her a fib.''

''You are *something*,'' Dale said and gave her a big smile as he drove away.

MAVIS WAS RIGHT. IT WAS still light just a little before nine o'clock, the sky a pale rose, shiny as satin, the mountains below already purple and deepening to brown. Dark birds, settling down for the night, rattled in the treetops, and a few wisps of fog stretched across the road like summer netting. Turning the piece of paper that she had written the address on towards the glow of the window, Mavis read it, and down the road Dale stopped at a Qwik-Pick to ask for directions. ''It's not far,'' he said when he got back in the car. ''The turnoff is just a little ways ahead.''

When Mavis saw the number and said, ''Stop!'' she wasn't at all sure it was the right place. RANDALL'S TRAILER COURT, PERMANENT ONLY, she read on a sign above the drive. "Reckon this is it?" she asked Dale.

"Why not? It's as good a place as any. You want me to drive inside?"

Bending forward, Mavis peered through the shadows. Well, it does look like a nice place, she thought to herself. The trailers were freshly painted, most all of them with additions—screened-in porches or little patios dwarfed by big barbecues off to the side—and a semicircle of brightly colored aluminum folding chairs. You could tell people had taken pains to make their tiny yards look pretty; rows of marigolds and zinnias stretched across the front, and painted plaster reindeer peeked from beneath the shrubs. "Go on," she told Dale. "I guess it's not much different from living anywhere else."

They could tell by the numbers on the mailboxes that Mamie Spence's trailer was five spaces down in the next-to-the-last row. After Dale parked under a weeping willow tree, they got out and started walking towards it on a white gravel driveway that seemed dazzling even in the low light. "They keep it up nice," Mavis said to Dale, carefully placing her feet so that she wouldn't trip.

He took her arm. "Yeah, and I bet they're real careful about who they let come here."

"What do you mean?"

"Haven't you seen the curtains moving? In the trailer windows, I mean. I'd bet anything there's somebody looking out of every one. They probably think we just escaped from the penitentiary and are wondering if they should call the police."

"Don't be silly," Mavis said. "They probably don't get many visitors. They're just curious, that's all."

But, despite her words, Mavis was beginning to wonder if coming here was the right thing to do. Suppose it wasn't the right person, even though the names were the same? And even if it was, maybe Mamie Spence wouldn't give them the time of day. Then she thought, well, we've gone this far, we might as well see it through, and she turned up the little path to the trailer.

Although they could hear a TV going inside, no one answered when Dale first knocked on the door. "Maybe they left the TV on to discourage a break-in," he said, but Mavis told him to try again. They waited another minute, but just as they were ready to turn away, the door opened a crack and they could see the vague outline of a figure behind the screen. "What do you want?" a low voice said. They couldn't tell whether it was a man or woman.

"How're *you?*" Mavis said, feeling a little silly smiling at someone she couldn't see. "We'd like a word with Miz Mamie Spence. Are you her?"

"You ain't none of them Jehovah's Witnesses, are you?" the voice asked without answering Mavis's question. "They pester the life out of me."

"No, ma'am," Dale said, taking a chance it was Mamie they were talking to. "I'm Dale Sumner, and this is my Aunt Mavis, Mavis Lashley. We're visiting here from over in Markham. You don't know us, but we know somebody you know and wanted to ask you a question or two, that's all."

There was silence again, but the door opened a little wider. "You're sure it's me, Mamie Spence, you want? I didn't know I was so famous."

"Yes, ma'am," Dale said, "if you please."

"Well, y'all come on in. You don't look too much like murderers, though you never know these days. I don't get many visitors and I'm tired of the silliness on TV, so if you want to sit and talk a spell, that's all right by me."

She opened the door wider, and they looked up at her, a tall woman, big-boned, gaunt, with no more softness about her than a pile of wood thrown into a corner. She wore her hair in a long gray braid twisted around her head, and was dressed in a woolen bathrobe that had seen better days. Dark brown splotches from too many years in the sun marred her skin. Though there was no doubt now about her voice, it had a rough edge, as if she'd smoked cigarettes most of her life and had given them up too late.

"Thank you kindly," Mavis said as she went past her through the door, vaguely aware of a medicinal scent coming from Mamie's body. Dale followed Mavis inside.

"Sit," Mamie said and nodded her head. Crossing to the other side of the small room, she sat down in what was obviously her chair, a huge recliner draped with an old chenille bedspread with a peacock pattern, the magenta feathers of its tail fanning out around her head. She clicked off the TV with the remote control. Dale pulled a plastic covered straight chair out from the dinette table, and Mavis sat in the only other easy chair across from Mamie.

"My, isn't this nice," Mavis said, looking around the room. And actually she thought to herself, it might not be too bad to live in a trailer like this, though she'd never known very well anybody who had. Everything fitted together, seemed to have its place, and there was certainly a lot less to clean. You could make it personal, too, the way Mamie had, with crocheted doilies on the chair backs, and a black velvet picture of Christ knocking at the gate on the wall. There were a whole slew of framed photographs on the partition between the living room and kitchen area, and several pretty cards standing there. Mavis bent a little closer, trying to read the names, and when Mamie spoke in that rough voice of hers, she almost jumped.

"Who is this here person that knows me?" Mamie asked. "Most everybody I know is dead."

Mavis was quiet for a minute, afraid to speak. Then she took a deep breath and said, "Eileen Hollowell, used to be Eileen Coates before she got married. You knew her a long time ago."

At first, Mamie had a blank look on her face, and Mavis wondered if she had made a mistake. Maybe this wasn't the woman who had attacked Eileen all those years ago—finding the name in the telephone book was just a coincidence. But then the pale skin beneath the dark splotches on Mamie's face became flushed, and she began to breathe faster, the sound like something loose rattling in her chest. Lord, Mavis thought, don't let her have some kind of spell! She bent over and said, "You need a glass of water or something?"

Mamie Spence shook her head; her breathing calmed a bit. Finally, she said, "I've been trying to forget that name most all my life," and shook her head. "It won't no use. Every time I picked up the paper, there it would be again. Eileen Hollowell did this or that at the schoolhouse, got awards. Or she'd be in the church news. I reckon I could have gone away, but why should I? Eileen Hollowell had made me leave once against my will when they dragged me off to prison. I wasn't going to let her do it again.'' She looked at Dale, then back at Mavis. ''Why in the world do you have to bring it up now?''

Mavis waited a minute before she spoke, almost holding her own breath, afraid that Mamie might suddenly turn them out, refuse to tell them anything. Her only hope was that this sick old woman (because she knew now that Mamie was dying) might have some need to get it all off her shrinking chest, to tell another live person what had been festering there all these years. When she spoke, her voice was very soft, and she stared into Mamie's eyes.

''There's been some trouble,'' she said. ''It may be that old business between you and Eileen has something to do with it. Could you tell us what happened back then? It might help.''

Mamie Spence leaned her head back against the peacock feathers. ''I've got no need to help out Eileen Coates,'' she said.

''It's not just her. Others are involved, too.''

The brown spots on Mamie's forehead seemed to pull together, as if she were in deep thought. Then, her head still tilted back, her eyes half closed, she said, ''I guess it don't make no difference now. Why not? I ain't talked about it in years.''

Suddenly, she dropped her head forward again and gave Mavis and Dale a big smile. Her forehead relaxed. ''It was all over my daughter Tula Mae,'' she said, ''cutest little thing you ever did see! Smart, too, though she never would mind, and you couldn't keep her attention for a minute. They had a time with her at school from the very first day. Her daddy could control her— she was afraid of him—but she didn't pay one speck of attention to me. Just one look from those pretty eyes of hers and I'd back down.

"Well, Eileen Coates got her in third grade, and I was glad at first 'cause they said she was a good teacher, strict and all, but the children learned. Then it started, notes coming home all the time complaining about Tula's behavior, papers she wanted me to make Tula finish at home since she messed around in school so much and didn't get her work done." Mamie shrugged her shoulders. "I didn't pay no attention, figured it was part of Eileen's teaching job to make Tula do what she was supposed to.

"Then one day, Tula came home telling me how Eileen had hit her. I still remember. I was standing at the sink washing beans for supper and I didn't pay her no attention at first. 'Mama, I got hit," she said, and I thought she meant some other kid on the playground. Then I looked around and saw it was something more. 'Miz Coates,' she said. 'Hit me in the head for talking.' She squeezed out a few tears. I should of known it wasn't much—Tula could lie like the Devil—and later, at the trial, Eileen said it was just a pat on the behind for talking back. If it was now, I'd probably pop her one, too, but back then, I just saw red."

Mamie paused a moment, then sat forward in the recliner, hands clutching the arms as if she were about to spring up.

"I didn't sleep a wink that night," she continued. "Got up at dawn the next morning, went out, hid by the road I knew Eileen took to school. I'd brought along this bull whip that belonged to my husband— he'd worked out west once and thought he was some kind of cowboy—and when Eileen come along, I called out her name. 'Eileen…' I can still hear the echo in that cold morning.'' Mamie sat back as if she expected to hear the sound again. "I didn't really mean to hurt her so bad, just teach her a lesson, but once I started, I couldn't stop myself, like something broke inside and let a lot more anger out than I'd ever intended. Finally, somebody must of heard her screams and came along and stopped me.'' Mamie paused again. To Mavis it seemed darker in the little room, as if clouds formed outside.

"What happened then?'' It was Dale's quiet voice, silent till now. He sat bent over on his straight chair towards Mamie, like a child listening to a story.

Mamie turned her head to look at him. "They took Eileen off to the hospital and me to jail,'' she said matter-of-factly. "Wasn't much else to do.'' She sighed. "They tried me in the courthouse and gave me three to five years in prison for attempted murder. I won't say anything about *that* time except it was a living hell. By the time I got home, paroled for good behavior, everything had fallen apart. My husband had found another woman—you know how they are, can't do without—and Tula Mae was well on her way to being ruint. While I was in prison, she lived with my mama, but she couldn't do anything with her, either, and Tula Mae ran wild. I tried to make her change after I come back, beat her far worse than Eileen ever would, but it didn't work. By the time she was teenage, I just gave up.'' Mamie looked back from Dale to Mavis as if expecting some word of condemnation. When none came, she went on.

"You don't even need to guess what happened after that. Tula Mae dropped out of school, got pregnant, thought she was going to lay up on me while I took care of the baby. But I told her she'd have to marry the daddy, work, or get out, and she chose the last. She left home then for parts unknown, and I never saw her again. Later I found out she'd died young—cancer—they cut off both her breasts.''

Mamie stopped talking, and there was silence in the trailer for what seemed a long while, the quiet finally broken by the sound of a motorcycle pulling up outside, and then, just as quickly, roaring away again. When the noise had faded away, Mavis asked, ''What about your grandson, Jordache?''

''How did you know about him?''

''The name. Not 'Jordache'—Dennis Spence, his real name. I connected it to yours after I found out. He goes with Eileen's granddaughter Tara. You must know.''

Mamie laughed. '''Course I do. That's my little revenge, my Jordache messing around with Tara. Eileen must want to die, her so high and mighty, thinking we're not worth dirt. But I can guarantee her that Tara is as hot to trot as Tula Mae ever was, and she's twice as trashy.''

''Maybe you wanted another kind of revenge.''

''What do you mean?''

''There's been a lot of things happening at Eileen's, mean things—a fire set on purpose, old treasures broken, animals killed—did you get Jordache to do that?''

Mamie's smile was gone. ''No, ma'am,'' she said. ''All I did was let nature take its course between Tara and him. I didn't do nothing on purpose.''

''How long has Jordache been around here?''

Mamie looked off, as if counting. ''Maybe six months,'' she said. ''Just showed up here one day knocking on the door like you two. He'd been roaming around—I didn't ask whatall he'd been doing, didn't really want to know—then decided for whatever reason he needed him some roots and looked me up. His mama had left some papers when she died. He was her last one, grew up in a foster home, the only one in the bunch that ever paid me any attention.'' She smiled again. ''He's been good to me, bought me that there TV set.'' She pointed to the partition. ''One of them cards was from him on Mother's Day, got the sweetest verse in it you ever did see. But I didn't get him to do nothing bad against Eileen. Tara was enough.''

Dale interrupted. ''Would he have anything to do with murder?''

Mamie pressed her hand to her chest as if she felt sudden pain. ''What in the world do you mean?''

''Brenda Trull, a girl that worked for Eileen, she was killed out on Eileen's place. Did Jordache ever mention her?''

''Nossir, not to my knowledge.'' Mamie continued to press her chest. ''Why would anybody suspect him?''

Mavis spoke up. ''He had to know of her, and she was pregnant, under age.''

''That's no reason to kill,'' Mamie said. ''That kind of thing goes on all the time these days. Anyway, I expect Jordache has his hands full with Tara.'' Suddenly a look of horror flashed across her face. ''Are they trying to say he done it because of me? Claim murdering runs in the family?''

Seeing her pain, Mavis wanted to comfort the other woman for just one moment. ''No, I don't think so. Far as I'm aware, nobody else knows about what happened between you and Eileen except us and her. Don't worry.''

Mamie began to struggle up from her chair. The peacock stared after her. "I've got to take my medicine," she said and stood. "Y'all learned all you need to know?" Her voice sounded bitter.

"I think so," Mavis said. "We'll go." She got up and Dale stood, too. "Thank you," she said and was about to walk to the door, but then, quite suddenly she began to cough. "Could I have a drink of water?" she asked Mamie who was already headed for the kitchenette.

"I ain't got no cold," she said as she reached up for a glass in the cabinet.

"That's just fine," Mavis said, leaning on the divider. She took the glass from Mamie, drank a few sips, then handed it back to her. "You take care now," she said but Mamie didn't answer her. Dale was already out the door, and Mavis walked over to where he was standing, and then followed him down two steps to the ground. If Mamie stood watching them through the screen, they couldn't tell. The sound on the TV set came back on before they were halfway down the path.

"You learn anything you didn't know before?" Dale asked as he helped Mavis into the car.

She waited until he'd gone around to the other side and got in. "I might have."

"What?"

She opened her purse and pulled out something that shone vaguely luminous in the dashboard lights. "This."

"What is it?"

"Turn on the overhead light so you can see. Mamie won't be looking up this way."

Reaching up, Dale switched on the light, and Mavis handed him what she had been holding. "For the sweetest grandmother in the whole wide world. Love, Jordache,'' he read out loud. The front of the card had ''Happy Mother's Day'' printed across the top, with a pretty picture of a flower basket down below. Jordache's message was written inside. ''You stole Mamie's Mother's Day card?'' he said, his eyes wide with surprise.

''Just borrowed. While Mamie was getting me that drink of water.''

''That was just a trick then? What in the world do you want the card for?''

''Look at the letters.'' Mavis took back the card and pointed at the writing inside. ''They're crooked, not much better than what a six-year-old might do. I bet anything they match the printing on the message Eileen got in her mailbox warning her not to open the B&B. That Jordache didn't even have enough sense to try to disguise his own hand!''

SEVENTEEN

NEXT MORNING, MAVIS HAD hardly set foot into the kitchen when Eileen turned from the stove where she was frying bacon and said, "I've got the best idea in the *world*," with a smile as bright as sunrise.

Gathering her robe around her, Mavis sat down on one of the stools at the counter. "What's that?"

"We'll go on a picnic. This is supposed to be a *vacation* for you and Dale, and all I've done to entertain you so far is to get you involved in a murder. For just one day, I want to take your minds off death. Tomorrow will be time enough for that. Brenda's funeral is at eleven o'clock, and I'll have to go. I shouldn't ask, but I wish you'd come along. Kevin will be there, but he's just a boy, and I'd appreciate a shoulder to lean on. I still feel responsible for what happened to that poor girl."

"Now you just *hush*," Mavis said. "You aren't to blame a-tall. And of course I'll go, Dale, too. You never know what we might find out there." Mavis got up, went over to the stove, and gave Eileen a squeeze, then went to the refrigerator to get out the bread for toast. Taking the loaf to the counter, she said, "Don't worry about entertaining us, either. Just being here with you is enough. But a picnic *would* be fun. I can't think when was the last time I've been on one. Where are you planning on going?"

Eileen poured the grease from the pan into a tin can, set it down again, and started to scramble eggs. "Jump-off Mountain," she said, "up in the state park. They have real nice facilities, and it won't be crowded on a weekday."

"Jump-off Mountain?" It was Dale, standing in the doorway in shortie pajama bottoms and a T-shirt. With tousled hair and sleepy eyes, he looked about five years old. "That doesn't exactly sound like a place to go to get away from death," he said, coming into the room.

"Aw, it's just an old tale," Eileen said. "A boy and girl were in love, their parents disapproved, so they hitched the horses to the carriage and drove right off the cliff to be together in eternity." She suddenly stopped stirring the eggs. "Oh, my Lord," she said, turning pale, "that story does remind me of Brenda's. I don't know which one has the worst ending."

"You said we weren't going to talk about that today," Mavis reminded her. She blew on her fingers after taking a piece of toast from the toaster. "I remember once before when you and I and John and Vance and a whole bunch of young-uns—yours, I think, and some neighbors—went up to Jump-off Mountain for a picnic. I've still got pictures somewhere. I remember how pretty it was. But I was afraid to get up close to the edge, even though John teased me and said we certainly weren't going to jump off together. I'm sure I'd still feel dizzy."

Dale came over and kissed her on the cheek and picked up one of the pieces of toast she had just buttered. "Don't you worry," he said, taking a big bite that left a shiny spot of butter on his chin. "We'll take care of you. You won't have a thing to worry about."

Claude came in then with a bucket of cucumbers and tomatoes that Eileen had sent him out to the garden for, and she told him to fill the cooler with ice and soda as soon as they finished breakfast. You could tell that the picnic was a special treat for him, too. He'd half-combed his hair and had on a clean shirt and while he ate, he had a little smile on his face, looking as pleased as he'd been when they first saw him down at the jail.

They finished breakfast quickly, and after the dishes were done, Eileen began to fry up chicken while Mavis made pimento-cheese sandwiches and Dale washed the tomatoes and sliced up the cucumbers. Claude asked if he could put some ice cream bars in the cooler, but Eileen told him they would melt, and he went outside to sit on the back steps. "Pouting," Eileen said and laughed. With fresh peaches and a cantaloupe packed for dessert, they had more than enough food, and they were out of the house, driving up to the road, by just past eleven o'clock.

Eileen drove. Turning right at the gate, as if going in the direction of the Trulls' house, she turned again in less than a mile into a narrow, twisting road that tunneled through the trees. "We'll hit the highway on the other side of the mountain," she said. "Then it's only a few miles to the park."

"I wouldn't mind riding through here a longer ways, it's so pretty," Mavis said, smiling at Eileen. Through the open windows, a cool breeze blew on her bare arms, and the light coming through the trees turned everything green so that it looked as if they were driving under water. If it weren't for the noise of the car, they would hear birds sing.

"Well, thank you, ma'am," Eileen said, laughing.

"What do you mean?"

"This is my land," she said, waving her hand. "At least on the right side of the car. The road's the line. Look there." She pointed just ahead to a tree stump where two tracks led off into the trees. "That's the back boundary, leads into the field where Vance once thought he'd build us a house. I haven't been back in there in years. I expect it's all grown up now."

Mavis looked closely and thought she saw weeds bent down, a broken branch on a tree, and though she didn't say anything, she wondered to herself, If Eileen hasn't been up in there lately, who has?

They hit the highway, and the road almost immediately started winding up. Eileen, always a skillful driver, Mavis remembered, shifted the old car into second and went steadily upwards without passing another vehicle. On one side of the car, the high banks still held the scars of the dynamite blasts used to shear off the mountainside to make the road, and on the other, thick trees blocked the view of the dropoff until they were halfway up. Then, quite suddenly, all they could see ahead of them was blue sky and when they rounded another curve, the valley spread out below them like a child's toy village. "I may get sick," Dale said.

"Don't you dare," Eileen responded, and they all laughed.

They went still further upwards, the air becoming cooler, thinner, then plunged into a thick grove of fir trees where the road leveled off. "Listen," Eileen said, and she let the car coast for a minute. They heard a rushing sound off to the right.

"What is it?" Mavis asked.

"Looking Glass Falls," Eileen said. "There, you can see it now."

They all stared in the direction Eileen pointed and saw the falls, a clear sheet of water at least thirty feet high that crashed on huge boulders and then went rushing away through the trees. Rainbow colors glittered in the spray. "Isn't that the prettiest sight?" Mavis asked. "I remember it from before," she said, touching Eileen's arm.

Eileen laughed. "Me, too. You remember the fun we had with Claude?" She turned around to the back seat and smiled at him. "He stood down there on the rocks for half an hour or more hoping to see his reflection. He really thought it was a looking glass. Nobody could make him understand anything different."

Eileen had been right about the park. When they pulled into the lot, every space was empty, and they had their choice of picnic tables. Choosing a spot next to a tall fir tree well away from the huge flat rock the couple had driven off ("Thank you," Mavis said to them, "I wouldn't have been able to eat a mouthful any closer to the edge"), they unloaded the car. The air smelled nice there, pungent, and the sun, breaking through the branches, gave just enough warmth. "Help me spread out this tablecloth," Eileen said to Mavis, handing her the corner of a bright, flower-printed piece of plastic. Whey they finished, Dale put the cooler on the tabletop. Claude started to walk away.

"Where's he going?" Mavis asked.

Before she answered her, Eileen called out to Claude, "Don't go far, we're going to eat in just a little while." Then she said to Mavis, "He's off to collect arrowheads, always does find a couple when-

ever we come here. They all go in his collection in the
playhouse.

The playhouse! The word passed over them like a
dark cloud, chilling their happiness. Even here, they
couldn't escape from all that had happened the past few
days. But nobody mentioned it further, and when Dale
said in a bright voice that rang out like bells in the
clear, crisp air, "Hey, anybody want a soda?" Mavis
and Eileen both told him yessirree! right away, hoping
to recapture the earlier joyousness of the day.

"How about a Mountain Dew?" he asked.

Eileen laughed. "Well, that seems appropriate. Not
that long ago, the woods around here were full of stills
that made a kind of 'mountain dew' that would knock
your socks off."

"Too bad we don't have some now," Dale said.
"We could have put a shot in the lemonade."

"Be ashamed of yourself," Mavis said, her voice
scolding though her eyes were all smiles.

They ate a little later. Eileen called Claude and he
came running, and they sat down on the benches on
each side of the table so that Eileen could ask the blessing. Remembering the woman who had led them in the
blessing in the restaurant where the bus had stopped
for lunch on the way up, Mavis thought, How different
this all seems, out here under the trees with the sun
shining down and me as near to God as I'll ever be in
this world, no need for show at all. She said a hearty,
"Amen!" when Eileen's words were finished.

Dale got the chicken gizzards and livers, his favorite
pieces, and Claude ate three drumsticks. Mavis was
glad for a piece of breast. Eileen praised the sandwiches, and they all told Claude how good the tomatoes were, he should enter them in the county fair.

When she cut the melon, Eileen said, "I hope it doesn't draw flies," but not a one came and they finished up the whole thing.

"I can't eat another bite," Mavis said, folding up her paper napkin.

Dale made an effort to get up. "Come on," he said, "we'll walk it off."

"Never in this world," Mavis said. "I'm going to stay right here." Then she pointed to the tree. "I've got a good mind to go over there and lie down on those needles and take me a little nap."

"Don't you ever do it," Eileen said. "You'll be full of chiggers tonight. And *that's* something you *don't* want."

"Well," Dale said, "Claude and I'll go exploring. Come on." He turned to the older man and told him, "We'll go down to the waterfall," then winked. "Maybe we'll see our reflection after all."

Smiling, Eileen and Mavis watched Dale and Claude disappear through the trees, then sat quietly for a long while without talking. A single yellow jacket swooped down, but Mavis waved it away with her napkin, and it didn't return. Neither one of them made any effort to pack up the food. With a yawn, Mavis said, "I can hardly keep my eyes open. I don't know when I've felt so satisfied."

"I'm glad we came," Eileen said and smiled. Then a frown turned down her lips. "But you know, I still can't get everything that's happened off my mind—so much meanness and now Brenda dead. I just don't understand it."

Mavis felt herself blush, a little ashamed that she had forgotten all about Eileen's recent tribulations. Sitting up straighter, she said, "I guess this is a good time for

me to confess. Maybe what I've got to say will clear
up things a little.''

"Confess what?''

"We made a little visit last night, Dale and I, after
he took me out to eat at the fish house.''

"Wherever to? I didn't know you knew anybody
else around here.''

Mavis waited a moment before she said, "Mamie
Spence,'' and then saw the sudden pain she feared
she'd cause rush into Eileen's eyes. Did she see that
country road where Mamie had waited with the whip
in her hands? Did she feel anew the stripes upon her
back?

"What for?'' Eileen asked. Her voice sounded as if
it came from some far-off place. "I spent years trying
to avoid her. When I'd see her in a store, at the Farmer's Market, I'd stop right in the middle of whatever
I was doing and leave. And, for a long time, I prayed
she'd move, though she never did. Since I hadn't seen
her lately, I'd begun to wonder if she was dead, maybe
wished it, however much a sin that might be.''

Mavis made no judgment. "I don't reckon she had
any place to go. Her only daughter, Tula Mae, the one
all the trouble was about, left home early on and, from
what Mamie said—she didn't try to hide it—was about
as sorry as they come.''

"But how did *you* know about Mamie Spence? I
never told you when we first met, and later it didn't
seem to matter.''

"That's what I have to confess,'' Mavis said. "I saw
the newspaper in the bottom of your dresser drawer. I
hate to tell you, but I caught Tara there reading through
anything she could get her hands on. I was going
to put it back, but curiosity got the best of me,

and I read the article. The name, 'Mamie Spence,' stayed with me, and when I heard it again, I thought there might be some connection.''

"Where did you hear it?''

"Right in your own yard. You did, too. When Sheriff Rhodes was questioning Tara and Jordache about the murder—Jordache gave his real name, Dennis Spence. He's Mamie's grandson, Tula Mae's baby son that was left after she died.''

Eileen brushed her hair back with both hands, then shook her head. "It sure escaped me. I guess I've closed my ears to that name so many years I didn't even hear it. But how did you ever find Mamie?''

"Easy,'' Mavis said with a smile. "Looked in the telephone book. She lives in a trailer court out off the highway.''

"I'm surprised she let you in.''

"Humph. She was right glad to see us, lonesome I guess, too old, too sick to worry about what happened in the past. Jordache seems to be her pride and joy, makes over her right much—at least that's how she tells it.''

"Maybe she's been trying to get back at me with all that's been going on.''

"I thought of that, too, but Mamie denies ever telling Jordache to do those things. It's enough for her that he's going with Tara, says it serves you right for being so high and mighty.''

Eileen's jaw went tight. "She's still a fool,'' she said. "I came from poor folks same as she did. I just decided I wasn't going to be ignorant the rest of my life and I put myself through school. But if it's not Jordache that's done all the things around my place— not to mention murder—then who *is* responsible?''

"Oh," Mavis said, "I didn't say he wasn't responsible. I just think he has a different motive. When I was at Mamie's, I borrowed a card with Jordache's handwriting on it. Soon as we get home, I want to look at it along side of that note you got in the mailbox warning you not to open the B&B—sure as anything they'll match. What we have to figure out now is why in the world Jordache should care."

You could hear Claude long before he appeared through the trees. "I found *three* arrowheads," he called out, trotting over the rocky ground in his bare feet, the delicate pieces of flint held out in front of him.

Dale was close behind. "He's got eyes like a hawk," he said. "You could set him up in business leading tourists on expeditions."

Beaming, Claude suddenly stopped, half turned, and held out one of the arrowheads to Dale. "Here," he said, "you take it. If it hadn't been for you, I might not of found a one."

"Thank you," Dale said, "but you keep it. Put it in your collection in the playhouse. That's where it belongs." Claude gave him a smile and carefully tucked the arrowheads into his overall pocket.

They packed up after that, poured the melted ice out of the cooler, put the garbage in the container, and carried the remaining food to the car. Taking one last look around before she got inside, Mavis thought to herself, It *has* been a nice day. Too bad we just couldn't stay here forever and forget about all that's happened. She almost hated to go home again, afraid that there might be more bad news waiting for them there.

They started down the mountain, and when they

passed the falls, Dale said, "We never did see our reflection," and even Claude laughed this time, as if he
understood the joke. Beneath the trees, the light seemed
to have thickened, and when they came out onto the
road that wound down the mountain, the sky had a
gauzy look; there might be rain. They passed only one
car, and when they turned onto the highway at the bottom, the traffic was light. "Well, here's your property
line," Dale said as Eileen signaled for the turn.

"Not quite yet," she said and headed into the tunnel
of trees.

It was Mavis who suddenly said, *"Stop!"* reaching
out to touch Eileen on the arm.

Eileen stomped on the brakes, the car stopped with
a jerk, and the cooler banged against the side of the
trunk. "What in the world?" Eileen said and looked
at Mavis as if she'd lost her mind.

"I'm sorry," Mavis said. "I didn't mean to scare
you." She pointed out the window. "I saw that stump
up yonder where you said the old road goes in, and all
of a sudden I felt I just *had* to go in there, I don't know
why. Maybe it's because I remember John and me listening to Vance talk about clearing off that spot in the
woods so many times." And if that wasn't quite the
truth, who was to know? She didn't want to tell them
that she'd seen a broken branch there and wondered
whether someone else had been down that road recently. She'd feel like a fool if they found nothing at
all. "Do you mind?" she asked Eileen and gave her a
smile.

"Of course not," Eileen said, starting up the car
again. "But it's probably all grown over now. I don't
know what you'll see." She turned the car into the
tracks, slowed even more as they bumped over rough

ground. Furry seeds drifted up from the weeds beneath the wheels, and tree branches slapped like hands against the windshield. When a thick wall of green loomed up in front of them, Eileen said, "This is about as far as we can go. You want to walk the rest of the way? It might be snaky."

Mavis shuddered but said, "I'll take the risk," so they got out of the car and began to walk single file through the woods, the leaves close about them, as if they moved through a dark hallway towards light ahead.

And sure enough, after no more than a three or four-minute walk, they emerged from the trees at the edge of a field bright as a sun-filled room. "Well, my goodness," Mavis said, her heart pounding, "it's not grown up at all."

"I'll say." Dale came up beside Mavis. "Somebody is cultivating a crop here."

Eileen had a look of amazement on her face. "Who in the world would do such a thing?" she said. But then she smiled as she reached out to touch the feathery leaves of one of the bright green, knee-high plants. "It *is* pretty, isn't it? I wonder what kind of plants they are."

"You don't *know?*" Dale's voice held a tone of amazement.

"Well, do you, Mr. Smarty-Pants?" Mavis asked him.

"Well, of course I do." He reached over and poked Eileen in the side. "You got a fine stand of marijuana growing on your back lot. It must be worth a fortune."

Eileen went pale. "Well, if this don't beat *all*," she said. "Who would have nerve enough to do such a thing? Do you think I'll be arrested?"

But before Mavis could say she didn't think it was very likely, Claude spoke up like it was as clear as anything to him. "It's Jordache's," he said. "I seen him working here. I hid in the trees and he didn't see me a-tall."

EIGHTEEN

As SOON AS THEY GOT HOME, Eileen had gone off to call Sheriff Rhodes and tell him what they had found in the woods, while Mavis and Dale put away the leftovers from the picnic and washed the few dishes they had used. Now, after hanging up the dishcloth to dry, Dale put the last platter away, then leaned against the counter and said, "No wonder Jordache wanted to keep the B&B from opening. He'd be scared to death that some of the guests might hike back that far in the woods and discover his secret little garden."

Mavis pulled off the bright yellow rubber gloves she'd been wearing. "He didn't know Eileen very well," she laughed. "It only made her more stubborn."

"I wonder how he knew about that patch of land in the first place."

"Tara, I bet anything. Vance was always going on about building him a house back there, and Tara probably heard it when she was a girl up here visiting. If Jordache was looking around for some spot to grow his dope and asked her, she'd be reminded," Mavis shook her head. "There's no reason to think she'd have any concern about Eileen a-tall."

"What are you two whispering about?" It was Eileen, coming through the kitchen door.

"Oh, nothing," Mavis said. "Just remarking that it

was no wonder Jordache didn't want you to open up the B&B, afraid his crop would be discovered.''

"That's what Sheriff Rhodes said. Jordache wouldn't likely be caught otherwise. They have plane spotters now—Jordache isn't the only one raising dope around here, it's replaced liquor stills—but they usually go further out into the mountains. Jordache was pretty safe this close to town, with all the houses around."

"Are they going after Jordache?" Dale asked.

"Right away, the sheriff said. They've been kind of keeping an eye on him anyway since the murder."

"Oh, Lord," Mavis said. "I had almost forgotten about that, with so much else going on. Is there any connection? Could Brenda have been involved?"

"I'd never believe it. Brenda wasn't that kind of a girl. And I never saw her say two words to Jordache when he was lying around here."

"Hey!" Dale stood up straighter by the counter, his eyes shining. "Maybe Brenda found out about the field. If she'd gone further in the woods blackberry picking, she might have stumbled on it. Maybe Jordache saw her and killed her to keep her quiet."

"Jordache is sorry as anything," Eileen said, "but I don't think he'd kill. Anyway, he'd never be up early enough to see Brenda picking berries." She stopped, a worried look on her face. "Still, I'm glad he didn't spot Claude peeping at him through the bushes. That fool! When I asked him why he didn't say anything, he said he didn't think it was important. Nobody else used the field—what difference did it make? Thank the Lord nothing happened to *him*."

THE REST OF THE AFTERNOON passed quietly. Eileen made a pound cake to freeze, ready for the church booth at the apple festival. "Don't tell a soul it's from a mix," she said. "It's easier and nobody can tell the difference, but I'd be ruined over at the church if anybody knew." Mavis washed out a pair of hose to wear to the funeral the next day. Dale slumped down in front of the TV set and dropped off to sleep in about two seconds. Smiling, Eileen said, "I wish I could go to sleep that easy. He's like a baby."

They were all startled when a car came rattling down the drive. Straightening up from the oven, Eileen said, "Who in the world can that be?" and walked out onto the porch. In just a minute, she said, "Why, it's the sheriff," and hurried over to the door and opened it. "Hey there!" she called out as she went down the steps to greet him, a little too loud, Mavis thought. She wondered if Eileen was worried about what might happen to Tara. Hanging up her apron, she walked out onto the porch.

"Who is that good looking man?" Dale asked her. He brushed his fingers through his hair.

"That's right," Mavis said. "You haven't met him. He's the sheriff. Lee Rhodes."

"*Sheriff!* Well, my goodness, I'd expect the sheriff around here to be pot-bellied and bald, with tobacco juice dripping off his chin. *That* one looks like something on TV. Do introduce us."

Eileen came up the steps with the sheriff just behind her. In her arms she carried a big bouquet of flowers wrapped in shiny florist's paper. "Look what the sheriff brought," she said, her eyes bright as new pennies. "Isn't that the *sweetest* thing?"

Giving them a big smile, Lee Rhodes said, "You

two ladies have been a big help. I wanted to do something to say, 'Thank you.'"

"What about *me?* I helped, too." Dale came up and put his arm around Mavis.

"Now, don't you pout," Mavis said with a laugh. She turned to Lee Rhodes. "This is my nephew, Dale Sumner," she said. "Always was the jealous type."

Lee laughed, too, offering his hand. "We'll say the flowers are for all of you. How about that?"

Hurrying to the china closet on the far wall of the porch, Eileen took out a cut glass vase. "Now you *will* stay for supper," she said to the sheriff. "I won't take no for an answer. All of you sit down at the table and I'll pour you a little glass of my scuppernong wine. I made it last summer." She almost giggled. "I guess you won't arrest me for *that,* will you?"

"Can I help?" Dale gave a dazzling smile.

"Why sure," Eileen said. "The wine glasses are over there." She pointed back to the china cabinet. "Use the pretty ones on the top shelf. This is a special occasion." She went into the kitchen, and they could hear water running in the sink. Dale busied himself getting the tinkling glasses out of the china closet.

Mavis couldn't stand it any longer. Here was Eileen running around like a sixteen-year-old before her first prom, and Dale not much better, like that bunch of flowers was the most important thing in the world. They seemed to have forgotten everything that had been going on. "Did you catch him?" she finally asked.

"Who?" The sheriff seemed to have forgotten, too. Then he said, "Oh, Jordache. Yes, ma'am, we went over as soon as Miz Hollowell called."

"What did he say?"

"Not much at first. I took several men with me, expecting maybe he'd put up a fuss. But he answered the door and let us in without any argument. He'd been sitting in his underwear, drinking a cola and watching TV. Tara was there with him." Lee looked over at Eileen who had come back quietly to stand in the doorway, the vase cradled in front of her. Then he went on. "They denied everything, of course, but we got a search warrant and went through the place. You've never seen such a mess. Clothes everywhere, a lot of expensive stereo equipment, jewelry, some other things I won't mention in polite company. And drugs, of course, hidden away. Not just what he was growing in that field, either, but a lot of other stuff, too—pills and cocaine.

"I guess at that point he decided it wasn't going to do him much good to keep denying everything, so he made a statement when we took him in." Lee looked at Eileen again. Mavis could tell he was embarrassed. "I hate to tell you," he said, "but he implicated Tara, said she was the one that told him about the field, though it was his idea what to plant. I guess she was responsible for some of the meanness around here, too."

Eileen half turned, as if she needed to check something in the kitchen, but Mavis knew it was to hide her tears. "She's made her bed and will have to lie in it," Eileen said after a moment. "Her daddy's got her out of trouble half her life. I knew it wouldn't do any good to have her up here this summer." She wiped her eyes. "Maybe we can hope this will teach her a lesson. Something needs to."

"Yes, ma'am," Lee said. "It'll help both of them if they cooperate. Jordache has been doing a lot of selling at that club on the highway, The Pit. We've been asking him about what else goes on there. We'd like to close the place down if we could.''

"Did he confess about the note?"

Lee stared at Mavis. "What note?" he said.

Mavis looked at Eileen. "You didn't tell him?" she asked.

"I guess I forgot, honey," Eileen said.

Mavis walked over to the china closet, pulled open the drawer, and reached inside. "Here," she said, coming back to stand in front of the sheriff with her arm stretched out. "Eileen found this note in her mailbox warning her not to open the B&B. Whoever it was didn't even try to disguise their handwriting. Now look at this." She gave him the Mother's Day card she had taken from Mamie Spence's trailer. "It's a known sample of Jordache's handwriting. If they aren't the same, I'll eat them both."

Taking the note and the card, Lee looked at them, then said, "They sure do look alike. But I expect we'll have plenty of charges against him to put him away for a long time. We won't need to worry about malicious damage to property and threatening notes."

"Well, what about murder?" Mavis said, her voice a bit sharp. She felt the sheriff should give her a little more credit for her sleuthing.

Lee Rhodes shook his head. "We don't have anything to tie him to it. The final medical report confirmed what we thought. Brenda was strangled, she was pregnant, but there's no way to say it's his child or come up with a reason why he'd want to kill her even if it was. Anyway, Tara says he was with her all that night and next morning."

Eileen's face flushed red. "Well, let's not stand around

here talking about sad things any longer," she said, changing the subject. "This is supposed to be a little *party*. I promised you some wine, and I'm going to get it right this minute. Mavis, you come help me." She started back into the kitchen, still carrying the vase, but then she turned around again. "You men sit down and enjoy yourselves," she said to Dale and Lee. "We'll have supper in a little while."

"Sure," Dale said, sitting on the sofa and picking up the remote control for the TV. "Maybe there's a ball game on."

Mavis had to laugh. It was the last thing in the world Dale would ever watch if he was alone. "If not, maybe you could get 'All My Children,'" she said as she turned towards the kitchen.

Dale gave her a hard look, then smiled.

FOR SUPPER, EILEEN COOKED a pork tenderloin with good country gravy, snap beans, and mashed potatoes. Five minutes before it was ready, Claude appeared, and Mavis went out onto the porch to tell Dale and Lee to wash up if they wanted to before they ate. Then they sat down. Except to tell Eileen how good the food was, nobody got a word in edgewise because Claude talked constantly about the three arrowheads he and Dale had found on Jump-off Mountain. Lee Rhodes listened to him with such a look of interest on his face that Claude might have been talking about the solution of the world's problems, and Eileen, who any other time would have told Claude to be quiet, sat smiling, her eyes blessing them all. It was a relief to forget all that had happened. Finally, after they had a piece of the extra pound cake Eileen had made, with fresh peaches and whipped cream on top, Lee Rhodes said he hated to eat and run but he wanted to check back by the office to see whether anything else had turned up on the case. There would be a bail hearing tomorrow for Jordache, he said, though he doubted that anybody would pay it.

They all accompanied him out to the car. The light had faded, and the sky was just one shade lighter blue than the mountain, but stars lit the yard as bright as day. Yellow flickers, like lightning bugs, came from the houses in the development next door when the wind blew through the trees. It was very quiet, and when they spoke, they kept their voices low, like children conspiring to stay up a little longer in the night. "Thank you again, Miz Hollowell," Lee Rhodes said as he got into his car. "I can't remember when I had such a good meal."

"You come again," Eileen said, peering to see his face through the windshield.

"Any time you ask me," he answered her. He closed the door and started the car. "I'll keep you posted on what's going on. We'll solve this case soon."

He drove off, and they stood in silence for a minute or two until the sound of the car finally faded, as if waiting for a spell to be broken. Then, laughing, Eileen said, "We'll turn into stone statues if we stand here any longer," turned and started back towards the house, and they walked after her single file.

Back in the house, Eileen headed straight to the kitchen, and Mavis began to stack the dishes. "You need any help?" Dale asked her.

"No, you go on," she said. "It won't take us a minute."

Dale gave her a wink and said, "I don't mind if I do. I think I'm going to have sweet dreams tonight."

He called out good night to Eileen and then walked out into the hallway.

Carrying a stack of plates, Mavis went to the kitchen. Eileen was standing by the sink with the water running, staring out the blackness of the window. "What is it, honey?" Mavis asked.

"Oh, nothing." Eileen shook her head and reached for the bottle of detergent and squirted some into the water. "I was just thinking."

"I can guess what about," Mavis said as she set the plates on the counter. "I'm real sorry about what's happened. About Tara." Eileen blinked back tears but didn't speak, and Mavis went on. "They don't have much on her. She's just an accessory from what Lee Rhodes said. If she testifies against that sorry Jordache, they might just give her a suspended sentence."

"I know. What hurts is the meanness. She had to be the one that broke all my bottles. Nobody else would have known about them. And she must have known, too, that Jordache killed Claude's ducks, even if she didn't have a hand in it. I hope it isn't born in."

"I don't think so. People can change. Like you said, maybe all this will teach her a lesson."

"I hope so, but I don't have the strength to be the one to change her. She's her daddy's responsibility now. He'll have to take care of her." Eileen suddenly fluffed up the suds in the sink. "Come on," she said in a louder voice. "Let's get these pots and pans done and get to bed. We've got other sorrows to face tomorrow."

NINETEEN

THE CHURCH WHERE BRENDA'S funeral was to be held
lay up a dusty unpaved road that cut off past the Trulls'
place and wound back into the mountains for a mile or
more. Leaning forward, Mavis peered through the
windshield of the car to see if she could see the building, but the overhanging trees and the dust Eileen's old
rattletrap churned up blocked her view. With a little
cough, she put her handkerchief to her mouth and
hoped she wouldn't look like she'd ridden through the
Sahara desert when they got there. Then she thought,
Maybe we shouldn't be going at all, but she didn't
whisper a word of it to Eileen.

Before leaving the house, Mavis and Eileen and Dale
had eaten a solemn breakfast—Claude already up and
out, no doubt prowling around somewhere, and then
had gone to their rooms to dress. No matter where she
went, Mavis always carried a good dark dress with her,
and if anyone ever asked her why, she would have told
them, You just never know when you might need it,
for a wedding or a funeral—wasn't today a perfect ex-
ample? When she'd left home she had no idea she'd
be attending services for some child who was a perfect
stranger to her, but here she was, dressing ready to
go to the church with her black patent purse and

white gloves laid out on the bed, waiting to complete her ensemble.

Even Dale had come up with a nice sport coat, a clean white shirt and a tie, and though he wore blue jeans and tennis shoes, he looked as nice as could be with his hair combed and smelling of cologne. Eileen had on her Sunday dress, navy blue, sandals instead of the usual thongs, but no hose. "I'd burn up," she had said. "Who's going to be looking at my legs anyway?" After Kevin came up on his bike, already sweating in a dark suit, they had climbed into Eileen's car, Mavis in front with Eileen, Dale and Kevin in back, and started out.

"Lord, we could sure use some rain," Eileen said, peering through the cloud of dust in front of the car.

"Let's hope not during the funeral," Mavis said, still unable to see much of anything out the window. "I expect the tears Brenda's mama sheds will be enough without a flood outside. And this road will turn to mud after two drops."

When the road finally dead-ended in the parking lot in front of the church, they saw several cars and trucks already parked there, dustier and even more dilapidated than Eileen's old Chevrolet. Eileen drove up and parked next to one of the trucks that had an old sofa in the back and a bumper sticker saying HONK IF YOU LOVE JESUS pasted to the fender, and they got out of the car. Mavis stepped carefully, hoping that she could keep the dust from covering her shoes.

"Well, they aren't exactly running out to greet us," Dale said in a low voice with a slight nod of his head towards the group of people who stood near the entrance of the church. When Mavis looked up at them, they seemed as still as a photograph, unmoving, their looks not particularly hostile, but not welcoming, either, maybe just curious, wondering why the four of them had come. They, too, had made some effort to dress for the occasion, Mavis noticed, the men standing a little away with suit coats carefully folded over their arms, the women hovering together in dark print dresses all made from what looked like the same pattern, not a sign of makeup on anyone's face, not a single piece of jewelry to brighten their clothes. A few children ran between the groups, tow-headed, with raw haircuts, pale and unhealthy looking. Mavis thought they might have worms.

They walked towards the entrance of the church, the eyes of the congregation following them. The building was old, covered in asbestos siding, mud-splattered, with a roof of flaking tin. In some better time, they must have started building a steeple, but it had never been completed and stood, unpainted now and rotting, a reminder of failed dreams. Out behind, a small cemetery stretched beneath the trees, some few graves displaying artificial wreaths as bright as neon signs. No grass grew there, not a flower. Poor Brenda, Mavis thought, to be buried in such an ugly place.

As they passed the two groups by the steps, several of the women smiled. Mavis nodded her head and tried to look friendly; there was no need to be ill mannered even if the others were a little standoffish. Once inside the vestibule they were greeted by a man with close-cropped hair and cuts on his face from shaving who said, "Welcome, brothers and sisters," but didn't offer to shake their hands. Behind him on a table Mavis saw a stack of religious tracts entitled "Will You Burn in Hell for All Eternity?" She thought it more likely they'd melt right there in church with the sun pouring down on the tin roof.

But when they went inside the sanctuary, it was pleasantly cool, the pale green glass in the half-opened windows tinting the light so that it was like forest shadows. "Let's slip in here near the back," Eileen whispered, pointing to a row of benches just a little ways down the aisle. They followed her and sat down on the hard seats, eyes focused a moment or so on folded hands before they raised their heads and looked around.

Well, the inside of the church looked just about as pitiful as the outside, Mavis thought. Not even the main aisle was carpeted and the bare wooden floor squeaked with every step as the other mourners began to file in and move towards the front. The walls near the ceiling were covered with dark water stains. Except for two stiff looking chairs sitting on the platform in front and an old upright piano, there was no other furniture, not even a table with waiting collection plates. To Mavis it looked as if only death had any place there, no trace of God's glory anywhere to be seen.

But maybe, she thought, as she looked at the rear wall where a crude painting stretched from the baptismal fount almost to the ceiling, that's how they see their God, a wild-looking Christ with bloody arms outstretched, one fist holding a mass of writhing serpents, evil cast out. They had no need for golden haloes and the brightness of angel's wings. Lord, the picture was ugly, Mavis thought. She hoped she didn't dream of those eyes staring down.

But then she caught her breath. Beneath the painting sat a pale pink casket—Brenda lying there. Mavis had almost forgotten why they had come. She was about to whisper to Eileen, what an awful place to lay that child, but before she could get the words out, Eileen turned to her instead and said, "We ought to go up and view the body," then stood up.

Mavis and Kevin and Dale followed Eileen down the aisle with Jesus's eyes following them to where a line had formed. The plain men and women of the church turned around, eyed them, then turned away again, slowly moving towards the casket. What in the world do they think of us? Mavis wondered. But she held her head high, feeling that she had every right to be there. She may not have known Brenda, but Eileen had, and it was enough that she was Eileen's friend there to support her.

They stopped by the casket, pink, a deeper pink inside, with a skimpy spray of gladiolus on top tied with ribbon that had "Love from Mama and Daddy" spelled out in golden letters. My goodness, Mavis thought, looking down, wasn't she pretty? and felt tears springing to her eyes as she remembered another pink casket, her own dead child. Brenda's hair was a pale honey color, curling over the pillow in the casket, her lashes darker against the delicate web of blue veins on her eyelids. Her skin was smooth, untouched by sun even though it was the middle of the summer, and the fingerprints on her neck (thank the Lord!) were not visible. Dressed in a little girl dress of white organdy with ruffles around the neck and a pale pink sash, it was probably the only pretty thing she had ever worn in her short life. She held a carnation in her hand.

"She does look peaceful, doesn't she?" It was Kevin beside her. Dale reached out and squeezed his shoulder.

Thinking again of her daughter, Mavis answered, "There has to be a special place in Heaven reserved for people like that,'' and Kevin looked up at her and smiled.

Mavis looked down at the clasped hands one more time. Then she stiffened. Suddenly, the memory of Brenda's arms flailing upwards when they had lain her on the ground in front of the playhouse passed before her eyes, the hands as pale and white then as they were now. And it came to her what had seemed wrong about that sight all along, though she had never been able to put it into words before. ''Oh, my Lord—'' she said aloud, then caught herself, remembering where she was, and tried to turn the words into a cough.

''You okay, honey?'' Eileen asked in a low voice, taking her arm. Perhaps she was thinking of Mavis's child, too.

''Just fine,'' she said and smiled, trying not to reveal her excitement. She couldn't wait to tell Sheriff Rhodes what she'd suddenly realized.

After everyone had sat down again, the family came down the aisle, Alton Trull in front, wearing a heavy gray winter suit that was too big for him, borrowed, Mavis would guess. His hair was slick with oil and a cowlick at the part flared upwards. He walked without looking left or right, as if led by the painted Jesus on the church's wall. Next came Wanda Faye in a dark blue dress that matched her eyes and almost made her tired plain face look pretty. She held the hands of the two little boys tightly, as if she was afraid they'd jerk away and start playing, and when they sat down on the second row, she tried to tuck their white shirttails inside their pants. Squirming, they pulled away from her and made a face. Last of all came Kristal, walking a little behind the others as if she didn't want to be seen with them, a smirk on her lips that said that as soon as she

could she would be gone from this place, never to return. The ugly plain dress she wore, Mavis thought,
must have belonged to Brenda, and she gave a sudden
shudder when it occurred to her that Kristal could end
up the very same way as her sister.

"Let's all sing hymn number twenty-nine, 'There is
a Fountain Filled with Blood,' said a woman who got
up from a front pew and walked over to the piano with
a slight limp and sat down. When she began to play—
boogie-woogie chords that reminded Mavis of Sunday
morning services on the radio, the only thing she could
ever get while she dressed for church—the congregation stood up and began to sing. Right away, a fat,
shiny-faced woman, almost dancing, grabbed a tam-
bourine from the top of the piano and began to bang it
with her hand. Pagan, Mavis thought, and kept her lips
tightly closed. She'd never liked that song anyway, and
certainly didn't think it was anything to sing at a sweet
child's funeral.

After they had all sat down again, the preacher came
in from a side door and stepped up to the pulpit. He
was a solid man, red from the sun, with hands like large
hams carrying a worn black leather Bible that he
slammed down in front of him. Staring out at the congregation with small eyes set too close together, he
rolled up his sleeves, wiped his brow (he was already
sweating), and began to read: "And he said unto them,
'Go ye into all the world, and preach the gospel to
every creature. He that believeth and is baptized shall
be saved; but he that believeth not shall be damned.'"

For what seemed like a long time, he was silent,
looking out at the audience, as if they were all in dan-
ger of damnation. Even the two Trull boys were quiet,
staring up at him. When he finally spoke, his voice was

so quiet that they had to strain to hear him, a singsong sound, lulling. But after his first few sentences his voice began to rise, and in no time at all he was shouting at them, the words raining down on their heads like hail on the rusty tin roof.

"Oh, that poor child," he shouted, "cut down in the flower of her youth. At least we can be comforted that she was baptized, she was saved, and today she lives up in glory with *Jesus.*" His voice softened for a moment, he may have shed a tear. "I remember how she came forward three years ago and said she had accepted the Lord Jesus Christ as her savior. I can still see the happy tears on her mama and daddy's faces. Back yonder," he pointed behind him to the baptismal fount, "I baptized her, washed her sins away, and she became a member of this flock."

He paused, wiped his face, then began to talk again, even louder this time, faster, making little grunts when he paused for breath. No one else in the building moved.

"But that wasn't enough to save her from the wickedness of this world. Her poor parents tried to lead her in the right direction, brought her here to witness with the rest of us, prayed over her, but the Devil—*Sin!*—attacked her, and she was not strong enough to cast him out. She was blinded by the glitter of clothes, jewelry, tempted by the Devil's own music, by *lust,* and instead of speaking with a new tongue of her love for Jesus, like the Bible says, she defied her parents and went her own way."

The preacher stopped then to catch his breath, his shirt soaked, his face redder than the sun's bright flush. Around the room several *Amens!* rose up, tentative at first, then louder, and down in front two

women suddenly stood, their eyes closed tightly and
their bodies arching, and began to jerk. A jumble of
sounds tumbled from their lips. "This is disgusting,"
Eileen said so that they all could hear. "How can they
dishonor sweet little Brenda in such a way?" She
wiped away tears. "Her mama and daddy ought to put
an end to this right now."

But instead of raising his voice against all that had
been said, Alton Trull jumped up, turned towards that
congregation, and with his Adam's apple bobbing up
and down, began to echo the preacher's words.

"That's right," he said, "we tried to keep her from
sinning, from turning away from the ways of our dear
Lord Jesus, but she defied us." His voice suddenly
dropped, as if to whisper; he wiped spittle from his lips
with the back of his hand. Then he almost shouted,
"*And they had help!* It won't just her own ideas that
led her astray. Other folks poisoned her mind, made
her think she was better than us. *They* gave her the
Devil's own books to read, taught her to paint her lips
and cover herself in shameful clothes. *They're* the reason she's lying dead in that there coffin with a little
bitty baby in her belly. And they've come here today
with no shame for what they done!"

Alton Trull pointed to the back of the church where
Eileen sat with the others, his arm outstretched and his
eyes as wild as those of the painted Jesus rising up
behind him. Everyone turned to stare, their own eyes
blank as stones; even the children cast hard looks.

Standing, Eileen put her purse under her arm and
said, "Come on, we're going," then moved out into
the aisle. The others followed her. Mavis reached out
to take Eileen's arm, but before she could touch her,
comfort her, Eileen turned and said in a voice that car-

ried into every corner of the building, "You should be ashamed of yourselves, carrying on like this. Brenda was a good girl, innocent. All she wanted was a little happiness. If anybody drove her away, it was you all. Here is where sin is, not in her heart."

She marched out of the church into the vestibule, the others right behind her. You could hear an intake of breath, like wind, back inside. Mavis felt a sudden moment of panic, wondering if the congregation would come rushing out ready to stone them in the parking lot. Dale hurried to open the outer door. Mavis noticed a sign on it saying, "Special Witnessing Service Tonight at 9:00." They walked outside.

The sky had grown darker. Wet spots as big as silver dollars lay on the dusty ground. "Come on," Dale said, putting his hand under Mavis's elbow. "Let's get to the car before it pours. You don't want to get your finery wet."

They all laughed then, suddenly released from the ugly little church and all the awful things that had been said there, and began to hurry over the dusty lot to the car. "Lord, I can't wait to get away," Mavis said, puffing from the run. "I've got to call the sheriff."

"What for?" Dale asked as he helped her into the car. Eileen, on the other side, looked at Mavis questioningly.

"I have to tell him something."

"What?" Dale slammed the door and climbed quickly into the backseat.

With her hands propped on her purse and a little smile of satisfaction on her face, Mavis said, "Brenda wasn't murdered there in the woods while she was picking berries for Eileen. Whoever killed her did it somewhere else, then brought her there and tried to make it look like she had died of snakebite.''

''How in the world do you know?'' Eileen said.

''I realized when I looked at Brenda's body today and saw her own sweet hands holding a carnation, pure white, unblemished. They were the very same the day she died. I saw them when they took her out of the playhouse. It's bothered me all along but I didn't know why.''

''I still don't understand,'' Dale said.

''*Stains.*'' Mavis gave the word special emphasis. ''Or the lack of them. Brenda hadn't picked any blackberries that day or her hands would have been stained with the juice. Somebody else filled that basket with berries and left it turned over by her body. The snakebite must have come after that.''

Just then, a bolt of lightning crashed somewhere behind the church, lighting up the dull tin roof. Eileen started the car. ''I hope those fools inside take that as a sign to stop their craziness,'' she said. ''And pray that it doesn't rain before they get that girl in the ground. She needs some peace at last.''

TWENTY

"WHY, ISN'T THIS A NICE surprise," Lee Rhodes said when he picked up the phone. Mavis had called the sheriff as soon as she got back home from Brenda's funeral. "What can I do for you?"

"I've just had a revelation," Mavis said.

After a pause, he answered, "Well, that's real nice, Miz Lashley."

Mavis suddenly realized he wouldn't know what in the world she was talking about. "At Brenda Trull's funeral. Something important came to me."

"What?"

"Her hands."

"Her hands?"

Mavis knew she would have to calm down or she'd never make him understand. She took a deep breath, then went on to tell Lee about the funeral earlier in the day and Brenda's pale hands. How they should have been stained the day she died but weren't, how it was likely she was killed somewhere else and brought to the woods. Lee listened quietly until she had finished. Then, after a moment, he said, "Well, that does make sense. We thought she'd been dragged. We found grass stains on her clothes but just assumed they got there when Claude was toting the body around. Maybe that explains the position of the body, too."

"What do you mean?"

"Well, Claude said he found Brenda lying on her back there in the leaves, but the way the blood had settled, it looked like she'd been more curled up on her side after she died. We thought Claude wasn't remembering correctly, but maybe he was right after all. She could have been transported there in a car, then spread out. That's something we hadn't thought about before. I'll have the lab boys examine the clothing more closely. They may find something from the car sticking to them."

Mavis smiled to herself. "So you don't think my 'revelation' is a piece of foolishness after all?"

"Oh, no, ma'am. I think it's real important. You keep right on having those revelations. We need them." He laughed and told Mavis goodbye and then hung up. Mavis went back to the porch.

"I'm fixing us some sandwiches for lunch," Eileen called from the kitchen. Kevin was there talking to Dale. After they had returned from the funeral Eileen asked him to stay on for lunch, but he had said he wasn't hungry after all that had happened at the church. Eileen told him, "Now, you stay. You've got to eat a little something or you'll be sick," and he'd seemed pleased and said he'd change his mind.

"I think I'll go to my room and just slip out of this dress," Mavis said. Nodding, the others smiled at her, and she turned and went out into the hallway. She *did* want to take off her good dress. Lord knows, given all that had happened she might need it again, but she had another reason for going to her room. The words of the preacher at Brenda's funeral were still ringing in her ears, not just the awful things he said about the dead girl lying there but the piece of scripture he had read at the beginning. Every year, Mavis read the New Testament straight through so that, by now, she could quote whole passages by heart, and she knew that the verses he had chosen led up to something else, she just couldn't remember what.

Changing quickly, she hung up her dress, then sat down on the bed and reached for her Bible on the stand beside it. When she looked in the concordance under "baptism," she found the passage she wanted with no trouble and reread the verses she'd heard at the funeral. She was almost afraid to look at the words of the next verse, but, with her breath half held, she went on, and with each new word that burned into her eyes, a terrible thought began to form in her head. She read the lines once more, then slammed shut the Bible. "But even if it's true," she said aloud, "what would it have to do with Brenda's death?" She didn't know then but, one way or another, she'd find out.

"Lord, I was about to send the Rescue Squad," Eileen said when Mavis returned to the kitchen. "You took so long."

"Just getting slow in my old age," Mavis said, walking up to the counter where Dale was opening a jar of Eileen's homemade pickles.

"Pshaw," Eileen said over her shoulder as she went out onto the porch with a pitcher of iced tea. "That'll be the day." Then she filled the glasses and called out to Claude and Kevin, who had gone down to the play-house to look at Claude's treasures, to come on in for lunch.

Quickly, before Eileen could come back, Mavis whispered to Dale, "Don't you make any plans for this evening. We've got another little trip to make."

"What is it this time?" he said, putting a round of cucumber in his mouth.

"Never you mind. I'll tell you later. But for now, it's just between you and me. Understand?"

He smiled and gave her a quick kiss on the cheek and then went out to the porch carrying the dish of pickles in front of him like they'd just been awarded first prize at the county fair.

ALL AFTERNOON MAVIS TRIED to think up some excuse she could give Eileen so that she and Dale could go off alone that night without raising Eileen's suspicions. If she'd told her what she suspected, surely Eileen would say, Have you lost your mind, Mavis Lashley. At the very least, I'm going along with you, and what you *should* do is call up the sheriff this very minute and let him do the investigating. But she couldn't do that. It was her idea and she had to find out for herself whether she was right or wrong. Finally, after they finished supper, she just said plain out, "Eileen, honey, I'd like to get a little fresh air. It's been real close all day. Dale and I are going to take a ride. You're welcome to come along, of course."

Eileen looked relieved. "You go ahead," she said. "I've still got some things to do if this place is going to be ready for guests by the weekend. I don't mind a bit."

"I *do* wonder what you're up to," Dale whispered as Mavis passed by.

"You'll see," she said, and went to her room to get her sweater.

Except for the few large drops that had pockmarked the dusty ground around the church that morning, there had been no more rain. Still, the sky had remained leaden all afternoon, and now, at a little past eight, it was dark outside, the air still, like breath held. Heat lightning glowed at the horizon. "You may get wet," Eileen called out as Dale and Mavis walked out to the car. "Be careful."

"Maybe it'll wash some of the dust off this car," Dale said back to her, and they both laughed. Then Dale helped Mavis inside, got in and started up the car, but stopped at the gate. Throwing up his hands, he said, "Well, now you'll *have* to tell me where we're going. I don't know which way to turn."

"Okay, smarty," Mavis told him. "Turn right. We're going back to that church. You think you can find it in the dark?"

"Sure, but I'm not real certain I want to. They didn't exactly give us a warm welcome this morning. And, anyway, won't the place be closed up tight as a tick tonight?"

"Didn't you see the sign?"

"What sign?" Dale briefly flashed the turn signal and turned into the darkened roadway.

"On the door. I noticed as we walked out, something about a 'special witnessing service tonight.' I want to see what that's like."

"My goodness," he said, "what if you get to shouting with that bunch of holy rollers? Don't count on me to pick you up if you fall out on the floor."

"Don't make fun," she said and gave him a little tap on the arm. He smiled back at her and drove on.

The road was as dark as a tunnel. They passed no other cars, and the only sign of life was a raccoon that shambled across the road, eyes flashing in the headlights before it disappeared beneath the trees. "You're sure this is right?'' Dale asked when Mavis indicated the turn-off.

''I think so,'' she answered, hoping they weren't lost.

When they finally did see the church up ahead (Dale complaining mightily about what the bumps in the road would do to his little car), Mavis told him to pull in beneath the trees and cut the motor. She got out carefully, glad she had worn her good walking shoes. The last thing in the world she needed to do was break an ankle in the dark.

Trying not to crunch on the gravel, they walked slowly past the few parked cars and trucks, but when they got closer to the church, they realized that they needn't be concerned about making any noise. From the brightly lit building came the sound of voices raised in song, accompanied this time by tambourines and the thump of an electric guitar. You could shoot off a cannon and no one in there would have heard. Still, when Dale seemed to be headed for the front door that led into the vestibule of the church, Mavis said, ''No!'' in a half whisper, then added, ''Come around to the side,'' and motioned for him to follow her.

''Lordy, Miz Mavis,'' he said, ''I never thought I'd live to see the day when you'd become a Peeping Tom!''

''Hush,'' she told him over her shoulder and went on.

Trying to keep their heads low, they crept up to a window tilted open halfway down the side of the building. A shaft of light slanted out and lit the ground. As she moved close to the wall, Mavis tried to avoid it, as if she would be immediately spotlighted for all to see if she stepped there. Slowly, she raised her head

up to the window ledge, then a little higher, then higher
still until she could look inside. Her heart gave a sudden leap and she almost yelled out—there was the
painted Christ with his arms uplifted staring straight
into her eyes. She must have made some sound because
Dale, coming up behind her, whispered in her ear,
"You all right, honey?" and then squeezed her arm.

"Yes," she said and swallowed. "Look." She
pointed to the little group gathered near the piano at
the front of the church.

A young man—boy really, one Mavis hadn't seen
before—played the guitar. Dressed in blue jeans and a
T-shirt with a faded emblem on the front, he looked
gawky as a young bird, head too big, legs too long, his
skin pale pink. He played with his eyes closed and
mouth half open, and Mavis could see that his teeth
were stained. The others she thought she recognized
from the service that morning, the two women who had
spoken in tongues, several of the men who were
dressed now in work clothes, their wild hair no longer
dampened down, arms upraised and eyes half closed,
strange sounds coming from their mouths. Alton Trull
moved among them shouting like the rest. In a front
row pew, sitting quietly, were several of the pale children who had been running back and forth earlier in
the parking lot.

"Halleluia!" cried the preacher as he came dancing
across the floor from the corner, his Bible held high in
front of him as if it was a rock that would save him
from drowning in his own sweat. It flew from his
flushed face, his shirt was soaked, and every time he
opened his mouth he sprayed the air with saliva. Mavis
thought, he's going to die of a heart attack right there,

but he continued to dance back and forth while the others jerked around him.

Then the music stopped. Mavis pulled back, alarmed, afraid someone had seen her and Dale outside the window. But no one looked their way, the people there suddenly calmed, as if waiting for some direction. The eyes of Christ seemed to have narrowed. When the preacher spoke, his voice was soft as that of a child. "It is time now," he said, wiping his damp face. "We must confirm our faith. *Jesus* has demanded it. This will be our witnessing for him."

He lowered his Bible, closed it, and placed it on the edge of the platform, his shoulders sagging, almost as if he felt great sorrow. Then, slowly, he walked a little further along the platform to four wooden boxes that sat at the edge, the others crowding around him, blocking him from view. Now where have I seen boxes like that before? Mavis asked herself, but the memory wouldn't come. She bent a little closer to the window, trying to see what was happening there.

"Praise the Lord!" came the voice of the preacher again in a roar. The music started up, shrieking, and after a moment the congregation fell back, eyes glazed, so that he was revealed with uplifted arms in front of the opened boxes holding a rattlesnake in each hand.

"Sweet Jesus!" Dale exclaimed. Mavis felt her legs go weak.

And while Mavis and Dale stood there in the darkness watching, the others inside the church seemed to waken from their trance as they gaily approached the boxes and picked up more snakes, holding them aloft while they crooned at the spitting tongues and draped the bodies around their heads. They strutted and swayed, handing the snakes back and forth with joyful smiles, shouting, "Thank you, Jesus! Thank you, Jesus!" while the children in their front row pew sat in wonderment with rounded eyes, as if they watched "Sesame Street" on TV. From high above, the hooded eyes of Christ looked down, a tangle of writhing serpents in his own hand.

"You seen enough?" Mavis asked, touching Dale on the arm. She realized she was trembling.

"God, yes!" he answered and started to say more, but his face was suddenly illumined by a silvery flash that lit up the entire church, the parking lot, the woods beyond, and any words he might have said were silenced by a crack of thunder that followed immediately after.

Mavis gasped, grabbed onto Dale with both hands. "Do you think they saw us peeping in?" she asked him. "What'll we do?"

"Run!" he said. "Come on." And, clasping her hand tightly in his, he lit out across the parking lot with Mavis just behind him, half flying she felt, no longer concerned about a misstep. She could feel her hose snagging on weeds, and there was a sudden sharp slap against her leg, but she didn't stop to look. All she wanted to do was get away from there, from the snakes and those fools handling them, from that awful painted Christ whose eyes she could still feel following her. Another flash of lightening came, thunder, and, this time, huge drops of rain that fell straight down, so that by the time they reached the car and jumped inside they were soaked to the skin.

TWENTY-ONE

"YOU *SUSPECTED* THEY WERE snake handlers?" Dale had said once they were in the car and away from the church, with no lights following along behind them in the darkness. "And you didn't *tell* me? I thought I would fall right out when they started waving those snakes around! You remember that time when we were out at Grandpa's and I snuck out to the scuppernong arbor and thought I saw a snake in the vines? I ran half a mile back to the house and couldn't sleep for a week. What if I'd fainted, or run off and left you back there by yourself?"

"You never would." Mavis shook her head, then gingerly felt her hair to see if the rain had taken all the curl out. "Maybe I *did* suspect, but suspecting wasn't knowing, and if I'd have told anyone and then it wasn't true, I'd feel like a fool."

"What *did* make you suspicious?"

"The preacher, the scripture he read at Brenda's funeral."

In the light of the dashboard Mavis could see Dale's lips turned down in a frown. "I don't remember anything special," he said. "What did I miss?"

"Nothing that he actually said, more what he left out."

"And you knew right away?"

"No, not immediately, just that something was left out. I didn't know for sure what it was until I looked in my Bible and found the passage and read the rest of it."

"What did it say?"

"I memorized it word for word," she said. "You want a recitation?" She laughed before he could answer, and then, sitting up straighter, with her torn hose and her clammy dress sticking to her back, she repeated the verses for him:

"And these signs shall follow them that believe: In my name shall they cast out devils: they shall speak with new tongues; they shall take up serpents; and if they drink any deadly thing, it shall not hurt them; they shall lay hands on the sick, and they shall recover."

"You get a gold star!" Dale looked over at her with a smile.

"Don't be smart," she said, but smiled back at him. Then she knew her look became more serious. "Those poor fools," she said. "They believe those verses exhort them to test their faith in God. If their faith is strong enough, then nothing can happen to them, and they handle deadly snakes and drink Lord knows what kind of poisons to prove it. Every now and then you see a piece in the paper about one of them dying, but the others keep right on as if they didn't have a lick of sense."

Dale shuddered. "I don't know that I'd pick any of them to cast out devils. Seems to me they've got more than enough of their own without worrying about anybody else's."

They were almost home now. Though lightning still flashed on the horizon, the thunder had become a low rumble and the rain had almost stopped. Through the windshield, Mavis suddenly saw the car lights reflecting on the white wooden fence and the B&B sign by the drive. "Don't tell Eileen anything about what we saw tonight," she said to Dale as he turned in at the gate.

"Why not?"

"We've got a little more investigating to do in the morning. I don't want her upset. She's got enough on her mind, with guests arriving on Saturday and Tara sitting downtown in jail."

"*What* investigating?" Mavis couldn't see but wondered if Dale rolled his eyes towards the roof of the car. "I'd think you would have had enough tonight."

"Never you mind," she said. "As soon as we get into the house, you can go right on up to bed."

Dale stopped the car and opened the door. "You want to come along with me and turn on the light? I'll be expecting a big snake to come slithering across the floor."

"Hush your silliness," she said. "You're not a little boy anymore. Of course there won't be any snakes."

But later, after she had walked inside and called out good-night to Eileen, thankful that she was still working in the kitchen and hadn't stuck her head out to see Mavis's wet, torn clothing, Mavis had gone to her room and, hating herself for it, had looked under her bed, the sight of Alton Trull and the others holding up the wiggling snakes still bright before her eyes. She prayed she wouldn't see them in her dreams.

EARLY NEXT MORNING, she told Eileen that she and Dale were going to the Farmer's Market to do some shopping. "I want to buy a few little gifts for folks back home," she said.

Eileen, wiping off the counter after they had finished the breakfast dishes, said, "I thought you bought those jars of jelly from Wanda Faye Trull for that."

"Yes, ma'am," she said and gave Eileen a smile. "I wanted her to think that. She looked so pitiful standing there. I thought it would make her feel better if I took a few jars. But, Lord have mercy, that jelly looks too bad to give anyone, and if I kept it for myself, I know I'd never feel safe eating even one bite."

"Well, you go on and enjoy yourselves. I've got work to do."

Dale took Mavis's arm, and they walked out to the car. "Are we *really* going to the Farmer's Market?" he asked in a whisper.

"Not directly," she told him. "If we get everything wrapped up, maybe we'll go to town and have a little chat with the sheriff. Then we can go to the market."

"Maybe we ought to have him with us if you're going to go poking around some more. I don't want to meet up with another bunch of snakes."

"Shoot," Mavis said. "You don't have to worry. We're just going on a little social call. Ask a few questions."

"Well, *you* give the directions," he said, starting the car. "Where to?"

"To the Trulls' house. Where else?"

"*That's* no social call."

"Hush up," she told him. "Just drive."

THE PLACE LOOKED DESERTED when they bounced down the road and stopped at the edge of the yard. The truck was gone, and though they waited a few minutes before they got out of the car, none of the children slipped out from behind the screen door to stare at them. "Maybe this was a wild goose chase," Dale said. "Looks like nobody's home."

"We'll see," Mavis said, getting out of the car. "Come on."

Dale shook his head. "You're not going to march into an empty house right in broad daylight, are you?"

"This is the *country*," Mavis said. "Used to be, if you left the front door open, it was an invitation for a visitor to go inside and wait around till somebody came home. You could even eat if there was anything on the table. Maybe the Trulls still think that way."

They walked across the yard slowly, the grass still wet from last night's rain making patterns on their shoes. On the steps of the porch sat several potted plants. Mavis wondered if Wanda Faye had put them out during the storm to wash the dusty leaves. At least the poor thing hadn't been at church handling snakes. They started up the steps, half expecting the old dog to slink from beneath the porch, but the house was still, only a bird sang, and the screen door, all shimmery in the early morning light, remained closed.

Dale opened it and shouted out, "Anybody home?" but got no answer. He called again but still there was silence.

"Go on in," Mavis said, coming up the steps behind him.

"All right, but if we get arrested for breaking and entering, don't blame me." With a little flourish, Dale opened the screen door, held it while Mavis went through, then followed her inside. They stood in the middle of the living room floor looking around. "Not exactly *House Beautiful*, is it?" Dale said.

"Be ashamed!" Mavis said. "They're *poor*. They can't help it. At least it's clean." But she had to admit that the room was depressing to her. Despite the morning light that came pouring through the windows, the room seemed drab, the furniture faded, the pattern of roses on the linoleum rug worn down in spots to the dark backing beneath. Not a picture hung on the walls; no curtains softened the windows. Why in the world didn't Wanda Faye cut some of her flowers and set them on a table there in a bright vase? At least it would bring one spot of color to that barren room. But then, Mavis thought, it would never occur to her, poor woman. Probably all her life, she'd had nothing, expected nothing, and the idea of taking one beautiful blossom from the garden to enjoy herself would have seemed a sin, like stealing.

The dining room was no better, no sign that anyone ever ate there, with two single beds pushed against one wall and an unfinished pine chest no one had bothered to paint across from them on the other side. It must be where the two little tow-headed boys slept, Mavis guessed, though there wasn't a toy in sight, not even a teddy bear to comfort dreams. Did they watch their daddy fondling snakes in that ugly church? Mavis shuddered at the thought.

She was about to go on to the kitchen when she saw the picture sitting on the mantel behind the space heater. Walking over, she picked up the golden frame and suddenly caught her breath—Brenda, photographed in her commencement gown. Mavis had seen only her dead body before, which had given her no real sense of what the living, breathing child had been like. But now, as she looked at the smiling face framed by pale hair nicely curled (Eileen had paid for that, she'd bet), set off by the light blue robe, eyes as clear and pure as morning light, perhaps with just a touch of added color on the lips, she thought, Oh what a loss! Her sweet life had hardly begun. And, with a rush in her chest like wind, she remembered her own vibrant daughter, almost heard her laughter in that deserted room, and sudden tears filled her eyes. When Dale asked her if she was all right, she shook her head yes, brushed her hand across her face, and returned the portrait to the mantel, turning it to the wall.

The kitchen was dark, and they stood a moment in the doorway waiting for their eyes to adjust. Dale started to speak, but Mavis raised her finger to her lips, then pointed. A figure sat there in the shadows near the old wood stove, hunched over in a rocking chair, unmoving. It had to be Wanda Faye—she wore the same faded sweater she'd had on at the market—but Mavis didn't say anything at first, standing close enough to Dale to hear his rapid breathing. Finally, she said in a soft voice, "Honey, is anything the matter? Can we help?"

Wanda Faye didn't answer at first, still sat with her back to them. Then she turned and they saw her stricken face; she'd been crying, her eyes were red-rimmed. Lord, I didn't mean to bring her more pain, Mavis thought to herself, but she had to go on, and she moved a little in front of Dale and said, "We're real sorry to disturb you. We wanted to come pay our condolences. At church we didn't get a chance."

With a weak smile, Wanda Faye turned up her face and said, "I'm awful sorry about that. Alton got carried away—he does that sometimes. He didn't mean half what he said."

"We hoped to see him, too."

"He ain't here." Wanda Faye looked past them towards the front of the house. "He took the young-uns to town to get them an ice cream cone. They've been good through all this, poor things.'' She seemed about to start crying again.

"Have you thought anymore about what happened? About Brenda's death, I mean? Any clue for the police?''

Wanda Faye shook her head, then said as if she recited a set piece, ''I was gone already that morning, to the Farmer's Market. Alton took me and come back home. I don't know what happened after that.''

Mavis was about to ask her another question, but before she could, Wanda Faye's body began to shake uncontrollably, as if a dam had burst inside her and her grief came pouring out. And with a wail that rattled the dishes drying on the sink, she began to say over and over again, ''Oh, Lord! Oh, Lord! Oh, Lord! If I'd only stayed home it might have been different.'' Then, quite suddenly, she calmed, her body stopped its shaking, and her voice was almost child-like when she spoke again. ''But it was already too late in one way, won't it?'' she asked Mavis with piteous eyes.

Walking over to the chair, Mavis knelt down beside Wanda Faye and took her hand. ''What do you mean?'' she asked her.

''What had been going on between Brenda and Mr. Trull. It must of been happening for a long time.''

''I expect so.''

''I'd swear on the Bible I didn't know!'' Wanda Faye said, her voice rising again. She grabbed Mavis's hand with both her own, as if Mavis could forgive her for some sin.

''How *did* you find out?'' Mavis asked, trying to get in a more comfortable position.

''From Kristal. She said Brenda told her what their

daddy had been doing to her.'' Wanda Faye turned her eyes away and relaxed her grip, as if she had no hope left. ''Now he's started in on *her*. She told me this morning. That's why he's not here. We had a big fuss about it and he told the young-uns to come on, he'd take them into town. I couldn't stop him.''

Mavis was nearly paralyzed, kneeling there, but she was still caught in Wanda Faye's grasp. ''There are other ways,'' she said and tried to slide her hand away.

Wanda Faye looked back at her with glazed eyes as if she didn't hear. ''The worst thing is, Kristal don't seem to care. 'Maybe I can get him to buy me things,' she said. Brenda didn't get a thing to show for what she done.''

Mavis had to stand. She'd heard enough of this sorry tale, though it was what she had suspected for some time now. She pulled her hands away from Wanda Faye's grip, pressed one on the arm of the chair and put her other hand on her knee, and slowly pushed herself up. When she heard a voice behind her, she thought at first it was Dale coming to her aid, but then she saw the look of horror on Wanda Faye's face and knew he wasn't the one who had spoken. She turned and saw Alton Trull standing in the doorway to the dining room with a hateful smile on his face.

''Well, ain't this a nice little visit,'' he said and gave a bigger grin. ''I don't know when we've had such fine folks in this house.''

''Where's the children?'' Wanda Faye asked in a fearful voice. ''We didn't hear you come up.''

'''Course not. Soon as I saw that little bitty red car parked in the yard, I stopped back under the trees. The young-uns are sitting down there pretty as you please dripping ice cream on them.''

"Have you been listening to our conversation?" Mavis asked.

Alton Trull lowered his arms from where he had propped them on the doorframe, walked around Dale to the other side of the stove, opposite Wanda Faye. "Oh, yes, ma'am," he said, looking from one to the other. "Wanda Faye been telling tales again?"

"I don't think it was tales, more like the truth she just found out."

Alton's Adam's apple dived down for a moment, as if he was looking for words to speak, and when they finally came out, the sound was harsh and ugly. "Well now, she don't need to do no more talking." He looked over at Wanda Faye. "You go on in yonder to the bedroom," he said. "I'll take care of you later."

She didn't answer him. With her head down, as if she'd already been beaten, she got up out of the chair, gathered her skirt about her like a little girl, and walked towards a door on the other side of the room. She didn't speak.

Dale took one step in her direction but then stopped and turned back to Alton. "Is that the way you treated Brenda, too," he asked, "ordering her around, making her do your bidding?" Mavis could see pure hate in his eyes.

Alton gave a little laugh. "I tried. It didn't always work. She was getting more and more uppity, threatening me. I told her nobody would believe her, but she said Miz Hollowell would, she'd tell her all about it if I didn't stop. She even claimed she was pregnant by me, said she'd tell that, too, and they'd be able to prove it with my blood."

"And you couldn't stand that, could you?" Dale's hands were clenched at his sides. "You'd already had trouble with the authorities from your preaching in town, you didn't want more. And even your snake-handling friends at church wouldn't have put up with incest, would they? That's why you killed her.''

If Alton was surprised to hear that Dale knew about the snakes, he didn't show it. Instead, his face became almost a blank and when he spoke again, it was in a monotone.

''I didn't mean it,'' he said. ''I went to her room that morning after I'd taken Wanda Faye to the market the way I always done, but that's when she pushed me away and said she'd tell Miz Hollowell what we'd been doing. I tried to reason with her. I told her I only did it 'cause I loved her better than anything. But she wouldn't listen, started shouting, and I was afraid she'd wake up the others. Then she hit me and my mind must of gone blank. I put my hands around her neck and squeezed, just to make her be quiet, but I felt some small thing break inside, like a chicken bone, and I knew she was dead.''

''That's when you had your idea, wasn't it?'' Mavis asked but went right on without giving him a chance to answer. ''You knew Brenda was supposed to pick berries for Miz Hollowell that morning, so you thought that if somebody found her there with a snakebite on her arm, they'd think it was just an accident and not do an autopsy. You had her bitten, didn't you, then carried her out to the woods behind Miz Hollowell's place and left her there. You even picked some berries and turned over the basket to make it look real. The one thing you didn't count on was Claude's finding the body and moving it away.''

''How did you know?'' Alton's voice was still flat,

without expression. He had moved further away into the shadows beside the stove.

"Hands." Mavis thrust out her palms. "Brenda's weren't stained the way they would have been if she'd been picking berries. Yours *were*—that morning when Eileen and I came over here to ask if Brenda was all right. You were hammering away, building something—I realized later it was boxes for those snakes—and I saw your hands. Maybe it was God's mark on you for what you did."

Mavis stopped, breathless. All she could see now of Alton Trull was the pale outline of his cheek, and when he spoke, his voice was almost a whisper. "The snakes..." he said. "Yes, they need a warm place, darkness, until we're ready to bring them into the light." Suddenly, he dipped down, merging with the shadows a moment, then rose up again with a shout on his lips—*"Halleluia, praise the Lord!"*—his arm thrust up towards the ceiling with four snakes, rattles whirring, clutched in his hand. He had moved from the shadows and they could see a look of ecstasy on his face. "*They* will make God's mark if you do not love him. Let us see if you pass the test."

He began to walk towards Mavis, his arm still held high. Already he was close enough for her to see the evil eyes of the serpents shining in the dim light that came from the window. Pulling back ready to run, she felt the edge of the table behind her blocking her path. Lord, help us! she prayed, harder than she'd ever prayed for anything before. Dale stepped in front of her. "Get away, you son-of-a-bitch!" he shouted, his hands up, as if he might grab the snakes and go dancing away with them like one of the worshippers at the church the night before.

But Alton Trull kept coming. "Take them," he said. "It don't matter which one of you goes first. You'll both be bit. I know. The Lord has spoke to me. Then there'll be two more bodies in the woods. Another accident. Folks'll grieve and say, Too bad them city folks didn't watch where they was stepping in the grass." He laughed, eyes glittering like those of the snakes, and Mavis thought of the wild face of the painted Christ hovering over the baptismal fount of the church.

The pellets from the shotgun took off the heads of the snakes and most of Alton Trull's hand. He stood there, arm still raised and the bodies twitching, and watched with a look of surprise on his face the fountain of blood that spilled down his arm and dripped onto the floor at his feet. In the doorway Wanda Faye stood cradling the gun. "I knew what he done in the night to Brenda," she said, "but not that he killed her. He deserves to die."

"Yes, ma'am, I agree," Dale said, moving towards Alton who had already sunk to his knees, his face pale as he looked at what was left of his hand. "But I think it's better if we call the sheriff and let other people make the final decision." He slipped a handkerchief out of his pocket. "I'll just make a little tourniquet, and then go to the nearest filling station and call an ambulance. Mavis, honey, you mind staying here with Miz Trull?" He pointed to Alton lying in the pool of blood. "He won't be going anywhere."

"Not a-tall," she told him, then walked over to where Wanda Faye still stood and took the gun from her and set it against the wall. "Come on, honey," she said. "The children must have heard the shot and they'll be running in here to find out what happened. You don't want them to see this, do you?''

Putting her arm around Wanda Faye's unresisting shoulders, she guided her through the house and out onto the porch. Dale dashed past them down the steps out across the yard to his car. Nearby, beneath the trees, Alton Trull's old truck sat, with the three Trull children lined up in front of it silently watching as if they were at the picture show. They stood there for the longest time after Dale had disappeared down the road, then turned and slowly began to walk single file towards the house.

Mavis felt Wanda Faye give a little shudder. "Is it over now?" Wanda Faye asked.

"I think so, honey," Mavis answered and gave her a big hug.

TWENTY-TWO

MAVIS LOOKED AT HER reflection in the small mirror above the dresser in her room. It seemed strange to be putting on her good dark dress to go to a celebration when, just two days before, she had worn it to Brenda's funeral. She ought to have something brighter. But after she finished buttoning up her dress, patted her hair into place beneath the spidery net, and then went to the porch where she found Dale making corsages out of what looked like half of Eileen's flower garden, she thought, With that thing on my shoulder I'll look festive after all!

"Eileen will skin you alive, cutting all her flowers," she said to Dale who was working at the dining table, so good looking in his crisp white pants and bright yellow shirt, setting off his summer tan (despite her warnings about cancer) that she had to smile.

"Will not," Eileen said, poking her head around the kitchen door from where she stood packing up food for her church's booth at the apple festival. "He asked me if he could, and I said, 'Of course, we all need something to brighten up our lives after all that's happened this week."

Well, wasn't that the truth! Mavis pulled a chair out from the table and sat down across from Dale. Drug dealers and snake handlers and murderers on the loose—it hadn't been quite the vacation she'd envisioned a week ago when she climbed aboard the bus with the others headed for Dollywood. Lord have mercy, wouldn't they be surprised to hear about all that had happened? "Won't it be dull up there in the country, just sitting on the porch and watching flies?" one of her neighbors had said. "You'd better stay on that bus and go on to Dollywood with the others for a little adventure." Well, she'd tell anybody who asked her, she'd had quite enough adventure for a while, thank you. She didn't need any more.

For a moment the memory of the scene in the Trulls' dark kitchen came before her eyes. Wanda Faye standing in the doorway with the gun in her hands, Alton turning pale, staring at what was left of his hand, four headless rattlers on the floor, oozing blood—she didn't know why she didn't faint dead away. After Dale had roared off down the road for help, she sat in the porch swing with Wanda Faye, still holding her, and waited for the children to come up the steps.

"There's been an accident," she had told them. "Your daddy's been hurt. Somebody has gone for help." None of them answered back. Kristal leaned against the porch rail chewing on her cuticle, and the two little boys stood where they were, staring at their mama and Mavis in the swing. It suddenly occurred to her that maybe they had never seen anybody holding Wanda Faye before (certainly not their daddy), no memory at all of when their own little hands clung to her neck in love.

They had stayed there on the porch until the Rescue Squad drove up into the yard, siren going loud enough to scare birds from the trees a mile around. For the first time, the children seemed interested. As soon as the attendants had started IVs and undone Dale's makeshift tourniquet and bound up Alton's hand, they rushed him out the door on a stretcher and slid him into the ambulance. Wanda Faye made no move to join him. They sped away, the siren blasting once again.

The sheriff came soon after, with Dale following behind, and once he'd nodded good day to Mavis and Wanda Faye, he said, "I reckon a lot has happened this morning," and Wanda Faye, still as a stone statue in the swing, told him all about what had been going on between Alton Trull and Brenda, and how he had now turned to her sister, the last straw for Wanda Faye before she shot him and the snakes he'd taken out to threaten the others with. Then, feeling Wanda Faye's trembling body beside her own, Mavis broke in to tell Sheriff Lee Rhodes the rest about Brenda's murder and Alton Trull's attempt to make it look like an accident.

"Did they arrest Wanda Faye?" Eileen had asked later, after they went back home and told her what had happened.

"Of course not," Mavis had replied. "She saved our lives, didn't she, shooting those snakes? It would break your heart, seeing her sitting there in the swing with her head hung down. We asked if she'd be all right, and she said she'd call her sister and maybe she and the young-uns would go stay with her a few days. When we left, they were all lined up on the porch like survivors on a stranded ship. I hate to think what will become of them."

Dale interrupted her thoughts. "Put this on and start feeling better," he said, coming around the table with the corsage in his hand. He bent over and pinned it on Mavis's dress.

"My goodness," she said, smelling the sweet scent of the flowers, "I look like I'm about to be installed in the Daughters of the Confederacy with that thing on my shoulder."

"Well, you deserve a prize, figuring out everything that was going on."

"You helped, too."

"Not much, drove you around."

Just then, Eileen came out of the kitchen. "Speaking of driving," she said, "we'd better get going. The apple festival won't wait."

"Let's get your corsage on," Dale said, picking up the other bouquet.

"Isn't that the prettiest *thing?*" Eileen said. "I couldn't make one in a million years."

"Nothing to it," Dale said. Then he stood back with his hands up in front of his face as if he focused a camera. "Smile! You two will outshine the festival queen."

"How about *you!*" Eileen said and gave him a little slap on the arm. "I've never seen anyone so good looking."

"I don't expect they'll have me up on any float."

Eileen laughed. "The parade's not tonight, anyway, just a street dance and speeches and fireworks afterwards. And the food, of course. Every church in town will have a booth selling something to make money."

"I'm already starved," Dale said. "Let's go." Grabbing them both by the arm, he started marching across the floor as if he was their escort for the senior prom, until Eileen, half doubled over with laughter, pulled away and said, "My food, it's sitting there on the counter!'' and they went back to the kitchen and helped her take the boxes out to the car.

THEY STOPPED BY FOR KEVIN on the way to town. Eileen had called his mother that morning and asked her if he could come along with them to the festival, and she had said she'd be mighty pleased if he could, he'd been so down in the mouth since Brenda was killed. Now, as Eileen pulled into the Farmer's Market parking lot, Kevin sat quietly in the back seat between Mavis and Claude, listening to some of Claude's foolishness. Though Claude had put up a big fuss at home about having to wear shoes and had pouted for a while when they first started out, he had begun chattering away as soon as Kevin had gotten into the car, and Eileen had to tell him twice to calm down, he'd be sick if he got over excited.

"Don't get lost," Eileen warned him as they got out of the car.

"I'll take care of him, Miz Hollowell," Kevin said. "We'll have a good time." And he and Claude went hurrying off ahead, while Mavis and Dale and Eileen strode more leisurely behind.

"I don't suppose Jordache will be doing much dancing in the streets tonight, unless it's in leg irons," Dale said, laughing, as they passed the jail. "Tara either."

"That mean thing," Mavis said. "Jordache. He's just as much of a killer as Alton Trull, only indirect, with drugs. I hope they send them both off to prison, unless, of course, Alton gets the electric chair. From what the paper said, he's recovering from the gunshot. They had to take off the rest of his hand."

They both noticed Eileen's silence. "Oh, honey,

I'm sorry," Mavis said, taking her arm. "Neither one of us was thinking about Tara and how you must feel."

Eileen brushed her hand in the air. "It's her life and she's made a mess of it. I can't change her," Eileen said. "But she'll be out of jail soon. I called her daddy, and he said he'd send bail money. Not on my doorstep, though—I told him I was through taking her in whenever she got in trouble."

"She'll probably get a suspended sentence," Mavis said. "Nobody can prove she had a hand in selling Jordache's drugs. At least that *place* got closed up, The Pit. Maybe they'll turn it back into a nice supper club again."

"How're y'all this evening?" Coming around the corner of a building, Boyd Wilkinson took off his cap, gave a little bow, and smiled. "How's your business going after all this scandal?"

"Just fine," Eileen responded sweetly. Sugar wouldn't melt in her mouth. "I've got my first guests coming in tomorrow, and we're booked up all through the fall foliage season. Seems like all the news helped us, people wanting to come to the scene of the crime."

Boyd put his cap back on and still retained the smile. "Well, if you ever *do* decide to sell the place, you know where to come."

"Not likely," Eileen said, giving him a slight nod. Then they passed on.

The streets were filled with people now, the crowd in a happy mood, though no one seemed out of the way. Mavis hoped the police would prevent a lot of drunkenness—so many things these days were ruined by a bunch of fools with a bottle in their hip pockets. After the storm two days before, the weather was just about perfect, the sky pale pink, fading to purple, with banners flying in a soft breeze. Mavis hardly needed the jacket of her dress. Every now and then, she would smell a whiff of perfume from the flowers on her shoulder, and she'd smile, thinking of Dale's thoughtfulness.

Going from one booth to another, they ate ham biscuits, fresh corn on the cob, deep fried mushrooms and zucchini. Dale insisted on paying for it all. "I hope you've got a big bottle of milk of magnesia at home," Mavis told Eileen. "We'll all be sick later."

"No you won't," Eileen said. "This is all good home cooking. Now, come on, I want to take you to my church's tent and get some of my pecan pie. With all the ruckus going on, I only made five, and they'll be gone in no time."

They pushed through the crowd, thicker now, lights bright around them, the sky darker, a little mysterious. Mavis thought of the old-fashioned carnivals she attended as a child. When they reached the church tent, all the ladies there gathered around Eileen, saying in chirrupy voices, "Honey, we read in the paper what happened. Isn't it just *awful?* I've never heard of such a thing!" But Eileen turned to Mavis and said, "This is my friend Mavis Lashley. *She's* the one that solved the mystery and almost got bit by snakes when Mr. Alton Trull went on his rampage."

The women looked at her with wide eyes, and Mavis felt herself blush as bright as the lights shining down, but she didn't say anything. "See, what did I tell you?" Dale said softly in her ear. "I told you you'd give the festival queen a run for her money. You're more famous than she is."

"Go eat your pie and be quiet," Mavis answered him.

"I already did. I'm ready for a second piece. If I get fat, I'll starve when I get home."

Just then the music started up. On the other side of the tent was a platform with a string band led by an old man with a harmonica, with a space out in front cleared off by the police for dancing. "Y'all grab you a partner and come on out here and let's *dance*," the man said, then gave a blast on the harmonica as the band started up. In no time, the street was filled with dancing figures, the music swelling through the night guided by the old man's raspy voice as he gave the square dance calls.

"Come on, honey, let's shake a leg." It was Dale, pulling at Mavis's arm.

"You know I'm not," she said. "I've never danced two steps in my entire life, and I'm not about to make a fool of myself now."

"Aw, come on. Just shuffle your feet back and forth like the others. I don't know the steps, either."

She tried to protest, but the music drowned out her words, and she felt herself being guided out into the street by Dale, sure she'd trip any minute, with every eye in the crowd on her ready to see her fall. But then, with Dale's strong arm around her shoulders, and the music providing a steady beat, she found that she could follow the couple in front of them as they circled around, even imitate their shuffling steps. Well, have mercy, she thought, this is not so hard after all, and she raised her head and smiled at Dale as they went whirling to the center of the ring.

"What?" she said. She thought that Dale must have asked her a question, but when she felt him stop and lead her out of the way of the other dancers, she turned and saw Sheriff Lee Rhodes standing there.

"I said, 'Can I cut in?' I'd like to dance with Miz Mavis."

"Well, my goodness, what are *you* doing here?" Mavis said, fanning her face with her handkerchief. Her heart was beating a mile a minute.

"Just wandering around, keeping an eye on things, but that don't mean I can't have a good time. Is it okay with you if I dance with her?" he asked Dale.

Dale moved away from Mavis and gave the sheriff the nicest smile. "Sure thing," he said. "I'll just go stand in the crowd and mope. Some people have all the luck."

"You go ask Eileen to dance," Mavis called out to him as Lee led her back to the circle. "She's probably a lot better than I am."

"You're doing just fine," Lee said, holding her tightly. "Just like a native." In the lights, his freckles merged into a dark tan, and his hair flashed like fire.

"Thank you kindly," Mavis said, and nothing more as they sped away into the crowd of dancers. But she thought, Lord, if only Zeena and the others over in Dollywood could see me now, dancing up a storm in the middle of the street in the arms of a red-headed policeman. Wouldn't they be surprised!

FOLLOW
THE
MURDER
CATHERINE DAIN

A FAITH CASSIDY MYSTERY

Psychotherapist Faith Cassidy believes her new client Natalie is simply working through her anger when she talks about killing her husband. However, when Natalie is charged with murder, Faith is stunned, especially since she may be sued for negligence.

Faith knows the only way to save her client *and* her career is to find out who killed Natalie's husband. Ignoring threatening phone calls, the sudden demise of one of Craig's cronies and the murder of his former girlfriend, Faith tries to sort out the dirty dealings and dangerous games—where following a murder leads to a date with a killer.

"Faith is a strong and gutsy heroine whose flaws make her even more likeable."
—*Booklist*

Available September 2003 at your favorite retail outlet.

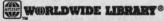

WORLDWIDE LIBRARY ®

WCD468

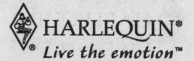

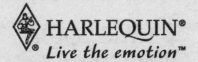

The Hydrogen Murder

Camille Minichino

A Gloria Lamerino Mystery

Gloria Lamerino is called in to investigate the murder of her former colleague, physicist Eric Bensen. Her understanding of Bensen's breakthrough research on hydrogen convinces detective and almost-beau Matt Gennaro that this is a high-stakes crime with no shortage of suspects.

Bensen's research has enormous potential for big business. Gloria is determined to expose the data tampering, deception and fraud by members of Bensen's team. When the person with the most to gain from Bensen's death is murdered, as well, it takes her most brilliant analytical skills to identify a killer.

"...a stunning debut..."
—Janet Evanovich

Available September 2003 at your favorite retail outlet.

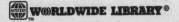

WCM467